STRANDED WITH EZRA
A PREQUEL TO THE WAGNER BRIGADE

ASHLEY A. QUINN

TCA PUBLISHING

ONE

"You want to go where for how long?"

Amy Preston couldn't help but grin at her friend Kasey Graham's incredulous expression. She'd just dropped a bit of a bombshell on her and hadn't expected anything less than the shocked response she'd received. Doing something wild wasn't entirely out of character for her. She could be impulsive. Though usually it was over what she ate for lunch or an outfit she bought at the mall.

"Australia. For a month," Amy repeated.

Kasey shook her head. "Why? What brought this on?"

Amy shrugged. "I just have some personal things I need to sort out and I need to get away from... everything to do it. If I take the time off but stay here, I'll just get distracted by my life. I need to step away from it, so that I can see it clearly. Does that make sense?" Getting away was something she'd been toying with for a while now. The last few weeks had really convinced her to do just that.

Kasey gave her a long look. "Yeah, I guess." She stepped away from the table she leaned against, moving closer to Amy.

"I just wish you weren't going so far away to do it. Can't you do your thinking in the continental United States?"

Amy smiled. "You know, I thought about going out west, but I've been there. I want to go somewhere I've never been. Australia sounds great. I haven't taken a real vacation in a long time."

"What about your job here?" Kasey's hand fluttered near her head as she gestured to the back room of the museum where they worked.

"I already talked to Rebecca. She's agreed to give me an unpaid leave of absence." For which Amy was grateful. When she talked to her boss, she wasn't sure the woman would grant her the extended leave. But Amy's request for most of her time away to be unpaid went a long way. She was only using a week of her vacation time.

Eyes bugging, Kasey blinked. "How can you afford that on top of the trip?"

"I don't have a wedding or a honeymoon to pay for now." Amy rubbed at the ache in her chest, the pain of her fiancé's betrayal still fresh. "I'm using that."

"Oh." Kasey tipped her head. "I guess that's true."

Amy reached out and put a hand on Kasey's shoulder. "Don't worry about me, Kase. I'm not crazy, I haven't gone off the deep end. I know what I'm doing. I just need a break. I've been working twelve-hour days, five or six, sometimes seven days a week, for the last four years. I'm tired, and I need to really think about what I want out of life."

Kasey's gaze narrowed. "You're not still pining over your idiot of an ex-fiancé, are you? Because he doesn't deserve any space in your thoughts."

Amy dropped her hand and stuffed it and her other one in the pockets of her oversize cardigan. Truthfully, she'd felt a deep sense of relief when things had ended with her now former fiancé, Andy Carrington. She definitely didn't miss having him in her life daily, but she did miss spending time with someone. "No. It's more about trying to get over the pain he inflicted."

Kasey opened her mouth, but Amy cut her off. "Ending that relationship has made me think about where I am in my life, and what I want as well as what's not there that I want. I need to figure out a few things. Like, do I really want to stay a curator here, or do I want to open my own antiques shop? And whether I want kids. And if I do, do I wait for Mr. Right or do I look at other options? I need to remove myself from my life so I can gain some perspective. Otherwise, I'll just get sucked back into things and never fully process all these thoughts." She gave Kasey an imploring gaze. "I'm not happy with the way my life stands, Kase. And I'm tired."

"I get that." Kasey sighed. "But Australia? For a month? Alone? I just wish you'd stay closer to home. Or take someone with you."

"I'll be fine." She knew the "by herself" part would be a hard-sell. Kasey was a few years older and tended to play big sister. Amy loved her to death for it too. "I'll be at a dude ranch and be able to keep in touch while I'm there. I'll be back before you know it."

Her friend let out a snort. "Yeah, right. The time might fly by for you. But I'll be here, working all by my lonesome and waiting for you to come home."

Amy grinned. "You should spend more time with that guy you met last month. Nate? He seems nice."

"He is. And I plan to. But I'll still miss you."

"I'll miss you too." Amy hugged the other woman. "Now, can we get back to work so you don't have to finish this project on your own?"

"Ugh. Fine. I suppose that's a good idea." Kasey wrinkled her nose, then chuckled.

Smiling, Amy picked up the next artifact on the table from

the collection they were cataloging. She felt lighter now that she had that conversation out of the way. She'd already told her parents about her plans. They'd been as concerned as Kasey, but it still didn't change her mind. She doubted anyone would. Now that Kasey knew, there wasn't anyone else to tell. Until Andy cheated on her and she kicked him out, she hadn't realized how isolated she'd become. It was past time for her to spread her wings. Was she going a little overboard with this trip? Probably. But she was hoping the shakeup would give her the boost she needed to make some hard decisions about her future. Because she couldn't continue with how things were now. She hadn't lied. She was tired and confused. Something had to give.

Two

Amy stowed her backpack in the overhead bin and took her seat next to the window on the airplane she just boarded. Settling her handbag on her lap, she folded her hands over it and glanced out at the tarmac. Nervous excitement made her twitchy, and she resisted the urge to tap her foot and twiddle her thumbs. The three cups of coffee she drank on her first flight might be partly responsible for her jitters too. This was flight number two of the day. Her flight out of D.C. this morning had been so early she'd been on autopilot and had gladly sucked down the coffee the airline offered. Now, though, she was wide awake and excitement coursed through her.

It still hadn't entirely hit her that she was leaving the trappings of her normal life behind and going to a foreign country. Alone. No griping bosses or whining co-workers. No hurried museum patrons upset they couldn't use the flash on their cameras. And definitely no memories of her ex cropping up when she passed his favorite coffee shop or the restaurant they frequented on date night. Nothing but peace and quiet for the next four weeks. It would all likely sink in once she got settled in at Black Diamond Station in Queensland.

Blowing out a breath, she opened her purse and took out her book. She debated putting her earbuds in, but decided to wait until they were underway. Once all the commotion died down.

She stowed her bag under her seat, then settled back and opened her book. One page in, a deep voice interrupted her from above.

"Howdy."

Amy looked up. Her eyes went wide as she took in the sight looming over her. He had to be six-foot-four or better with the most piercing blue eyes she'd ever seen. A shock of short, dark hair with just the faintest hint of gray set them off even more. And he was beautiful.

Suddenly realizing she was staring, she tried to arrange her mouth into a smile. "Hi." Dear God, she sounded like a frog. Clearing her throat, she tried again. "Sorry, hi." That was much better.

The man stuffed his carry-on into the bin above, muscles rippling beneath the light blue t-shirt he wore. He sat down next to her, shoving a black backpack under his seat, and nearly blinded her with a grin. Amy's eyes rounded again. That smile took him from beautiful to stunning. She'd never been so close to a more gorgeous man. And she got to sit next to him for the next eighteen hours. Holy crap.

He held out his hand. "I'm Ezra."

Amy shook it. "Amy. It's nice to meet you."

"So where are you headed?"

"Brisbane. Actually, to a ranch a few hours from there. You?" She clenched her book, amazed she was able to form a complete sentence. The rest of the plane had faded away. She felt like she was in a tunnel with him at the end. He'd completely short-circuited her brain.

"My sister's place. Her husband owns a cattle station a few hours from Brisbane by air."

Amy smiled. "That sounds nice. Getting to visit family."

He nodded. "She just had a baby, her first. And I haven't seen her in quite a while, so I figured it'd be a good time to go for a visit." He pulled a book of his own out of the backpack by his feet.

"That sounds great." Offering him a smile, she turned back to her book, attempting to regain her focus.

Her eyes strayed to his long legs, so close to her own. The denim covering them stretched to within an inch of its life to cover his thick, muscled limbs. She was glad they were in an exit row. She couldn't imagine how he would have coped being in a regular coach seat. The man's legs were a mile long. Their seats weren't any wider, though, and they were scrunched close. His broad shoulders nearly touched hers. She had a feeling trying to fall asleep tonight would be difficult. She was very aware of how near he was.

Wrenching her gaze away from the hunk of pure masculinity next to her, Amy concentrated on her book, but still had to reread sections. With a sigh, she marked her page, then bent over to dig into her bag for her earbuds. If she had any hope of ignoring the underwear model next to her, she needed a bigger distraction than just her book.

"Ladies and gentlemen, may I have your attention, please?"

Amy glanced up at the flight attendant's perky voice over the intercom, her hand closing around her earbuds. Bringing them out, she listened to the woman's safety spiel as she connected them to her phone, then frowned as she realized she'd need to wait until after takeoff to put them in. She flew often enough, she should know that. Biting back a low growl, she stuffed everything, book included, into the pouch on the back of the seat. Her seatmate had her all sorts of flustered.

Their wait to taxi wasn't long, thankfully, and soon they were moving. Amy stared out the window, watching the hustle and bustle of the airport. The plane turned onto the runway and paused for a long moment before the engines ramped up and they shot forward. In moments, they were winging through the air.

Once they were safely off the ground and the flight crew gave them the okay to use electronics, Amy dug her phone and book out of the seat back and popped her earbuds into her ears. Turning on her favorite reading playlist, she opened her book and immersed herself in late-nineteenth-century Plains culture. Before she knew it, they were well over the Pacific.

Several hours passed, and she only looked up once, and that was to request a water and cookies when the flight attendant came around with the drink cart before dinner. She'd made it halfway through her book before the crew came around again. With a glance at her watch, Amy was surprised at how long she'd been reading. And by how hungry she was. She readily accepted the meal the woman handed her and cut into it. It wasn't the best chicken parmesan she'd ever had, but it wasn't terrible.

Her eyes strayed to her seatmate. He'd opted for the same meal. The muscles in his jaw worked as he chewed. She turned her gaze back to her tray table. Watching him eat was creepy. So what if he had a jaw carved from granite or cheekbones that could cut paper? She knew she'd be uncomfortable with someone staring at her for no reason while she ate.

"So, are you by yourself?"

Amy jumped. She'd been so caught up in not staring and in her own thoughts, his voice startled her. She glanced at him. He cut off another piece of chicken and ate it while he looked at her, waiting for an answer.

It momentarily crossed her mind that she probably

shouldn't divulge that she was by herself, but her mouth over-rode her brain. "Yes, I'm alone."

His forehead wrinkled. "Why? I mean, there's nothing wrong with a woman traveling alone, but it just seems a bit crazy to me that anyone would travel halfway around the world by themselves for vacation." He tipped his head, a curious light entering his eyes. "Unless, you're on business? You said you're headed to a dude ranch, which says vacation to me, but I could be wrong."

She smiled softly. "No. I'm not on business. I'm running from my business."

One of his perfect eyebrows shot skyward.

Amy laughed. That hadn't come out sounding quite right. "What I mean is I'm taking a much-needed break from work. I've been working way too much for the last few years and needed to get away. I'm not some crazy lady who embezzled from her company or something."

He smiled that killer smile again. "Good. But why by yourself? Why not with a family member or a friend?"

Amy shrugged. "I needed some space to think. My best friend would try to talk me into staying in my current job since we work together and she doesn't want to see me go, and my mother and sisters would harp on me every day to just make a decision. I wanted to have the time and space to come to my own conclusions."

He nodded slowly. "Makes sense. So, what do you do, anyway?"

"I'm a curator at a local history museum just outside of Washington D.C."

That perfect eyebrow shot up again. "Really? That sounds fascinating. What kind of history do you deal with there? Is it all local to D.C.?"

Amy couldn't help but smile. Most people automatically

assumed she worked with general historical items when she told them she was a curator. They didn't realize how specific curatorial work could get. "It's actually dedicated to the Potomac region. I'm on the colonial side of things. We're gearing up to open a new exhibit on the Siege of the Potomac. We had one, but it was—well, inadequate."

"That sounds neat. Military history of any kind is interesting to me, though. I don't get to many museums nowadays, but when I do, those types of places are where I gravitate to."

Amy turned toward him, her dinner pretty much forgotten now. "We've done several updates to our exhibits in the last few years, thanks to some grants. It's been exciting."

"It sounds like you really like your work. Why are you running from it if you love it so much? Is it just the long hours?"

That was a great question. One Amy didn't have a ready answer to. "I do love it, but it's also very stressful. I put in a lot of hours. I have a background in military and cultural history, but I also love to delve into antiques. Actually, I've been contemplating opening an antiques store. I guess it's more of whether I want to be a slave to the museum's work schedule or my own. I'm hoping this vacation will help me sort that out." Among other things.

Ezra nodded thoughtfully.

"So, what about you?" Amy asked, wanting to get the focus off herself and her problems. She had the next four weeks to contemplate that. "What do you do for a living?"

"I'm a pilot in the Army," he replied.

Amy smiled. "No wonder you like military history."

He laughed. "Probably."

"How long have you been in?" she asked.

"Twelve years."

"I take it you're a career man, then?"

He nodded. "Most likely. I love being up in the air. And where else do you get to play with the newest and best stuff? It's great."

Amy smiled. "Very true. What do you fly?"

"Choppers. I've got a civilian certification for light planes too."

It was Amy's turn to arch an eyebrow. "You fly in your down time too?"

Ezra laughed. "What can I say? I'm a junkie."

Amy glanced down and saw the book sticking out of the seat pocket and laughed. She picked it up so he could see the title. *Shifting Winds: The Story of a High Plains Family, 1880-1945.* "I guess I can't say too much."

"Now that's just pathetic." He pointed a finger at her, biting back a smile and losing.

Their meals forgotten, Amy and Ezra fell into deep conversation, passing the hours until the flight attendant came by again, offering pillows and blankets.

Ezra looked at his watch, taking the items. "I guess we should try to get some sleep, so we're not totally off kilter once we get there." He passed a pillow and blanket to Amy.

Amy nodded. "I hate jet lag." She stuffed the pillow behind her head and spread the blanket over her legs, then hit the button on her seat and laid back. Ezra flipped off his overhead light and reclined his seat.

A hyper-awareness pricked Amy's skin as they settled down. He was *so* close. Even scrunched against the window, she could feel his presence. The darkness and quiet descending in the aircraft didn't help matters. It enveloped them like a cocoon. She could feel Ezra's body heat and the brush of his arm against hers as he moved.

She shifted, turning away, and curled her legs under herself. Drawing the blanket up, she adjusted the tiny pillow.

For once, she was glad she was small. It meant she not only fit on the seat like this, but could put some space between them.

Ezra moved, sending a wave of heat and a cloud of his spicy male scent toward her.

Amy widened her eyes, staring out the window at the darkened sky, and sighed. It was going to be a long night.

THREE

Clouds floated through an endless blue sky as Ezra walked through a field. The smell of lilies and sunshine filled his nose and brought a smile to his face. Warmth permeated his chest.

Though it was warmer on just his right shoulder. He frowned.

Slowly, reality intruded, and he realized he was dreaming. Taking a deep breath and coming awake, he blinked, seeing the back of the plane seat in front of him. The warm weight on his shoulder registered a moment before Amy snorted softly and snuggled deeper into him.

He blinked again and looked over at the woman using him as a pillow. Her thick, dark hair was tucked up close to his face. Sometime in the night, she had shifted to face him and was now tucked into his arm.

Ezra studied her face. She really was quite beautiful. She had skin so creamy and smooth it resembled porcelain. Her high cheekbones gave her a slightly exotic look, and her nose turned up ever so slightly on the end, making her look like a pixie. And she was tiny enough to be one. His fingers itched to touch her full, soft pink lips. It was a shame they were going different ways once they landed. He wouldn't mind finding out more about this intriguing lady. She had fascinated him last night with her quick wit and intelligence. It was a rare day he met a woman with whom he could talk so freely. Especially one so beautiful.

And she smelled wonderful. Ezra inhaled once more. There was that lilies and sunshine fragrance again. He closed his eyes, savoring the scent.

Amy shifted and her eyes fluttered open. He could tell the moment she realized her pillow wasn't down-filled. She stiffened, going hard as a board, and sat up. Ezra raised his seat back and smiled at her. "Good morning."

She blushed. "Good morning." Lifting a hand, she pushed her hair away from her face and cast a quick look at him. "Sorry about that. I guess I rolled over in my sleep."

Ezra's smile grew. "I didn't mind. You make a nice blanket." He'd been toasty warm and had pleasant dreams, thanks to her.

Her cheeks reddened further, and she looked away, shifting in her seat.

"Did you sleep well, though?"

She nodded, turning her head to cast him a quick glance. "Very."

"Good." He had too, surprisingly. When he boarded the flight, he'd already resigned himself to tossing and turning, never really falling asleep. He didn't like flying if he wasn't the one piloting. But her warmth and lovely scent lulled him into a state of bliss, and he'd slept better than he ever had on a commercial flight.

She pushed her blanket off. "I'm going to go use the restroom before they come around with drinks."

Ezra tipped his legs to the side so she could get past. His gaze followed her as she walked away. Those leggings she had on hugged every curve she possessed. The woman was stunning, and he doubted she even saw it. There was a wholesomeness about her that drew him in. Just as much as her looks and smarts. Again, he couldn't help but regret they wouldn't see each other after the plane landed.

Yawning, he stretched, already feeling more relaxed than when his first flight took off from Nashville yesterday. If this was how his trip started, he couldn't wait to see how it evolved.

Four

Amy stared at herself in the bathroom mirror. Her face was still red. She couldn't believe she spent the night asleep on Ezra's shoulder. Handsome or not, she had just met the man. She blew out a breath, making the hair hanging around her face flutter. At least they both slept well.

She turned on the faucet and splashed some water on her face and used her finger to try to scrub some of the sleep from her teeth. They weren't perfect, but it would do until she got to the ranch and could settle in. She planned to take a nice hot shower before she did anything else. Flying always made her feel grungy. It was the stale air. No matter what scrubbers the airlines claimed to use, plane air always smelled weird, and it just made her feel icky by the time they landed.

What she really needed, though, was a hairbrush. Amy tipped her head, looking at her hair. While not a rat's nest, it was tangled and sticking out in many different directions. She plunged her fingers into it, wincing as they caught in the tangles. Working out the worst ones as best she could, she took a hair band out of her pocket and hastily scraped it back into a ponytail. Checking to make sure there weren't any weird bumps, she nodded at her image. That was as good as it was going to get.

After using the facilities, she washed her hands, then flipped the lock open and stepped back into the cabin. The flight attendant was coming around with breakfast as Amy took her seat.

"What can I get you to drink?" The woman smiled expectantly at them.

"Coffee," Ezra said.

Whoa, buddy. A shiver went down Amy's spine. Ezra's voice was low, still thick with sleep. She crossed her legs and kept her eyes on the attendant. If she looked at the man right now, she might melt. "I'll have the same, please."

The attendant nodded and poured two cups of coffee. "Sugar or cream?"

Amy shook her head. So did Ezra.

"What would you like to eat?" She handed them the cups. "I have toast, scrambled eggs, sausage, yogurt, and fruit. You can pick two items."

"Eggs and sausage for me, please." Ezra indicated the hot tray on her cart.

"I'll just have yogurt and fruit." Amy laid a hand over her stomach. She wasn't all that hungry. Flying upset her stomach to a degree.

Pulling the items from her cart, the woman passed them the food and some utensils, then moved on.

"I should have sprung for a bigger meal."

Amy glanced over at Ezra's grumble. He had a scoop of eggs and two sausages. She grinned. "You want my yogurt?" She held up the cup.

He waved a hand. "No. Thank you, though. If I get really hungry, I have a protein bar in my bag. I imagine there will be food right outside the gate when we land. I'll hit up a fast-food place when we get there." He stabbed a sausage with his plastic fork and put it in his mouth. In one bite, it was gone.

Amy rolled her lips in, holding back a smile. That wasn't breakfast. Not for a man his size. It was barely a snack. "Are you sure? I'm not that hungry."

"I'm sure. You eat it."

Peeling back the lid, she unwrapped her spoon and dunked it in. After a few bites, she set the cup down, needing to give her stomach a break. If she wanted it all to stay down, she'd need to eat slowly. Amy reached for her coffee and took a sip. The warm liquid—while it didn't taste the best—soothed her stomach. And it provided some much-needed caffeine. It would combat the jet lag she would no doubt suffer from later.

She settled back, holding the cup, and looked out the window. The sun was up, but all that met her gaze was water and some thin clouds. "Do you know how far we have to go yet?"

Ezra looked at his watch. "We should be landing in a couple hours if we're on time."

She sighed and grabbed her book out of the pouch under the tray, not really wanting to talk. The caffeine hadn't kicked in yet, so she was still in a bit of a fog. Maybe reading would help engage her brain and wake her up.

The remaining flight passed quickly. Ezra seemed to be in a similar boat to Amy and buried his nose in his own book. As they neared the Australian coast, Amy finished her breakfast and cleaned up around her seat. Stowing her book in her bag, she watched Brisbane come into view. Those excited nerves she felt when she boarded in Los Angeles were back. She couldn't wait to start her adventure.

For thirty minutes, the plane dropped steadily in altitude, and soon, the pilot made a smooth landing at the Brisbane airport. Amy's gaze stayed glued to the window and the vista beyond as they taxied to the gate.

"Ladies and gentlemen, we have arrived at our destination. The current weather here in Brisbane is beautiful with a temperature of twenty-four degrees centigrade. Please stay in your seats with your seatbelts fastened until we arrive at the gate and the seatbelt light goes off. The crew and I hope you had a good flight. Thank you for flying with us."

In minutes, they were docked and the seatbelt light went out. Amy grabbed her bag and stood, waiting for Ezra to step into the aisle.

"Which of these bags is yours?" He dipped his head to look at her.

"The purple backpack."

He pulled it down and passed it to her, then grabbed a black rolling case. Slinging his olive green backpack over his shoulder, he stepped back so she could exit the row. "After you."

"Thanks." Offering him a smile, she stepped into the aisle and headed for the door. He followed her off the plane.

"I'm guessing you have bags to claim?" He put a hand on her back to steer her through the crowd streaming around them.

She nodded.

"Me too. Come on. I'll walk with you to the carousel." He turned, heading for baggage claim.

It didn't take long for them to get there. Ezra's large frame cut through the crowd with ease. People parted like the Red Sea, and she was glad to be with him. She would have been pushing and shoving her way through.

Ezra elbowed his way into the throng around the baggage carousel. "Holler at me when you see one of yours." He glanced over his shoulder at her.

"They're crazy colors, so they shouldn't be too hard to spot. One's neon green and the other is orange."

Ezra smiled. "What on earth made you buy luggage in those colors?"

Amy shrugged. "I had normal colored luggage when I graduated college. But once I started working, I started traveling more, and I could never find my bag. It looked like all the others. I finally got sick of it and went out and bought the craziest looking stuff I could find." She grinned. "I've got a pink leopard print duffel at home that I use for short trips."

Ezra laughed. "You know, I think I can imagine you with that." He tapped her nose with a finger. "You've got a funky streak, I think."

Amy tipped her head, a crooked grin on her face. "Maybe just a little." She glanced back at the carousel. "Oh! There's my suitcase."

Ezra stepped forward and snagged the bright orange case off the belt. Two suitcases behind it came his black duffel. He set both at her feet, then stepped back to the belt to grab a large black rolling suitcase and her green one.

Amy pulled the handle up on the orange one and was reaching for the smaller green one when Ezra grabbed it and swung it up to rest on top of his suitcase. He slung his duffel over his shoulder and reached to take the orange case from her.

Amy stared. She'd never expected him to help with her bags. "You don't have to carry my bags, Ezra."

He shrugged. "No biggie."

Amy could tell arguing with him would get her nowhere. There was something in his eyes that was dead set on carrying her bags. Apparently, chivalry wasn't dead.

"Thank you, then."

"You're welcome." He set his small carry-on atop her orange case, then turned, reentering the crowd.

He wove through the throng toward customs, where they entered the twisting queue. Thankfully, the line wasn't too long. Amy found her passport and entry card as they shuffled forward. Once through, Amy paused, looking up at the signs to see which way she needed to go.

"Where do you want me to drop you?" Ezra asked, stopping beside her.

Amy gestured to the sign pointing the way to the car rental counters. "That way. I need to pick up my rental."

He nodded and turned, leading the way to the car rental counters. Amy did her best to keep her eyes forward and off the bulging muscles in his arms as he carried all their stuff. She was going to miss looking at him when they parted ways soon.

"Which one?" Ezra tipped his head toward the counters as they approached.

"That one." Amy pointed to the company through which she'd booked her car.

Ezra crossed to the counter and plopped her bags down. "You want me to stick around and help you to your car?"

Oh, she was so tempted just so she could look at him a little while longer. But common sense told her she could handle it. She smiled at him. "Thanks, but I can get them."

One perfect eyebrow rose. "You're sure?"

She nodded.

"Okay." He took a step closer. "Well, I hope you enjoy your vacation, Amy. It was very nice to meet you." He bent forward and dropped a kiss on her cheek.

Momentarily stunned, she gaped up at him. Her cheek tingled where his warm lips had touched. Not for the first time, she wished she could get to know him better. It figured she'd meet someone interesting while she was here, only to have him going in a different direction.

Not that she was looking for someone special. She wasn't.

Amy cleared her throat and shook herself out of her stupor. "Thank you. It was nice to meet you, too, Ezra. I hope you enjoy your time with your sister."

"I will." He grabbed the handle of his suitcase and tipped his head to her. "Take care."

Amy nodded and waved as he turned and walked away. She watched him go until he disappeared into the crowd. She sighed, wishing again they were heading the same way.

The clerk at the counter cleared her throat and Amy turned, realizing she'd been standing there watching Ezra for much longer than necessary. Blushing furiously at being caught daydreaming about the man, she stepped forward and gave the woman her name. The clerk typed it into the computer and pulled up her reservation.

"We have you down with an economy car for a month. Is that correct?"

Amy nodded. "Yes." She handed the woman her credit card and international driver's license.

"That's a nice chunk of time. You'll be able to see a lot while you're here. Where are you headed first?"

"Black Diamond Station," Amy said.

The clerk frowned. "Wait. That's a dude ranch, right? Outside of Miles?"

"Yes." Amy cocked her head, hearing something in the clerk's tone. "Why?"

The woman's frown deepened. "Ma'am, that place closed last week. It was all over the news. The owners were caught guiding illegal hunting parties, and the ranch had to shut down. Weren't you informed? The report mentioned that customers were being contacted."

"What? No, I was not informed." Oh, this was just fantastic. Her entire trip hinged on that ranch. Because of the length of her stay, she'd gotten a special rate. At least she hadn't paid anything besides a deposit in advance. Which meant she could stay in the country if she could find a decent hotel in her price range.

Amy groaned. This was not what she needed. "Um, okay.

Can you recommend a place to stay locally tonight, so I can come up with a new plan?"

"Why do you need a new plan?"

Amy whirled at the deep voice that spoke behind her. "Ezra."

FIVE

The main doors leading outside loomed when Ezra turned back. He couldn't in good conscience leave Amy alone here without a way to contact him if she needed help. He knew she could go to the U.S. Embassy, but it wasn't the same. Sometimes, the help a person needed wasn't something the government could provide. Plus, he'd kick himself for the rest of his life if he didn't get her number. When they got back to the States, he didn't care how far apart they were; he wanted to see her again.

He was much relieved to see her still standing at the rental counter when he reached it, but the droop to her shoulders and the pinched look on the clerk's face told him something wasn't right. Amy confirmed it when she asked the woman for a local hotel. Now, he stared down at her pretty face and wide brown eyes.

"Is everything okay?"

The surprise on her face morphed into one of dismay, and she seemed to fold in on herself, making her already small frame look even smaller. "No. The clerk says the ranch I was supposed to stay at closed down last week."

"Closed? Weren't you notified?"

Amy shook her head, smoothing her hand down her pony-tail. "No. I don't know what I'm going to do now. I'll probably stay in Brisbane tonight, then go from there."

"There aren't a lot of rooms left in any of the better hotels," the clerk interjected. "There's a big convention going on this week, so a lot of places are booked up."

Amy's shoulders fell. "Great." She turned back to the clerk. "I guess I'll just head out and stop somewhere along the coast tonight, then. Save myself calling around to find a room."

Alarm bells went off in Ezra's head. He did not like the idea of her running around a foreign country by herself without a concrete plan. There were too many unknowns, and even a well-developed nation like Australia could be danger-ous, especially for a lone female tourist.

He put his hand on her shoulder. "You can't just head off to no-man's-land. It's not safe, and you don't know the area."

She turned and looked up at him. Her brown eyes flashed fire. "You think I don't know that? But what other choice do I have? It's not like I plan to go to the seedy side of town and check into some pay-by-the-hour motel. I'll find a decent place. It just might be a few miles up the coast. I'll be fine. And who knows? Maybe this will turn out to be a good thing. I was debating going to the beach instead of the dude ranch before I booked things. Maybe this is fate's way of telling me what I really needed was a beach vacation. So, don't worry about me. I'll be okay."

Ezra shook his head. "I still don't like it. You're by yourself in a populated area. At least at that ranch, you could build relationships with the staff, who would help look out for you. But here? Any cretin out there could take advantage of you. You're such a slip of a thing they wouldn't have any trouble at all forcing you to do whatever they wanted."

Fire blazed to life in her eyes. Ezra realized he'd hit a nerve commenting on her size. But it was worth her wrath to watch the flames erupt. She was beautiful when she was happy. Spitting mad, she was one of those women who turned vibrantly gorgeous.

"I'll. Be. *Fine*," she growled through clenched teeth. She turned back to the clerk, who had been avidly watching their exchange. "I'll take that car now."

"No, she won't." Ezra stepped forward. He couldn't let her run off to parts unknown by herself. It'd haunt him forever.

"Ezra." She turned those fiery eyes on him again. "You cannot make decisions for me. This is my vacation, and I—"

"Come back to my sister's place with me."

Wait. Where did that idea come from?

He bit the corner of his mouth, but didn't retract the words. She looked as astonished as he felt. He wasn't even aware he was contemplating that idea until he said it aloud.

"I'm sorry, what?"

"You heard me." Though the idea surprised them both, it was what he wanted. It meant he got to spend more time with her, and it meant she was safe. "Come back to my sister's with me. She's got a huge place and she won't mind another guest. She'll probably be glad to have you, what with the new baby around. She could use the extra hands." He held out his hands and waved them, eyes widening. "Not that you'd be there to work." Ezra straightened and pinched the bridge of his nose, closing his eyes. "That didn't come out right."

Amy stared at him. "You think? And I barely know you, so why would I leave here with you? Were you not just cautioning me about all the 'cretins'"—she made air quotes—"out there who could take advantage of me? How do I know you aren't one of them? Just because you're gorgeous and claim to be in the military, doesn't make you safe."

Ezra's jaw worked, and he glanced away, gathering his thoughts. When he looked at her again, she had her hands on her hips and stared up at him like some pissed off fairy. "You're right. But first, I'm not lying about who I am." He reached into his back pocket and withdrew his wallet, opening it to take out his military ID. He showed it to Amy as well as the clerk, knowing it might make Amy feel better to have a witness. "And second"—he shoved the card back into his wallet—"look in my eyes and tell me you don't trust me. Tell me you don't see that all I want is for you to be safe."

A beat of silence passed between them as Amy searched his gaze. Ezra tried to put everything he was feeling into his eyes. Determination. Sincerity. Assurance. Passion. He did *not* want her wandering around by herself. It didn't matter that he'd only known her less than a day or that she shouldn't matter so much to him. He was having visions of her being attacked by some piece of scum that thought she was an easy mark.

She huffed. "So you are who you say you are, and you seem to want to be my protector. But why should I trust you? Conversing on a plane is one thing, but letting you take me to parts unknown? I just can't, Ezra."

He ground his molars, staring at her as he contemplated what to do. Letting her stay in Brisbane alone wasn't an option. "Fine. I'll call my sister and stay here for now."

"What? No, you can't."

"Of course I can. I can do whatever I want."

Amy's eyebrows drew down, forming a vee. "Don't be obtuse. You know what I mean. You're here to see her. Not babysit me. I'll be fine."

Ezra crossed his arms and shifted his feet, cocking out a hip. "I'm not leaving you in Brisbane with no plan. I'm staying at least through tonight. Until you make a plan."

She glared at him; her hands curled into fists at her sides.

Pops of color bloomed on her cheeks. She stamped her foot. "Fine."

A smile spread over his face as she whirled around and faced the clerk.

"I'll take my vehicle now," she said through clenched teeth.

Wide-eyed, the woman nodded. She sent a look at Ezra, amusement lighting her eyes. He knew they would be the talk of the office for the rest of the day. But he didn't care. Amy wasn't alone, and that was all that mattered.

While he waited on the rental agent to process things, he phoned his sister. Anna would be disappointed at the delay, but she'd understand.

The line rang several times before her cheery voice sounded in his ear.

"Hey, big brother. Are you on Australian soil?"

He couldn't hold back the grin at hearing her voice. "Yeah. We landed about half an hour ago. Hey, so, there's been a change of plans."

"Oh? What do you mean?"

"So, I met a woman on the plane. When we got here, she found out that the place she was supposed to stay at closed down unexpectedly, so now she's trying to figure out what to do, and she's by herself. I'm going to stay in Brisbane for a day or two and keep her company until she figures things out."

A beat of silence went by, then Anna chuckled. "I would say I'm surprised, but I'm not."

Ezra echoed her laugh. "I tried to convince her to come with me to your place—I know you have plenty of room—but she threw the 'you're a stranger' card at me."

"Good for her. If you manage to change her mind, though, she's welcome. It might be nice to have another woman to talk to. How old is she, anyway?"

His gaze strayed to Amy, and he looked her up and down,

his eyes lingering on her perfect backside highlighted by her black leggings. "I don't know. Late twenties, thirty. Younger than me, but not by much."

"Oh, yes. Definitely bring her. What does she do for a living? And why is she by herself on holiday?"

"She's a museum curator. And she said it's because she needed some time alone to figure things out."

"Oh, boy."

He could hear the misgivings creeping into his sister's voice. "It's nothing bad. She's contemplating a career change."

"To what?"

"Antiques dealer."

Amy glanced at him, the frown still on her face, but more curious now. She was listening to his end of the conversation.

Anna laughed. "I have to say, that is the kind of woman I never imagined you with."

His forehead wrinkled. "What do you mean?"

"I mean, most of your girlfriends are fellow officers. Or uniform chasers. You don't typically go for the serious, intellectual types."

He did when they looked like Amy. "Liz was serious and intellectual," he said, reminding her of his last girlfriend. They'd dated almost a year before calling it quits when she was assigned to a new base.

Anna scoffed. "Yeah. Serious about her career and how far your reputation could advance hers."

Ezra's lips pursed. She wasn't wrong. "Maybe, but she was still on the intellectual side."

Amy stepped away from the counter, keys in her hand.

"Hey, I need to go. I'll call you in a day or two and let you know what's happening."

"All right. Let me talk to this woman before you hang up. And don't put me on speaker."

He bit back a groan. God only knew what she'd tell Amy.

"Fine." He pulled the phone away from his ear and held it out to Amy. "It's my sister. She wants to talk to you."

Amy blinked, then looked at the phone, then back at him. "Why?"

"Probably to tell you I'm an overprotective caveman, but not to let that put you off."

The first inkling of a smile since he walked up twitched her lips. She took the phone.

"Hello?"

Ezra strained to hear, but only caught the low murmur of Anna's voice. He tapped his foot and shoved his hands in his pockets, waiting.

Amy's smile bloomed, and she cast a quick look at him before glancing away, chuckling softly. Ezra blew out a breath. At least whatever Anna said was putting her at ease.

A moment later, she hung up and handed him back the phone.

"What did she say?" He took the device and slid it into his pocket.

She looked down her nose at him, amusement shining in her eyes. "Nothing you need to know."

He groaned and shook his head. "Women." Reaching for the handle on his suitcase, he took a step toward the door. "Are you ready?"

"Yes."

"Perfect. Where are we going?"

The amusement on her face died. "I'm not quite sure. The clerk gave me a list of hotels nearby. How about we find my car, then see about finding some phone numbers?"

"Sounds good to me." He held out an arm behind her, urging her toward the exit.

Outside, they took the shuttle to the car rental lot and found the two-door compact Amy rented. They stowed their luggage—having to use the back seat as well as the trunk—then got in.

"Whew. It's hot in here." Amy started the engine and turned on the air-conditioning.

Ezra folded himself into the passenger seat, his knees pressed to the dash. With a grimace, he reached under the seat to find the release bar and lifted it, shoving the chair back as far as it would go. He still felt a bit like a pretzel, but it wasn't as bad.

"And it's still morning too." He fiddled with the vents, pointing them at his chest.

"I was hoping to avoid the worst of the heat, but apparently, October has other plans."

"It'll be hotter in the interior, too, if that's where you go. There won't be a breeze coming off the ocean."

She shrugged. "I packed shorts. Let's find a hotel. Maybe it'll have a pool." She took out her phone and opened her internet browser, typing in something.

Ezra took out his cell. "You read the number off and I'll call."

With a nod, she told him the first phone number. Ezra dialed and worked his way through the menu to reservations. It didn't take him long to discover the hotel was booked solid. Thanking the woman on the line, he hung up. "Next one."

They went through several major hotel chains with no luck.

"Maybe we should try outside of Brisbane." She switched to her map app. Her fingers flew over the screen as she typed. "Sunshine Coast has some decent places."

He lifted a shoulder. "Wherever."

She nodded. "Try this one." She rattled off a number.

Ezra dialed and went through the menu to get to reservations. "How many nights? I probably should have asked that before."

"One for now."

He nodded just as a male voice came over the line.

"Reservations. How may I help you?"

"Hi, I'm looking to book two rooms for tonight. Do you have any availability?"

"We do, yes." The man gave Ezra options and prices.

"We'll take two king rooms." He covered the receiver and glanced at Amy. "They were the cheapest."

She nodded.

"Can I have your name, please?"

"Ezra Chastain."

"Great. And I just need a credit card to hold the rooms."

Ezra lifted his hip and dug out his wallet.

"You can't pay for my room," Amy hissed.

He held up a finger, then opened the wallet and took out his credit card. Paying for both rooms was easier than trying to split them now over the phone. She could pay him back later. He read his card details to the man on the phone, then thanked him and hung up once the reservation was confirmed.

"You can't pay for my room," Amy repeated.

"You can buy lunch and dinner for me. Or just pay me back in cash. It was easier to book them with one card than to try to book them separately."

Her lips twisted, and she stared at him a beat. "Fine."

His mouth lifted on one side. He reached for the infotainment screen. "What's the address of that place?" He tapped the setup icon, found her phone, and connected it. She typed her password into her cell, then he went to the map app on the screen.

Amy read him the address. Ezra typed it in and directions appeared. "All right. We're all set. Are you ready for the beginning of your adventure?"

Amy huffed a laugh, her ire fading. "Yes." She sent him a bright smile. "Buckle up, flyboy."

Six

Amy drove out of the lot, trying not to notice the man squeezed into the passenger seat of her compact rental. She needed all her focus to be on the road. Driving on the left was new, and she didn't want it to end in disaster. Nerves made her palms sweaty, but she maneuvered them away from the airport and onto the highway heading north. Once they were in the flow of traffic, she relaxed a bit.

"You could have let me drive, you know. I've driven on the left before."

She glanced at Ezra. "Can't. Rental is in my name." A frown crossed her face as a thought occurred to her. "Wait. You were supposed to go to your sister's. How were you going to get there? You didn't mention the need to cancel a rental car."

"I was going to fly."

Her eyes widened. "You missed your flight for me? Oh, man."

He chuckled. "Not exactly. Anna's husband, Wayne, owns some small aircraft. He had one brought to Brisbane for some updates and repairs. I'm going to fly it back for him."

Owned some aircraft? "You said he owns a cattle station, right?"

Ezra nodded.

"Just how big is his place?"

He lifted a shoulder. "I'm not real sure. I know he runs about three thousand head of cattle, though."

Amy felt like her eyes were googling out of her face. Three *thousand* head? "That's a lot of cows." Amy knew a bit about cattle ranching from her studies. It took several acres to sustain one animal. She quickly did the math in her head. He had to have close to fifteen thousand acres of land to sustain that many cattle.

"It's a family business, I guess. Been in his family for generations, so they've got quite a spread built up."

"Still. That's nuts. How did your sister meet him?"

"She studied abroad here for a semester. Marine biology. He was going to school for agri-business. They just hit it off, and she applied to transfer. It took about a year, but she was accepted and granted a visa. They've been married about three years now.

"Did she finish her degree?"

"Yes, but she changed her major. She has a Ph.D. in wildlife biology. Now, she runs a rehabilitation center on the ranch."

"Really?" She glanced at him. "That's neat."

"Yeah. And she loves every minute."

"What do your parents think?"

"They're proud of her. Obviously, they wish she were closer, but they FaceTime a lot, and they visit. Anna goes home once a year, and they come to see her once a year."

"How come you haven't seen her in a while, then?"

"Because I live in Tennessee just over the border from my base in Kentucky, and our parents live near New Orleans. I haven't been able to get home when she's there."

"Oh." That made sense. "Do you have any other siblings?"

He shook his head. "You?"

She let out a little laugh. "I have three sisters."

"Oh, wow. Are you all close?"

"Yes. We're all spread apart, though. We try to do a group FaceTime a few times a month. We get our snacks and wine and close ourselves away from everyone and just talk."

"That sounds fun."

"It is." She hadn't been sure she'd be able to do that while she was here and it had been one of her few misgivings about the trip. But now that she wouldn't be at the dude ranch with its limited bandwidth, she might get to participate.

"Where do you fall in the age line?"

"With my sisters?"

He nodded.

"I'm the second oldest. Tess is about eighteen months older than me. Kylie is two years younger, then Eden is the youngest. She's about eighteen months younger than Kylie."

"Wow, you guys are pretty close in age. Anna's four years younger than me."

"So, early thirties?"

His head bobbed. "She's thirty. I just turned thirty-four in August."

"Oh, she is close to my age. I'll be twenty-eight in a little over a week."

His eyes widened. "Seriously? So, was this a birthday trip too?"

Her mouth twisted. "Not exactly." She changed lanes, going around a slow-moving truck, then glanced at him, debating whether to tell him the rest of why she was here. It wasn't a secret, but she didn't want to come off sounding pathetic.

Ezra raised an eyebrow. "There's more to your story. I can

see it on your face. But you don't have to share. I'll listen if you want to, but you don't have to."

Amy blew out a breath. Oh, hell. Why not? "I dumped my fiancé. He cheated on me, so I ended things. But we still see each other occasionally—not on a personal level." She held up a hand. "He's a park ranger, and sometimes, our jobs connect when we do outreach programs."

"Oh. Well, the man's an idiot. Are you—" He broke off and looked out the window, his mouth opening, then closing again.

Amy chuckled, knowing he was trying to come up with a tactful way to ask how she felt about her ex. "I don't still have feelings for him, if that's what you're wondering. Nor am I here trying to forget him. I meant what I said on the plane. I'm just trying to figure things out. Our breakup sort of precipitated something I was already contemplating. It just made me consider it more seriously."

He tipped his head. "Makes sense. Sort of like a mid-life crisis, but a smidge earlier."

She laughed. "Something like that."

"Would you stay in D.C.? If you opened a shop, I mean?"

"You know, I don't know. My parents and my oldest sister live in Georgia. Kylie's in Nashville. Only Eden is further away. She's in Texas, finishing her Master's degree. So I might go home to Georgia. That's something else I need to figure out." She waved a hand. "But enough about me. How did you manage to get a month's leave from the military?"

Ezra let out a snort and rolled his eyes. "Because I never take time off and have a bunch saved. I had to use it or lose it."

"Ah. A fellow workaholic."

A smile slashed over his face. "Something like that. I was getting burnt out, though. So, this break is about more than just visiting my sister and meeting my niece." He shifted, a cloud coming over his face. "Too much on the go. I'm an adrenaline junkie, but the constant barrage of dangerous missions was getting to be too much. I needed a break."

Amy could see how that could wear on a person. She wouldn't want to always be keyed up. It would make her a basket case.

"So, what did my sister say to you?"

She glanced at him with a coy smile. "Nothing bad."

"Oh, please. I know my sister. She probably told you all sorts of things. I'm surprised she didn't text you embarrassing photos of me."

Amy laughed harder. "I got that vibe, yes. And you're safe. She just told me to trust you. That she understood where I was coming from, but you're one of the good guys."

"Is that why you let me in your car without question?"

"Partly. I also wanted help navigating." She shot him a sheepish smile. Truthfully, she wasn't that upset he'd stuck around. She might have talked a good game and said she'd be fine on her own, but the thought of not having a plan—or even knowing where she would go once she walked out of the airport doors—was daunting. It was nice having an anchor, even if she was a little leery. He hadn't given her any creeper vibes on the flight over. He actually seemed quite nice. But riding in a car—which she controlled—was much different from jetting off with him in a small plane to the interior of Australia.

He gave a soft laugh. "Well, I'm glad to be of service." He cleared his throat and sat up, looking at the screen. "You need to turn in approximately five miles."

Chuckling, she shot him an amused look. "Funny."

"I try." He laid a hand on his chest.

Mood lightened significantly from when they left the airport, Amy concentrated on the traffic and soon navigated them off the freeway and onto surface streets to their hotel.

She pulled into the parking lot and found a space near the entrance.

"If you want to wait here, I'll check us in."

She lifted an eyebrow. "I'll come with you. See if they can split the rooms onto two different cards."

He raised a shoulder. "Suit yourself." He pulled on the door handle and got out.

Amy followed him, stopping long enough to flip the front seat down and yank her orange suitcase out of the backseat. Ezra grabbed his duffel. She popped the trunk, and they took out their last two bags and their backpacks.

"Here." Ezra hooked a hand around her backpack strap and pulled it down her arm. "Give me that." He put it over his shoulder, then held out his hand. "The suitcases too."

Amy blinked several times, staring. "You know, I've got two hands." She held them out for his perusal.

He smiled. "You can get the door." He tipped his head toward the hotel.

"It's automatic."

His smile grew. "You can close the trunk, then."

She sighed, gave him another look, then put one hand on the trunk hatch and closed it. "Happy?"

"As pie. Let's go." He spun her stacked suitcases around and headed for the door.

Amy gave a short huff, staring at his broad back. Men.

She followed him, shaking her head. Though she didn't know why she was complaining. It was kind of nice to have a man offer to carry her things. Andy never did.

And she couldn't help but admire the view as they walked. His muscles bulged beneath his t-shirt as he carried all that weight. *Yum*... And that butt! Whoever invented jeans was a genius. Ezra's hugged his ass like a second skin. She deliberately walked at her normal pace rather than scurrying after him just so she could watch him walk. He really was a stagger-ingly handsome man.

Get a hold of yourself, Amelia!

She rolled her eyes at herself and hurried to catch up. Fantasizing about Ezra wouldn't solve any of her problems. It would just create more.

The hotel doors swished open, admitting them to the building. They walked to the check-in desk, where a young man with sun-bleached curly hair greeted them with a smile.

"Hello. Checking in?"

Amy nodded, but Ezra spoke first.

"I called about an hour ago and made a reservation. Ezra Chastain?"

The man typed his name into the computer. "Yes, I have it here. Your rooms aren't ready yet, but you're welcome to leave your luggage with us and come back in a few hours. I can offer you some maps of the area and some recommendations on places to eat."

Amy bit back a groan. She just wanted a shower and to sit somewhere she wasn't moving.

Ezra glanced at her, the downward tilt to his mouth telling her he'd sensed her displeasure. Or that he was also unhappy they couldn't go to their rooms. He turned back to the clerk. "That sounds fine."

"Are you able to separate the rooms into two reserva-tions?" Amy asked. "I'd like to pay for my own."

"I can, but it will incur a cancellation fee on his card."

She grimaced. "Never mind." She glanced at Ezra. "All your food and drinks today are on me." Her gaze returned to the young man behind the desk. "Could you print two copies of the receipt, so I know how much it was? This one"—she pointed at Ezra—"will probably fold it up and stuff it in his pocket before I can see it and then refuse to show it to me."

An amused glint lit the man's eyes. "Of course. Give me just one moment." His fingers worked the keyboard, entering information, then the printer behind him spit out two sheets of paper. He took them from the tray, then wrote on one before passing them over the counter. "I've written on here that you need keys and that we have your luggage. I'll give you some valet tags for the bags as well. When you come back, show that to whoever is at the desk, and they'll finish your check-in process."

Ezra nodded. Amy took the paper and glanced at the total. It wasn't bad. But it was more than she was paying per day at the dude ranch. She would need to find cheaper accommodations.

The young man came around the desk with some paper tags in his hand. He attached one to each suitcase, then tore off the bottom and handed those to Ezra. "You're all set. Our normal check-in time is three o'clock, but your rooms might be ready as early as two. You can call and ask before you come back, if you'd like. The hotel's direct number is on your receipt."

"Great, thank you." Ezra offered him a smile.

"You're welcome. And don't forget your maps." The man rounded the desk and took several brochures from a rack on the wall. He passed them over the counter. "We have lots of things to do in the area, and today's weather is gorgeous, so you shouldn't have any problems staying occupied. You're also welcome to come back and hang out in our lobby until your rooms are ready if you just want to sit and relax."

Amy picked up the pamphlets and leafed through them. There were indeed many things to do. But right now, the beach sounded great. She stepped back, lifting the brochures in a wave. "I'm sure we'll find something. Thank you."

The young man nodded, coming around the counter again to collect their luggage. Amy turned and headed for the door, Ezra on her heels.

"So, anything look interesting in those?"

Amy lifted the flyers in her hand and leafed through them. "Kinda. Can we hit up the beach, though? Sand, sun, and waves sound fabulous."

"Sure."

They made their way back to the car and used the map the clerk gave them to get them to a local beach. It was only a couple of miles away. Amy pulled into the parking lot, which was only partially full. Despite the heat, it was mid-morning during the week. She imagined this place was much busier on the weekends.

Getting out of the vehicle, they walked toward the path that led down to the beach, pausing at the top to remove their shoes and socks and roll up their pant legs. With their socks stuffed in their shoes and their footwear hooked over their fingers, they walked down the narrow boardwalk.

Warm sand squished between Amy's toes. Peace washed over her, and some of the tension lining her shoulders disappeared. She was in Australia. *Australia*. It was finally hitting. A joyous laugh bubbled up. She tipped her face to the sky and let it out. "This is amazing!" Spinning around, she bestowed a bright smile on Ezra. "Last one to the water is a rotten egg!" She took off, not waiting for him to respond.

"Hey!"

Laughing, she glanced back at his shout. He wasn't far behind; his long legs ate up the ground much faster than hers. In moments, he passed her, splashing into the surf.

"I'd say you owe me lunch, but since you're already buying..." He flashed her a grin.

Amy rolled her eyes, reaching the water. "How about you get to pick the next place we go?"

"Deal." He nodded. A moment later, a devilish gleam entered his eyes.

She held up a finger and backed away, seeing the mischievousness blossoming on his handsome face. He wanted to dunk her. "No. Don't you dare. All my clothes are at the hotel."

Grinning, he reached down and scooped a handful of water in her direction.

Amy squealed and put her hands up, blocking the spray. "Oh!" Laughing, she splashed him back. The water was warmer than she thought it would be. The spray felt good on her skin.

But still, she didn't want to get too wet. Dashing out of the water, she stopped at the edge of the wet sand, waving her hands. "No more. I don't want to walk around in soaked clothes."

He pouted, but straightened, jogging toward her. "Party pooper. Fine. No more water play. Do you want to walk? Or just sit?"

"We can walk." Now that reality had hit, her earlier fatigue was gone. She was ready to explore.

His head bobbed in a short nod. "Lead the way."

Amy turned and headed down the beach. They strolled in silence, letting the crashing waves fill it. With every step, she felt more relaxed. She still needed to figure out where to go, but the beauty surrounding her helped calm her anxiety. All would work out fine, she was sure.

"You know..." Ezra glanced at her. "We never formally introduced ourselves."

Her eyes rounded, and she stopped. "We didn't, did we?"

He shook his head, holding out a hand. "I'm Ezra Chastain."

"Amelia Preston." She took his hand. Warmth raced up her arm the moment their palms connected.

A corner of his mouth curved up. "Amelia, huh? I like that."

Amy felt her cheeks heat as a blush stole over them. She let go of his hand. "Thanks."

"Why the nickname? Amelia is pretty."

She lifted a shoulder. "It's what my parents always called me. Amelia was saved for when I was in trouble."

He chuckled. "I always got my middle name added to my first."

"Oh, I did too. For when I did something extra egregious."

Another deep chuckle rumbled from his chest. "Well, it's nice to meet you, Amelia. I'm glad your plans got screwed up." He flashed her a sunny smile.

She couldn't help but smile back. "You know, I'm not that upset. Not anymore, at least. I wanted adventure. I guess I've found it."

"You certainly have."

They resumed their walk, lapsing back into silence. When sweat broke out on her skin, Amy moved out of the wet sand. "How about we take a break?"

"Sure."

She sat. Ezra sank down beside her, close enough their shoulders brushed. Amy found she didn't mind. He was growing on her.

"So, what do you want to do next?" His low voice rumbled in her ear.

The wind blew the fine hairs around her face free of her ponytail, whipping them over her eyes. She scooped them back and looked at him. "It's your turn to choose. Though I'm happy if we stay here a while." She squinted at him. "I don't think you are, though." He had his knees drawn up and his arms wrapped around them. The fingers of one hand drummed against the back of the other.

A sheepish smile flitted over his mouth. "I'm just not used to sitting still. I was dreading the flight over, but having you to talk to made it bearable."

Heat returned to her face. "Oh, well, we can keep talking." She chewed on her bottom lip. "I like talking to you."

His smile grew. "Yeah? Well, good. What should we talk about?"

Amy shrugged. She drew up her knees, mimicking his pose. "Tell me about your job. It sounds interesting."

"It can be. A lot of it I can't talk about. It's all classified. But I meet some interesting people and go to some really cool places. I've seen more sand than I ever thought I would. And I'm from coastal Louisiana, so that's saying something."

"It's a different kind of sand, though. This—" she scooped up a handful of sand and let it fall through her fingers. "This is the good kind. Where there are ocean waves and a warm breeze. Desert sand—" She broke off and shook her head. "I couldn't imagine living in some of those places you've been. That's a hard life."

He nodded. "They're resilient over there, I'll give them that."

"What's the coolest place you've been?"

"South America."

She chuckled. "Boy, you said that fast."

Ezra smiled. "Because it's true. I've flown several missions with the SEALs in some of the northern South American countries. The Amazon is unlike any other place on Earth. And Carnival in Rio is—" he lifted a hand, fluttering it through the air. "It's incredible. Mardi Gras is amazing, but Carnival?" He shook his head. "Nothing could beat it." He leaned closer and lowered his voice. "Don't tell some of my friends back home I said that."

Amy grinned. "Sacrilege?"

"Oh, yeah."

"I went to Mardi Gras once." She stared out at the water, thinking about her time in New Orleans several years ago.

"Really? What did you think?"

"That it was an amazing experience, but not one I'd want to repeat." She gave a soft laugh. "Too many people for my taste. And booze. Too much booze. I'm not a big drinker." She wrinkled her nose. "But my friends kept shoving pints into my hand. Stupid me kept sipping. I've never been so drunk."

"You stayed safe, though, right?" His bright blue eyes shone with concern. "Nothing happened to you?"

"Yeah, I was fine. We stuck together and stayed close to our hotel. Most of the night, we were at a bar right around the corner from it. When the party ended, we stumbled back and all of us passed out. I went with a group of girls my senior year of college."

"Good. The bar scene can get pretty wild, from what I've heard. I haven't actually been to Mardi Gras as an adult. I'm glad you played it safe."

She turned her head to stare at him. "Really? You've never been drinking on Bourbon Street during the biggest party of the year?"

"Really." He nodded. "I left for college and could never get away to go back. After I graduated, I went straight into the military. They've kept me busy ever since. The only reason I went to Carnival was because I was already down there."

"Huh." She stared at him. "Who'd have thought a local boy wouldn't party at Mardi Gras?"

His quiet laugh joined hers. "Right? I guess I'm just not much of a partier."

"Me, either. That was the wildest I'd ever been. And the most adventure I'd ever had. Until now."

A long beat of silence passed.

"Have you thought about where you want to go?"

Amy shook her head. "Not really. I need to get online and do some research. I just know I can't stay at the hotel we booked. It's more per night than the ranch."

"Well, my offer still stands. You're welcome to come to Anna's with me."

She nodded, staring at the waves. "I appreciate it. I still think I want to go my own way, though." But why did that idea make her heart hurt?

Her gaze strayed to the man next to her, knowing he was behind a lot of it. She didn't want to leave him behind. Which was ridiculous. Someone she just met shouldn't have such an effect on her. Sure, he was gorgeous. And nice. And easy to talk to. They could exchange phone numbers and continue to talk. She was here for herself. Not to start something with a guy. But she'd be damned if she didn't get a thrill thinking about spending time with him over the next month—what that could lead to.

Suddenly warm again, Amy shot to her feet. "I'm ready for our next stop. How about you?" Not waiting for an answer, she took off down the beach the way they came. She strayed back into the water lapping the sand, hoping it would cool her off. But she knew that while it might cool her body, it wouldn't cool her developing feelings.

Honestly, though, did she want it to? Because how often did a man like Ezra come around?

She didn't have an answer for that. It was just one more thing for her to add to her list to figure out.

SEVEN

Buzzing woke Ezra. He lifted his head from his pillow, raising an arm to slap at the alarm clock, only to realize it was his phone vibrating on the nightstand. Groaning, he reached for it and blinked, clearing the sleep from his eyes so he could see the screen. It was his sister.

He slid his thumb over the screen and answered. "Hello?"

"Ezra, do you know when you'll be headed this way?"

Something about the tone of Anna's voice caught his attention. He shifted, sitting up. "Not yet. What's wrong? And don't say nothing. I can hear it in your voice."

Her shaky inhalation came over the line. "Wayne. He—" She stopped and sniffed, taking another breath. "He was checking livestock this morning and got trampled. He's been air-lifted to Darwin. I need you, Ezra. Please, can you come?" Her voice wobbled.

A surge of adrenaline wiped away all traces of sleep from Ezra's brain. "Of course. I'll be on my way in the next couple of hours. Do you want me to fly to you or meet you in Darwin?"

"Come here. It'll be faster to wait on you and have you fly

us to Darwin than it would be for me to drive there. I'd ask one of Wayne's parents to fly me, but they're out of town. So is his brother, Jericho. There isn't another pilot here."

"Don't worry. I'm on my way. I'll text you when I'm getting ready to take off."

She sniffed again. "Okay."

Ezra closed his eyes, his heart clenching at the pain in her voice. He clutched the phone tighter, wishing he was already there. "You hang in there. I'll be there as soon as humanly possible, all right?"

"I know. Thank you."

"You don't need to thank me, Anna. I'll see you soon."

"Okay. Fly safe."

"I will. Love you."

"Love you too. Bye."

He echoed her goodbye and hung up, then launched into action. Getting up, he threw on his clothes, then hurried through brushing his teeth. Not bothering to shave, he tossed all his toiletries into their bag, then stowed it in his backpack. Next, he wadded up his dirty clothes and shoved them into the laundry sack he brought and pushed it into the corner of his duffel. With a quick glance around the room to make sure he didn't miss anything, he grabbed his room key and ran across the hall to Amy's room. He hated to leave her before she'd decided where she was going, but he had to put Anna first.

Knocking on her door, he called her name. When she didn't answer, he tried again, louder. "Amy? It's Ezra. Open the door."

He heard her fumble with the lock, then the door swung open. For a moment, he forgot why he knocked. She had on a long t-shirt that just skimmed the tops of her thighs, and from the looks of it, not much else underneath.

"What? It's not even eight o'clock yet. We weren't supposed to meet for breakfast until nine."

"I know." When they parted ways after dinner last night, they'd agreed to meet for breakfast in the hotel restaurant this morning. "Anna called. Her husband's been injured in a farming accident. I need to go."

Amy's eyes widened. "Oh no. Badly?" She waved her hand. "Of course it's bad. You wouldn't be waking me up and telling me you're leaving if it wasn't." She bit her lip. "Hang on."

The door shut in his face. Ezra blinked. He raised a fist and knocked again. "Amy."

"Just a second. I'm putting some pants on."

Lord have mercy. He did not need that visual.

A moment later, the door swung open. She'd donned another pair of leggings and pulled a sweater over her t-shirt. "Sorry. Standing in the doorway and having such a serious conversation in my pajamas felt weird." She grabbed his arm and pulled him inside. "You're leaving now?"

He nodded. "I'm all packed. I just stopped to tell you I was going. I wish I could stay, but—"

She waved her hand again. "No, I get it. You need to go. I'll be okay." She sucked that bottom lip between her teeth again.

Despite her brave words, Ezra could tell she was nervous to be on her own. "You can call me whenever you want. If I don't answer, I will always call you back or text you to let you know I can't talk." So long as he had a signal. He would in Darwin, but Dalton Creek was pretty remote. He made a mental note to text her his email address. It might be a better form of communication.

"I know." She added a finger to the chewing action, biting the nail.

"Did you come up with a plan for where you're going?" When he dropped her at her door, she said she intended to come up with an idea of how she would spend at least the first week of her time here before she went to bed. He'd feel better leaving her if he knew she had a solid plan.

"Sort of. I thought I'd stick around here for a week. Soak up some sun. Although—" she broke off and paced toward the window, glancing out.

Ezra's brows dipped, wondering what she was thinking. "Although, what?"

She turned to him. "Maybe I should come with you."

His eyes widened. "I thought you didn't want to jet off with a stranger."

"Right, but if you were going to hurt me, you'd have done it already. You had ample opportunity yesterday. And maybe I could help?" She raised her hands, palms up. "I mean, she'll have a baby and an injured husband to take care of once he's home. You'll be there, obviously, but it's always better to have extra hands when you need them."

"Oh." Ezra squared his shoulders and tipped his head as a thought struck. "You're not running from making decisions about your life, are you?" He'd noticed while they were out yesterday that every time he brought up her life, she steered the conversation to something else.

"No. I'm sure I'll have plenty of downtime to think about things." She put her hands on her hips. "Why are you arguing with me about this? You wanted me to come with you. Now that I've agreed, you're trying to convince me to stay?" She narrowed her eyes. "Are you having second thoughts?"

"No." He'd be thrilled to have her along. It would be one less thing for him to worry about. "I just want you to be sure."

She crossed her arms. "Well, I am."

Ezra studied her for another long moment, then gave a short nod. "Okay. Get your stuff."

Amy dropped her hands and walked to her suitcase. Digging inside, she pulled out several items, then zipped it closed. "If you want, to save time, you can take all our stuff down to the car except for my orange case and my backpack and check us out. It won't take me long to change."

He reached for the handle of her bright green bag. "Works for me." He needed a minute alone, anyway. The sight of the balled-up lace in her hand was threatening to derail his thoughts. Despite the situation, she set his blood on fire. The warmth wasn't unwelcome, but now wasn't the time or place for it.

Spinning on his heel, he grabbed the car keys from the dresser and marched toward the door. "I'll see you downstairs."

Eight

Amy smoothed her damp palms over her thighs as she left the airport terminal for the second time in two days. They'd just turned in her rental car and were headed for the shuttle station to take a bus to the private hangars.

What was she doing? Was it lunacy to be getting into a plane with Ezra at the controls? She wasn't questioning his ability to fly. She doubted the people they were about to meet would let him in the cockpit, let alone off the ground, if he didn't have the right credentials. But she was putting her life in his hands. Being in a foreign country with no plan was bad enough, but now she was about to fly into the Australian interior with a man she met two days ago. Her family would flip if they knew.

But she trusted him. She knew it was crazy, but he'd given her no reason not to. The entire time they'd been together, he'd never once tried anything untoward. He was always the perfect gentleman. If it wasn't for the spark of—something—she saw in his eyes every once in a while, it would give her a complex. No woman wanted a man like him to look at her and not feel something. He was the kind of guy women chased.

Not her, though. No. She didn't chase men. But if she were the type, he'd be one she would chase.

A white shuttle bus pulled up. Ezra stepped onto the first stair and told the driver where they needed to go. The man nodded and motioned them on. Amy followed Ezra aboard and sat down by the window behind the driver. Her body went on full alert when Ezra sat next to her, leaning over to get out of the way of people boarding. When he finally sat up, she was dizzy from the increased blood flow to her brain, courtesy of her rapidly beating heart. She turned her attention to the view outside the window and tried to slow her heart rate and her breathing.

The bus lurched forward, and they were off, making a circuit through the various parking lots, divulging passengers and picking up new ones along the way. Finally, they reached the private hangar entrance, where she and Ezra got off.

"How are we supposed to get in?"

Ezra took his passport and a laminated card from his back pocket. "Wayne left my name with security. You're my passenger." He walked up to the small building beside the gate and knocked on the door's window.

A man in a black uniform emerged from a door inside. He opened the outer door. "Hello. Can I help you?"

"Yes." Ezra held out his passport and the card. "I'm here to fly a plane back to Dalton Creek for my brother-in-law, Wayne Dalton."

The man looked at Ezra's identification, then ducked inside the guard shack. "Just a moment."

Amy saw him pick up a binder and leaf through it, then set it down and come back out.

"You're good to go." He held out Ezra's ID. "She flying with you?"

"Yes. As a passenger."

"Ma'am, do you have ID?"

Amy dug into her purse and produced her passport. The guard examined it, then handed it back.

"The plane's in hangar seven. Do you know the tail numbers?"

Ezra nodded. "Wayne said the keys would be with the mechanics who worked on it. Are they in the same hangar?"

The guard nodded.

"Okay, great." Ezra offered the man a smile.

"Yep. Have a safe flight and tell Wayne Eric said hello."

"I will."

The guard stepped back into the building and pressed a button. The metal gate blocking the drive slid open. Ezra motioned for Amy to proceed him, and they rolled their luggage through. It was a hot, five-minute walk across the tarmac to the maintenance hangar from there. They entered through a side door. Amy blinked, trying to bring the darker interior into focus. The sun outside was bright.

"Can I help you?"

Amy turned at the male voice to her right. A man in a gray work shirt stepped away from a plane with the engine exposed.

"Hi." Ezra held out a hand. "Ezra Chastain. I'm here to pick up a Piper M350 for Wayne Dalton."

"Ah, the brother-in-law. Right." The man nodded and shook Ezra's hand. "Follow me." He led them to a small office on the right side of the hangar. Inside, he snagged a set of keys off the pegboard on the wall. "I just need some photo ID and your signature on some paperwork."

Ezra handed the man his passport and the laminated card, taking a clipboard in return. He flipped through the papers, stopping to study several things, then scrawled his name on the last page.

"Did you understand the work we did?"

"Yep. Seemed pretty straightforward. You'll give me copies of that to give to Wayne, right?"

The mechanic nodded. He took the clipboard and gave Ezra his documents. "Give me a moment to make copies."

"Can we load up?"

"Sure." He passed the keys to Ezra. "It's out front on the left, near the bay doors."

"Thanks."

Again, Amy followed Ezra, this time to a plane painted white with a gold stripe down the side and a logo proclaiming the cattle station's name stamped in the middle.

"It looks brand-new." She eyed the gleaming aircraft.

"It does. But it's not. It's just been well-maintained. Wayne had it here to get routine work done on it. The paperwork said they also replaced a hydraulic line for the rudder." He looked at the keys in his hand and chose one, using it to unlock a compartment on the side of the plane. Pocketing the keys, he lifted their suitcases into the hold, then shut the door. "You can get in while I do my pre-flight." He took the keys out again and unlocked the door to the cabin. Lowering the steps, he backed away.

Amy climbed inside, glancing around. Tan leather seats and wood trim decorated the cabin. In here, too, it looked new. It was hard to imagine a cattle rancher flying in such a nice plane. When she thought of that occupation, she thought of dirt and manure. This plane was spotless. And it was nicer than her car.

She let out a soft snort. Why that surprised her, she didn't know. It shouldn't. It was a plane. Not everyone owned a plane. Of course it would be elegantly appointed.

Settling into a seat, she looked out the window. Planes taxied beyond the hangars. Across the field, larger jets moved, and she watched a jetliner land.

Movement at the rear of the plane caught her attention. She turned, trying to see better, and caught a glimpse of Ezra inspecting the tail section. The murmur of his voice reached her as he spoke to someone, then a few minutes later, he climbed inside.

"You can sit up front with me, if you'd like. But I completely understand if you want to stay back here. The cockpit isn't the place for everyone." He moved toward the front of the aircraft.

"Actually, that sounds like fun. I like to fly." She moved up behind him.

Ezra pointed to the right. "You can sit there." He moved back to let her get in.

"Thanks." She squeezed between the seats and sat down, careful not to touch anything. Ezra folded his long frame into the seat beside her.

"I need to let Anna know we're on our way, then we can go." He removed his phone from his pocket and sent a text, then put it in the pocket on the wall to his left. "You ready?" He looked at Amy.

She nodded. "Yes."

"Okay, then. Let's get rolling." He started flipping switches. The single propeller spun to life, filling the cockpit with a roar.

"Here." Ezra reached over her to pluck a headset off the wall to her right. "Put this on."

Amy took it and settled it over her ears, adjusting the microphone.

"Better?" His voice came through her headset, and she nodded.

"Good."

Over the next few minutes, he checked gauges and entered information into the flight computer. When he radioed the tower for permission to taxi, she jumped when static and then an unfamiliar voice filled her ears. Smiling sheepishly, she looked at Ezra. She hadn't expected to be able to hear anyone but him.

The controller gave Ezra permission to taxi to the runway. Amy gripped the arms on her seat and stared straight ahead. She was excited, but also nervous. While she liked to fly, she'd never been in a plane this small or seen take off from this perspective.

"You doing okay?" Ezra glanced at her.

She nodded. "I'm fine."

It took them several minutes to reach the runway devoted to light aircraft. Ezra radioed their position to the tower and asked to take off. The controller gave it, and he pushed the throttle forward. The engine revved and their slow roll shifted to high speed. She dug her nails into the rich leather and watched as the ground disappeared beneath them as they went airborne.

In what seemed like no time, they were high above the Australian countryside, leaving Brisbane far behind. Amy stared out the window, fascinated by what she saw below. Winding rivers bordered by lush forests would suddenly give way to a tan landscape dotted intermittently by trees and scrub brush, then return to a deep emerald green. Every once in a while, a town would pop up below, tiny dots of life on the landscape.

The first part of their journey passed in silence. She was too busy soaking up the sights to talk. Before long, they were passing from the lush forest to mountains, the tall rocky peaks jutting toward them. The mountains soon gave way to rust red sand dunes and plains sparsely dotted with trees.

"Have you ever had this vantage point from a plane before? From the cockpit?" Ezra asked.

Amy tore her gaze away from the ground below to answer him. "No. I've only ever flown commercially. This is awesome. I can see now why you're such a junkie."

Ezra chuckled. "It is pretty great."

Amy turned back to the window. "How long have you

been flying? I know you said you've been in the Army twelve years. Is that when you started flying?"

Ezra shook his head. "Since I was in high school. I was fifteen when I started taking lessons. I got my small craft license the same week I got my driver's license."

"What made you choose the military? Why not fly for a private firm? Or just for fun?"

"I knew as soon as I started taking lessons I wanted to be a pilot. It wasn't something I wanted to do just in my spare time. As for the military part, I figured out by the end of high school that I wanted to play with all the latest gadgets and that I loved flying helicopters. I got that license just before graduation." He glanced at her. "When I took my chopper lessons, I got the chance to go up in a Huey. I was a goner from there. Military choppers are a million times more fun to fly than civilian ones."

"Why the Army, then? Why not the Air Force?"

"I figured if I was going to be a chopper pilot, I should shoot for the elite, you know? I wanted to be one of those guys who could hover at the edge of a cliff to extract special operators from sketchy situations." He lifted a shoulder. "Night Stalkers are the best of the best."

He turned to look at her. "What about you? What made you want to become a curator?"

Amy smiled, thinking back. "I didn't start out wanting to be one. I was an I.T. major when I started college. Then I took a history class on early American history as an elective and I was hooked. The professor I had made it seem like history was a living, breathing thing. I knew I wanted to be like that. I wanted to show others how history could come alive. I switched my major and never looked back."

Ezra frowned slightly. "Why curatorial work, then, instead of teaching?"

Amy laughed. "I'm horrible at public speaking. Even now,

anytime I have to give a presentation at a staff meeting, I um and uh my way through it."

Ezra chuckled. "I guess I'd pick museum studies, then, too."

Amy looked out the window again as Ezra banked the plane to the left. "So how much further do we have to go?"

Ezra glanced at the instrument panel. "About another hour or so." He looked at her. "You wanna fly for a bit?"

Amy's eyebrows shot skyward. "Seriously?"

He nodded. "I need to check the map and make sure I have the right heading to line us up with the station's airstrip."

"Okay. What do I do?" Amy sat up a little straighter in her seat. Her eyes roved over the gauges and dials in front of her. She didn't know what any of them were for. Except the one with the plane and the horizon line and the one that said altitude.

"Take hold of the yoke and just keep it steady. It's like driving a car, just with four directions controlled by the wheel instead of two."

Amy wrapped her hands around the yoke in front of her. She loved to fly, but she never thought she'd actually get to fly a plane on her own. Palms sweating, she readjusted her grip, her nerves tempering her excitement.

"Good," Ezra said. "That's good. Now, there's a little ball instrument in front of you that has a pair of wings on it. You want to make sure you keep the wings level."

Amy nodded. Her gaze bounced between the view outside and the instrument. She could do this. Like driving a car. Right. The yoke moved a little more than the wheel of her car, but it wasn't that different.

She spared a glance at Ezra. He was bent over the map with a pencil in his hand and some kind of instrument laid over the map. It didn't take him long to figure out what he wanted. He made a notation in a small notebook and looked up at her.

"Relax." He chuckled. "We won't fall out of the sky."

Amy frowned and looked down at her hands. Her knuckles were white from gripping the yoke so hard. She made a conscious effort to loosen her fingers, then rolled her shoulders, trying to release some tension. *Driving a car. It's just like driving a car.* She repeated the mantra over in her head, then shot him a self-conscious smile. "Sorry. It's just a bit nerve-wracking to be flying a plane for the first time."

Ezra nodded. "It can be, yeah." He gestured out the window. "The weather's good, though. As long as you don't lean way forward or pull way back on the yoke, we'll be fine." He sat back in his seat and tossed the map and notebook in the pocket beside him. Propping his hands behind his head, he spread his feet wide. "You're doing great. I'm going to just sit back and relax for a while. You can fly us the rest of the way. I'll take over when we need to start turning." He paused for a beat. "Unless you want me to take over?"

Amy quickly shook her head. "I'm good. This is fun. Especially now that I'm relaxing a bit. You're right, it's not much different than driving a car. The steering's a little looser, but other than that, it's not too bad."

They flew in comparative silence for the next few minutes. Amy concentrated on what she was doing while Ezra watched the scenery.

And her.

Every so often, she could feel his eyes on her. She knew part of it was because he was checking to make sure she was doing alright. But that wasn't all of it. She could feel the heat.

She looked over at him and caught the fire blazing in his eyes. It was simmering just under the surface of his contemplative expression. Amy turned her eyes back to the controls. What she wouldn't give to know what he was thinking.

This was going to be an interesting vacation.

Suddenly, the plane shuddered and Amy heard a sputtering noise. Ezra sat up in an instant, his eyes scanning all the dials and gauges in front of him.

"What's going on?" Amy asked.

"We're losing fuel. Quickly." He put one hand on the yoke and gestured at the fuel gauge with the other. The needle was rapidly heading toward empty.

Amy let go of the yoke and sat back, not wanting to get in his way.

Ezra peered out the windshield to look at the ground below. "We're going to have to land."

"What? Out here? There's nothing. For miles and miles." Amy couldn't believe what she was hearing. Other than meeting Ezra, this vacation was turning out to be a disaster.

"We either land out there"—he pointed out the window —"or we crash a little further away. The ground looks fairly flat and there certainly aren't any trees we have to worry about, so we should be fine."

Amy pressed her fingers to her temples, trying to absorb what he was telling her. They were going down. Literally in the middle of nowhere. "I can't believe this is happening. Didn't you say this plane had been repaired recently? Why is it leaking fuel if that's the case?"

Ezra continued scanning the ground as he answered. "I'm not sure. Maybe a loose fuel line. I checked for leaks before we took off, but didn't see anything. Engine vibrations could have loosened it until it came free." He spared her a glance. "Tighten your seat belt. It's gonna get bumpy."

Nine

Amy started praying fervently as Ezra pushed the yoke forward. As they descended, he called out a mayday, but no one answered. All she heard was static.

The engine gave one last hiccup, then completely died. Without the engine noise, it was deathly quiet inside the plane. All she heard was the whoosh of the wind rushing past and the thud of her own heartbeat.

The plane went into a dive, and Amy gripped the armrests so hard she left deep dents in the leather with her nails.

"Sorry." Ezra's voice was tight. "We need to land. I don't have any engine thrust to reduce the propeller to slow us down. That's the river." He nodded toward the horizon. "We're descending too fast to make it over it, but I still need room to stop us."

Amy glanced out the windscreen, but quickly turned away as the ground rushed ever closer. Watching Ezra's face was much less nerve-wracking than watching the ground come up to meet them. She analyzed the hard planes of his face and the clench to his jaw. His intense concentration on the task of putting them safely on the ground calmed her. She could almost see the gears turning in his mind as he calculated how much space they'd need to land and where would be the best place to put down.

He reached between them and pulled a lever. Amy heard the landing gear come down.

She closed her eyes and prayed harder than she ever had in her life. The plane's nose lifted, then a moment later, the back wheels touched the ground. The aircraft bounced like it was on a trampoline. Amy's eyes popped open, and she bit back a scream.

Ezra fought for control and set the back wheels down again. This time, they stayed. He eased the nose down. They had rolled about a hundred yards when Amy saw a wide crack in the earth twenty yards in front of them. There was no way to avoid it. She clutched the armrests tighter and squeezed her eyes shut.

The nose gear hit the crack, slipped down, and stuck. The plane pitched forward, throwing Amy against her seatbelt and pushing the air from her lungs. She slammed back into the seat as the nose rammed into the ground. The screech of shearing metal drowned out her scream, and the nose gear ripped free of the plane; the fuselage continued to slide along the ground. She kept her eyes closed, waiting for it to end.

After what seemed like a lifetime, they came to a halt. Ears ringing from the noise and now the sudden silence, she swallowed hard and blinked.

Thick gray tendrils of smoke drifted up from under the front of the plane. The friction from their slide had lit the fuel residue on fire. Eyes wide, she stared at it.

"Amy. Unbuckle. We need to get out."

She blinked again, gaze still locked on the rising smoke. Ezra's voice registered, but his words didn't.

"Amy!"

A large hand landed on her shoulder and shook her. She turned to Ezra, her brain fog lifting.

"We need to get out of the plane. Now. Unbuckle." Ezra already had his seatbelt undone.

Amy's hands went to hers, fumbling with the buckle. She got it undone and shrugged off the straps.

"Here, take this." He shoved the map in her hands, then grabbed her forearms and lifted her from her seat, pushing her toward the main cabin and the door.

She stumbled between the seats, falling into the cabin and crawling toward the door, clutching the map. Fear made her ears ring. She could smell the smoke now.

Ezra came up behind her, motioning for her to move to the side. He reached for the door handle and wrenched the door open. "I'm going to lower you down, and I want you to run. As far and as fast as you can."

Amy barely had a chance to nod before he pulled her forward and helped her through the door. Her feet hit the ground with a thud, and she took off running. After several yards, she glanced back to see items flying out the door. A survival bag and both of their backpacks.

By now, flames had licked back toward the wings. It wouldn't be long before the last dregs of fuel caught fire and engulfed the plane. Panic made her heart skip. Ezra still wasn't out of the plane. She cupped her hands around her mouth and yelled. "Ezra! Hurry!"

His broad-shouldered frame emerged from the cabin and dropped to the ground. She didn't feel relieved yet, though. He still needed to get away from the plane.

Stooping, he picked up all the items he'd tossed out, then ran toward her. "Go! Keep running!"

She turned, not questioning his orders, and took off again. Amy was fifty yards from the plane and Ezra nearly upon her when a boom rocked the desert solitude. The shockwave knocked them both to the ground.

Moaning, she rolled to her back and sat up, glancing at the aircraft. Flames engulfed it, sending thick, black smoke into the sky.

She felt a hand on her face.

"Are you okay?" Ezra's sapphire eyes bored into hers.

"Yeah." She lifted a hand to cover his. "Other than being a little shocked at it all, yes, I'm fine." She quickly scanned his face and body, looking for outward signs of injury. "Are *you* okay?"

He nodded and pulled his hand back, swiping it over his face. "Yeah." He pushed to his feet and held out a hand to her, helping her stand. "Let me see that map."

Amy handed it over, her gaze fixed on the plane, watching it burn. It didn't seem real.

Ezra dug through the survival bag and withdrew a compass. After a few moments, he stuffed it and the map into his backpack and slung both bags over his shoulders. He handed her backpack to her.

"What? You're not going to carry it this time?" She shrugged it over her shoulders, sending him a smile as she tried to inject some levity into their situation. If she didn't laugh right now, she'd cry. And once she started that, she was afraid it would be a while before she could stop.

A slight smile cracked his stern features. "Not this time, Tinkerbell." He tipped his head forward. "Let's go."

"Tinkerbell?" She stared at his back, now walking away from her. "And go where?" She hurried after him.

His long legs ate up the ground, and she had to double her stride to match his. Maintaining this pace wouldn't last long. She was in good shape, but she was practically running. He was so intent on going—well, anywhere but where they were

—that she didn't ask him to slow down. It'd become apparent soon enough.

"So, you gonna... tell me... where... we're headed?" Her words came out on short puffs as she scurried along behind him.

Ezra glanced back and saw her struggling to keep up. He slowed his pace. "I want to get across the river and find shelter before nightfall. It might take us some time to find a place to cross."

Amy nodded, falling into step beside him. She gulped in air, glad he'd slowed. "Okay. Where are we headed in the long run? And why can't we stay near the plane? In case someone heard your mayday? And surely someone will see that fire."

He shook his head. "I doubt my transmission went through. We should have heard breaks in the static, at the very least, if someone tried to reply. And no one's going to see that fire. Not out here. We're hiking to a large cattle station. It's the closest settlement shown on the map."

She frowned at his gruff tone and the cold look in his eyes. Where did this hard version of Ezra come from? Granted, they'd been in a plane crash, but he seemed—angry. More than he should be. She was upset, but not angry.

"And how far away is that?"

"Two to three days' walk."

Amy stopped dead. "Two to three *days?* There's nothing closer?"

"Nope."

Amy ran to catch up and grabbed his arm, pulling him to a halt. "You can't be serious. There *has* to be something closer."

Ezra wrenched his arm away. "I can't make a village magically appear. Look around, Amy. We're in the middle of the Outback. The closest place that will have a phone is that station—unless we stumble upon a hiker with a sat phone or a homestead not on the map. I can't change how it is. We're stuck out here, so deal with it." He stalked away, leaving Amy staring after him open-mouthed.

What was that all about? That was not the man she'd gotten to know.

She shook her head and ran after him again. "Hang on a second, here. Why are you so angry? We could be a lot worse off. Yeah, we crashed, but we're alive and uninjured."

"I don't want to talk right now." Ezra stared straight ahead, refusing to look at her as he walked. "Let's just keep walking. We really need to find shelter before nightfall. It gets chilly here at night and the dingoes and other creepy-crawlies will come out once the sun goes down. We need to build a fire to keep both at bay."

"No."

Ezra's angry gaze snapped down to her. "What?" His voice seemed to drop an octave.

"No." Amy straightened to her full five-foot-two-inch height and stopped. "I'm not moving until you tell me what's going on. We need to be able to work together to survive the next few days. If you aren't going to talk to me more than to say one-word answers, how is that going to happen? You apparently have some grand plan in your head, but you're not sharing much. If we get separated, I might as well stand in front of a dingo den and paint myself with blood, I'm as good as dead." Amy saw a flicker of something cross his features. "Now tell me why you're so upset. And don't give me any bullshit about, 'Oh, we were just in a plane crash, so I'm mad.'" She leveled a look on him. "The truth, Ezra."

He clenched his jaw and turned away, staring out over the landscape. She crossed her arms and waited. She meant what she said. She wasn't going anywhere until they talked.

"It was my fault." His low voice finally broke the silence. He glanced over his shoulder at her. "The crash was my fault."

Amy dropped her arms, staring at him with wide eyes. "How? You didn't do anything. If you want to blame someone, blame me. I was flying. Wait." She dropped her arms and straightened. "Are you blaming yourself because you let me fly?"

"No," he growled, looking away again. "I should have seen it." His voice grew in intensity and volume. He whirled to face her, anger flashing in his bright blue eyes. "I check every inch of every aircraft I fly before I fly it, and I never miss problems. I missed this one and look where we are." He threw his hands up and gestured to the surrounding landscape. "I screwed up. And do you know why I screwed up? Because I was distracted. My focus wasn't where it should have been, and that's unacceptable. It's what gets pilots killed. It's what almost got you killed." He turned and took several steps away.

Amy blinked, shocked. She had not expected that. Though she should have. It was natural for the person behind the wheel to blame themselves for a crash. She likely would have if the situation were reversed. But as he said, he checked the aircraft. And it had just been through maintenance. If there was an obvious fault, someone would have noticed.

She closed the gap between them and put her hand in the center of his strong, broad back. "Ezra, whatever you may think, the crash was not your fault. How many eyes have been on that plane lately? And no one noticed a problem? It could have been internal—a cracked housing or something—in a place no one could see without taking things apart."

He continued to stare off into the distance, not saying anything.

With a huff, she dropped her hand. "Stop blaming yourself." Her anger surged at his stubbornness. She rounded him to look up at his face. Grabbing his arms, she shook him, but he still wouldn't look at her. "We are alive because of you. *You* got us down safely. *You* noticed the terrain and made sure we had plenty of room to land. *Your* experience and attention to detail is what saved our lives."

Growling when he still refused to react, she shoved his chest. He turned startled eyes on her. She held his gaze. "Stop blaming yourself and use your experience and the survival skills I know the Army taught you and get us the hell out of here."

That intense blue gaze held hers. Amy barely breathed, awaiting his response. She did not want him to blame himself for their crash. If anyone really was at fault and it wasn't just a sudden failure of a part, it would be the maintenance crew. And they might never know the cause. It would depend on whether investigators could piece together the burned wreckage. And if they were alive to hear the results.

Ezra's jaw twitched. "Getting rid of the guilt isn't so easy, but you're right. I can get us out of here." Suddenly, his arm snaked around her waist and pulled her close in a hug. "I'm sorry." His voice ended on a whisper.

Amy swallowed hard. Tingles raced through her from the full-body contact. "It's okay."

He drew back, but didn't let her go. She swallowed again, tamping down the urge to frame his face in her hands and stand on her toes for a kiss. Adrenaline was doing funny things to her emotions, and she was seriously hanging onto them by a thread.

Need ignited in his eyes, and his hold on her changed. One hand came up to stroke her hair and cup the side of her head. "I like this fire flashing in your eyes."

The gravel in his voice fanned the flames now burning in her belly.

"Makes you even more beautiful."

She was helpless to get away from his intense sapphire gaze. Not that she wanted to. No. Those emotions she held back broke free of their reins, and she lifted her hands to his shoulders. Muscles moved beneath her fingertips, like silky steel alloy. He dipped his head, hovering just millimeters away, giving her time to back out of his embrace. When she didn't, he closed the gap.

Shock reverberated through her brain. She felt her bones melt as a fierce rush of pleasure went through her, building on itself like a wave in a storm. Her fingers dug into his hard biceps. She clung to him, afraid she would end up in a puddle at his feet if she didn't. The adrenaline still coursing through her from the crash wasn't helping.

Ezra broke the kiss, staring at her as his breath sawed in and out. Thankfully, he didn't let her go right away. She wasn't sure she could stand on her own. Her bones needed a chance to solidify again.

He cleared his throat. "We really do need to get moving now." He let her go, running a hand through his short hair.

"Right. Yes, we should." She swiped her hands down her leggings and licked her lips.

Desire licked in the depths of his eyes again, and his gaze went to her mouth. Closing his eyes, he turned away with a soft moan. "Come on. Let's get walking."

TEN

Hot and sweaty, Ezra led Amy to a copse of trees near the river. They'd been further from it than he thought. He was doubly glad he'd put down where he did. They wouldn't have made it over the river, and the ground turned hilly the closer they got. Though he wished he'd missed that crack.

Sliding his pack off his shoulders, he took out the map and stared down at the line marking the river. Thankfully, it was an aeronautical navigation map, which showed the width of the river. He scanned it, looking for the thinnest part. It would be quite the task to get across. It had at least a dozen small tributaries running alongside it they would have to cross first. The rainy season wasn't upon them yet, so Ezra hoped most of them would be dry or very shallow. The main river, though, they would have to forge.

He looked over at the tiny woman sinking down to the ground at the base of a tree. She was something else. They had crashed a plane in the middle of the Australian Outback and it barely fazed her. In fact, she'd pulled him out of a funk.

He still couldn't believe he'd missed whatever it was that brought them down. The news of Wayne's accident had thrown him more than he realized. Not to mention the distraction of his pretty passenger. But it didn't matter. Whether it was a crack in the tank or a loose line, he should have seen it. Losing his focus nearly cost them their lives. He couldn't let it happen again.

Ezra's gaze traveled the length of Amy's petite form. Need stirred once more. He clenched his teeth and shook his head, turning back to the map. His jaw worked as he tried to regain his focus once again.

What was the matter with him? Was it the adrenaline? It had never had this effect on him before. But he'd also never been in a situation like this with a beautiful woman. People reacted in all kinds of ways to adrenaline. Add in the relief of walking away from the crash, and he could definitely understand the need for that intimate connection.

He didn't like it. It made him feel out of control. And right now, he needed to be in control.

Ezra pressed his lips together, trying—and failing—to hold the memory of their embrace at bay. It had been a mistake. He should have kept his lips to himself. But that fire flashing in her eyes was like a beacon, drawing him home. Keeping his focus with her around would be difficult. He'd met more beautiful women—had even dated more beautiful women. But there was something about Amelia Preston. Her pixie face and tiny frame belied a strength that ran miles deep. And she was interesting. He could talk to her for days and never get bored.

Growling softly at himself and his train of thought, he gave the map a shake and forced his mind back to finding them a way across the river. If they walked northwest along the bank about a mile, according to the map, the river narrowed, and they'd be able to cross.

Before they started out again, though, they needed to see what they had in their packs. He'd been so intent on getting them out of this mess, he'd forgotten one of the principle rules of his survival training. Know what you have.

"Amy? What all do you have in your backpack?" He walked over to her and crouched, setting his bags on the ground.

"I'm not sure." She pulled her pack in front of her and unzipped it, dumping the contents onto the ground. Ezra did the same, then took stock. They both had two bottles of water, plus the full half-gallon jug that was in the survival pack; a change of clothes; some toiletry items; and some snacks as well as Amy's purse, which she'd stuffed down inside her backpack. They also had the other basics from the survival kit—matches, ponchos, flashlight, first-aid kit, protein bars, water purifying tablets, a Swiss Army knife, and a flare gun with two flares. Normally, Ezra carried a single-blade pocket knife, but he'd left it at home. What he wouldn't give for a longer and stronger blade.

"Do you have anything of use in there?" He pointed to her purse.

Her eyes widened. "My phone." She grabbed the bag and unzipped it, quickly locating the device. Touching the button on the side, the screen lit up. Her eager, hopeful expression fell. "No service."

Ezra grunted. "I didn't expect otherwise. Turn it off and save the battery. It won't be of any use to us out here. Is there anything else in there?" He gestured to her bag.

She shook her head, doing as he said. "No. It's just my wallet and some tissues. And my book." She tossed her phone into her bag, then spread it open to show him its contents.

He nodded. "Okay. It looks like with what we have, our biggest issue will be staying hydrated. Normally, out here, they recommend about a gallon and a half of water per person per day." He picked up the tablets, shaking the bottle. "These will make the water drinkable, but they don't always kill everything, and we could still get sick."

"Great." Her nose wrinkled.

He flashed her a smile and reached for the empty survival bag. "Hopefully, the water we find will have minimal germs and the tablets will take care of it all. If not, well, we'll deal with it." He put the bottle in the bag, then reached for the first-aid kit.

Amy shifted, then moved again a moment later. Ezra frowned. "You okay?"

"Um." She grimaced. "I need to, um, relieve myself, so could you..." Her voice trailed off as her cheeks flamed.

Ezra nodded, understanding, and turned around. He didn't want to add to her embarrassment. He had no problem using the wilderness as a restroom, but for most people, it was a new experience.

She moved behind a scraggly tree, and he heard the rustle of her clothing. Ezra hummed a song in his head and stuffed their packs, putting most of her things in his to lighten her load. When he finished, he moved several feet away, out of earshot, and stared at the muddy river.

He tipped his head, watching the current. It was a shame the map couldn't tell him how deep the water was.

Amy shrieked. His heart jumped, then raced, and he spun, taking two running steps.

"I'm fine!"

He slowed, still walking toward her, but at a more sedate pace.

"I just lost my balance. This isn't the easiest thing in the world to do."

Ezra heard more rustling and scuffling. He could picture her getting up, dusting herself off and righting her clothing.

She stepped out from behind the tree, looking frazzled and annoyed.

"'Kay. Now that I have that embarrassing experience over with, can we get moving?" She picked up her backpack and slung it over her shoulders.

Ezra bit back a smile, once again admiring her spunk. "Sure. But drink some water first."

Frowning, she spun the bag around and unzipped it, grumbling about how drinking would just make her have to pee again. He opened his mouth to remind her staying hydrated was necessary, but she waved a hand at him.

"I get it. Doesn't mean I want to repeat that experience, but I get it." She unscrewed the cap and took a long drink.

Grinning, he picked up the other two bags and walked past her. "Come on, Tinkerbell. Time to go."

ELEVEN

What Amy wouldn't give for a bottle of sunscreen or a hat. She was going to look like a lobster before they reached that village. The Outback sun was relentless. She felt like an egg frying in a skillet. If it weren't for what could be lurking in the river, she would relish crossing it. The water would feel glorious on her hot skin. Thankfully, she had the foresight to wear leggings and to tie a light zip-up hoodie around her waist in case she got cold on the plane. They now shielded her arms and legs from the sun, not to mention from all the bugs and other creepy-crawlies out here. She wouldn't mind a pair of hiking boots, though. Her old sneakers were easy to slip on and off, but they weren't meant for walking over the Outback's rough terrain. She sighed. At least they weren't sandals. That would really suck.

Amy ran her gaze over the man walking in front of her. He wore jeans, but no jacket or long sleeves. His arms, though deeply tanned, were already showing a pink tinge from the sun. Sweat ran in rivulets down his neck and soaked the neck of his rust-colored t-shirt and the middle of his back. A light breeze blew and molded the shirt to his sculpted body. He was so handsome it made her ache. Especially since he'd kissed her. There was a fire between them that wanted to be let loose. She just hoped they survived this so they could unleash it. It promised to consume her, and she was all for that.

She probably shouldn't be, but after what they just went through, she didn't care that she'd known him just three days. Her life flashed before her eyes when they crashed, and it made her realize her time on this planet was much too short to live with regrets. And she would regret it if she didn't let whatever this was sparking between them erupt.

Her foot snagged on a tuft of grass, and she stumbled. Gritting her teeth, she forced her thoughts onto her current situation. She needed to concentrate on where she was going, so she didn't step on a snake or something equally dangerous. Australia was littered with dangers. And out here, without help close by, getting bitten by something or falling and injuring herself could mean death. She'd been close enough to that for one day, thank you very much.

"So, where are we going?" She kept her eyes trained on the ground as she followed behind him.

Ezra glanced back. "A narrow spot in the river, so we can cross."

"Is it much further?"

He shook his head. "Not too much."

Amy paused and squinted at the water, looking for a place where it seemed to be thinner. It twisted, like a snake slithering along the desert floor, making it hard to judge the width from a distance. The ground shimmered with a mirage from the heat, distorting the landscape. She shaded her eyes with a hand.

"Is that the narrow spot?" She pointed.

Ezra stopped and studied the river. "Maybe." He pulled out the map, looking at the river's course drawn on it, then at the actual river. "Yeah, could be."

Spurred on by the thought of getting across their first major hurdle—well, other than surviving a plane crash and running away from said plane as it exploded—Amy quickened her pace. As they neared the point in the distance, it became obvious the river did, in fact, narrow.

She stopped at the bank of the muddy river, gazing across to the opposite bank only fifty feet away. The water moved along like it had nowhere to be, but Amy knew the current was stronger than it looked. Eddies swirled near the middle as the water flowed around underwater obstacles.

"I don't suppose your wonder-map shows how deep it is, does it?" Amy asked, staring out at the mucky water.

"Nope." He shrugged off the survival kit and stuffed the map down inside the waterproof bag. "Only one way to find out." He sat down on the ground and started to pull off his boots. "Take off your shoes and socks. Stuff your socks down in your shoes and tie the laces together and loop them around your neck. It'll hopefully keep them dry."

Amy did as he said and soon stood nervously next to him at the edge of the river. She did not want to get in that water. Heaven only knew what was lurking under the surface. Trying not to think about it, she kept her gaze trained on Ezra's face as he scanned the water. She knew that look. It was the same one he'd given the map after they'd climbed out of the plane. He was searching for the best way across and any obstacles in their path.

He looked down at her. "You ready?"

"No."

Ezra's grin flashed, and he grabbed her hand. "Just stay close. Our biggest problem is going to be making sure you don't float away."

Amy rolled her eyes. "Hardy-har-har."

Ezra's grin only grew. "You can swim, right?"

"Yes, Great Leader, I can swim. Rather well, actually."

She'd spent most of her youth in the pool every summer, even lifeguarding at the local aquatic center for several years in high school. "I'm more worried about crocodiles."

He tugged on her hand. "I think they're further north. Closer to the coast." He walked down the bank, pulling her with him. "Come on."

Amy held tight to his hand and followed him down to the water. She said silent prayer after silent prayer as they waded in, and she carefully placed each foot on the river bed. The last thing she needed was to slip and soak herself. It would be bad enough most of her clothing would end up wet and smelly; she'd rather her hair escaped that fate.

Not quite halfway across, the water reached her ribcage, and she felt herself start to float. She would have to start swimming or float away. "Ezra. I'm starting to float."

He stopped, turning around and pulling her close. "Hook your hand around my belt."

She let go of his hand and hooked it around his waistband.

"Let me have your shoes."

She unwrapped them from her shoulders and handed them over. He looped them around his neck. His chest and head were still well out of the water.

The lucky bastard. Sometimes, she hated being short.

"I'm going to walk. Hang on tight, okay?"

She nodded.

Amy hooked her hand into his jeans and held on, doing her best to stay semi-upright so she didn't have to do more than paddle a little. The water got slightly deeper at the midway point, but Ezra was still able to easily touch the river bed. Her toes skimmed the bottom, but the current kept her from maintaining her footing. She clutched his belt and let him tow her to shallower water.

It wasn't long and she was able to reach the bottom again. She released her grip on Ezra's jeans and headed for shore.

She saw the log a moment before it slammed into her thigh. Unprepared, it knocked her sideways. Muddy water surrounded her as she went under. The log glanced off the top of her head, and she sucked in an involuntary gasp from the pain; except instead of air, her lungs filled with water. She coughed, trying to expel the fluid, and fought to surface as blackness edged her vision. The river's current, while not swift, pulled her downstream and into deeper water. Pain screamed through her thigh and lungs, and her body grew limp. Her feet hit the bottom. With her last ounce of strength, she pushed up. Her head broke the surface, and she sputtered, then sank, already too weak to stay afloat.

This is it. I'm going to die in a dirty Australian river. Me, the former lifeguard, is going to drown.

TWELVE

Amy's quick shriek was Ezra's only warning that something was wrong. When he turned around, it was to see the splash as she went under. He took a step toward her, but waited, thinking she'd pop up on her own. The water was shallow. But she didn't.

"Amy?" His long legs cut through the water as he walked to where she went under. A log popped up a few yards downstream, but there was no sign of Amy.

Alarmed, he waded into deeper water. "Amy!" His heart thundered in his ears as he scanned the water's surface, looking for any sign of her; bubbles, a strange eddy—anything. But there was nothing.

No, no, no. This wasn't happening. Ezra scanned the water again. "Amy!"

In front of him several yards to his left, her head broke the surface. Just for a moment; then she sank again. He dove toward her, using his long, powerful arms to reach the spot in just a few strokes. Diving beneath the surface, he strained to see anything in the murky water. He waved his hands, hoping to connect with some part of her.

His hands passed through something soft and silky. A surge of adrenaline hit. That was hair. He kicked, getting closer, and bumped her arm. Hooking a hand under it, he pulled, tugging her limp body into his. He pushed off the bottom and brought them to the surface.

Hauling in a lungful of air, he looked at the woman in his arms. Pale, except for the blood running down her face, and virtually lifeless, she sagged against him. Her head lolled onto his shoulder, and her eyelids fluttered.

Sweet Jesus. "Hang on, Tinkerbell. I got you." He floated her on her back, putting an arm around her torso, and side-kicked to shallower water. Once he could stand and walk easily, he hooked his hands under her arms and pulled her out of the river.

"Amy." Ezra knelt next to her and patted her cheek. Her eyelids fluttered again, but he got no other response. She wasn't breathing. "Amy, sweetheart, you need to breathe." Urgency punched him in the gut. Cursing under his breath, he rolled her onto her side. Water dribbled out of her mouth, but she still didn't take a breath.

Gulping back the panic that he was losing her, Ezra focused on his first-aid training. Rolling her onto her back, he pinched her nose and blew two quick breaths into her mouth.

Her response was swift, the influx of air doing the trick. She coughed, expelling water. He turned her onto her side again, so the fluid could drain. Hard, wracking coughs shook her body. He supported her small frame as she rose to her hands and knees, retching into the dirt.

Slowly, the bone-breaking coughs and dry heaves abated. When she would have collapsed to the ground, he scooped her up and held her close.

Ezra's heart thumped in his ears and chest, and his hands shook as he held her. That had been close. Too close. "You're all right, baby. You're okay." He smoothed a hand over her wet hair, reassuring her and himself that she was fine.

She lifted a small hand and laid it against his neck, turning into his chest. Sobs shook her slight frame. Ezra held on tighter, murmuring to her and stroking her head and back until her cries turned to soft hiccups.

"Let's not do that again, huh?" He put a hand under her chin, tipping her face up so he could look into her eyes.

"No." Her voice was low and raspy. "Thank you." Tears shimmered in her eyes.

He leaned down and pressed a long kiss to her forehead. "Don't thank me. I'm just glad you're all right." He pulled back to look at her again. "Do you remember what happened?"

She put a hand on his chest and pushed, sitting up. "I got hit. By a log." She touched her leg and cleared her throat, coughing again. Taking a shaky breath, she continued. "It knocked me off my feet, and I went under. Then it smacked me on the head." Lifting a hand, she touched the spot still oozing blood.

Ezra wiggled out of the backpack straps and dug into the survival bag for the first-aid kit. "Let's fix that." He moved out from under her so he could access her wound. She propped herself up on one hand, but her elbow buckled.

"Whoa, there." He grabbed her arm to keep her from hitting the dirt. "Let's prop you up." Glancing around, he spotted the trees up the bank. Shifting her, he scooped her into his arms.

"Where are we going?"

"Just to the top of the bank." He carried her the few feet up the embankment and set her against a tree. "Hang tight." Turning around, he went back to the river's edge to retrieve his things, then returned to her side.

"Okay. Let's fix your head." He opened the first-aid kit

and took out some gauze and some alcohol wipes. Tearing open the gauze packages, he separated her hair to look at the wound. It could probably use a few stitches, but he didn't have that out here.

"Well?"

"You've got a laceration that could use some stitches. I'll try my best to close it." He reached for the kit, rummaging through it. Tucked in one corner were some small tubes of superglue. He took one of the tiny tubes from the package, then grabbed the bottle of hydrogen peroxide and a syringe full of sterile saline.

"This might sting." He opened the hydrogen peroxide and poured some on the wound. It bubbled, and she winced. Ezra glanced at her. "You doing okay?"

"Yeah." She let out a hard cough.

He frowned, not liking the sound of that. He'd need to keep a close eye on her for the next twenty-four hours. She was at risk of a lung infection or even secondary drowning. He prayed fervently the latter didn't happen. There wasn't anything he could do to help her if that happened.

Using the saline, he washed the wound, then poured more peroxide on it. After rinsing it once more, he dabbed the area dry, then cracked open the superglue tube and squeezed it into the wound. With the steri-strips he found in the kit, he did his best to hold it closed so the glue could dry.

"Okay. That's about as good as it's going to get for now. Are you hurt anywhere else?"

"Just my thigh, where the wood hit me initially." She motioned to her right leg.

Ezra probed the area with his fingers.

She hissed. "I think it's just bruised, but it hurts."

"Do you want me to take a look?"

"No. I think it's fine." She moved her leg, flexing her toes. "It only hurts when the skin pulls, so I should be all right."

He nodded. "Okay." Picking up the first-aid kit again, he rifled through it and came up with some painkillers. "Take these." He handed her a couple of paracetamol tablets—Australia's version of acetaminophen.

She took them, then swallowed them with water from the bottle in her bag. Coughing again, she sagged against the tree. "What now?"

"The plan's still the same. We need to find a place to make camp." He gazed out over the landscape, assessing the area beyond. They were in the floodplain of the river, so the vegetation was decent. Copses of trees poked up here and there with lots of scrub grass scattered between them. The ground rose quickly on this side of the river in a gentle slope about two hundred feet before leveling out. They really needed to get to the top of that. They would be less vulnerable to predators and insects away from the water.

"Can't we stay here?"

"No. I know you're tired and hurting, but we need to get away from the river. It's too dangerous in the dark. We won't go far."

"Okay." She lifted a hand. "Just let me rest for a few minutes."

He sat down next to her, having no intention of rushing her. Ezra glanced skyward. The sun was dipping lower, but they had about two hours of daylight before they needed to be secured somewhere.

"You doing okay?" He turned back to her.

"Yeah. Just shaky still." She coughed. "That was intense. I could hear you, but I couldn't really see. My vision was dark and fuzzy. Right before the river left my lungs after you hauled me out, even your voice faded to practically nothing." She shook her head. "That was scary."

A fine tremor ran through her. Ezra reached out and took

her hand, needing to touch her. "Yeah, it was. I'm glad you're all right." He squeezed her fingers.

She offered him a tremulous smile, then closed her eyes. "I feel like I could sleep for days."

Ezra frowned, hoping it was just fatigue talking and not her head injury. "Do you remember what day it is?"

"Um, Monday, right?" She didn't open her eyes.

"Yes. And you know where you are and what happened?"

"Australia. The river tried to kill me."

A smile played with his lips. He was glad to see her near-death experience hadn't hampered her sense of humor. "Good. I'll keep asking you silly questions tonight. For now, you seem fine."

Her lower lip trembled, and a tear slid free of her eye. "Yeah."

He squeezed her hand again, then stood, needing a moment himself. She'd been extremely lucky. "I'm going to scout for a campsite. Stay put, okay?"

She cracked her eyes open to look at him. "Don't worry. I don't plan to move until you make me."

Again, a smile toyed with his mouth. "Good. I'll be right back."

She lifted a hand in farewell and closed her eyes again.

Ezra walked away, his gaze trained on the landscape. But his mind was on their near-miss. Another few seconds and she'd have been gone. If she hadn't managed to get her head up so he could see her, he wouldn't have found her. This wasn't the first life-threatening or emergency situation he'd ever been in—he was a special forces pilot—but it had the most profound impact. Maybe because he wasn't expecting it. They'd nearly made it across when she went under. It shouldn't have been so dangerous.

He shook his head, attempting to clear his thoughts. Worrying about what could have been wasn't helpful. She was alive and relatively unharmed. He needed to focus on getting them out of here. That was his priority.

Climbing the hill, he stopped at the top. Up here, there was less vegetation, but he saw several spots that would offer them shelter. The trees weren't necessary—it wasn't supposed to rain—but it would be nice to have their backs to something should a predator find them overnight. Without a tent, they would be particularly vulnerable.

With a location in mind, he turned around and went down the hill. Amy was still where he left her and in the same position.

"You awake?"

"Yeah," she croaked. "Do I have to get up now?"

"Not yet. Rest a little longer. I found us a spot at the top of the hill. We have time yet."

"Awesome."

He sat down beside her. "Do you want something to eat?"

She shook her head. "I'm still queasy from the river water."

Leaning against the tree, he stared out over the river. She wasn't the only one feeling the aftereffects of their misadventure. With his adrenaline gone, fatigue was setting in. He glanced at his watch. A short nap wouldn't hurt. He pushed some buttons on the casing, setting the alarm so he wouldn't sleep too long, then crossed his arms and closed his eyes.

Amy shifted, rolling into him. He glanced down, then put an arm around her shoulders and tucked her close. She curled into him. One tiny hand came to rest on his chest. He settled against the tree again and let his eyes drift shut. He could feel her breathing slow and her body grow heavy.

"Sleep, Amy. You're safe." He intended to make sure she stayed that way.

THIRTEEN

Beeping drew Ezra from a sound sleep. Yawning, he shut off the alarm on his watch, then looked down at Amy. She still laid curled up in his arms, her face tucked into the crook of his neck. Her soft breath puffed warmly against his skin. Her color was good and her breathing sounded normal, which made him happy. He leaned down and pressed a kiss to the top of her head. She smelled overwhelmingly of river water, but beneath it, he could still detect the sunshine and lilies that haunted his dreams. He didn't want to move. If it weren't for the cold, clammy clothes they both wore, he could almost pretend they were on some exotic vacation instead of stranded in the Outback.

She sighed into his neck and curled further into his body, her arm sliding up over his shoulder to hook around his neck. Ezra's libido stirred, but he tamped it down. He'd let it have free rein another time. When they weren't in danger of dying and she wasn't injured.

He wrapped a hand around her wrist and peeled her arm off. "Amy. Honey, it's time to wake up."

She groaned and tugged her arm free of his grip, tucking it close to her body as she snuggled into his side.

A smile lifted one side of his mouth. She was cute; he hated to wake her. "Come on, sleepyhead. We need to conquer the hill, then you can rest again."

"No." But she opened her eyes and yawned. "That felt like a minute."

"More sleep is incoming, I promise." He shifted her so she sat upright, then got to his feet.

She looked at him with those liquid brown eyes. Something shifted in his chest, and a wash of emotion hit him. Even bedraggled and smelling like the river, she was beautiful. He swallowed hard and glanced away.

Rubbing sleep from her eyes, she got up. Her knees buckled, and he shot out a hand to catch her. Tucking it under her elbow, he wrapped his other hand around her back. "Whoa. You all right?"

"Yeah. Dizzy." She blinked at him, her eyes unfocused. After a moment, they cleared. "It's fading."

"Good. Let's take your pack off. I'll come back down and get it." He hadn't bothered to remove any of her gear when he pulled her from the river, and she hadn't either. But the weight would make it harder for her to climb the hill.

She shrugged out of the backpack and set it in the dirt.

"Ready?" He gave her an expectant look.

"Yes."

"Okay. Put your arm around my back and lean into me."

Doing as he asked, she tucked herself into his side. Ezra wrapped an arm around her waist and turned, heading for the hill. It wasn't too steep, thankfully, but it had enough of a grade it would be slow going for her. Watching his step, he picked a path up the hill, pausing when she needed a moment to catch her breath. Her coughing increased the further they climbed. So did her fatigue level. By the time they reached the top, his arm was the only thing holding her up. She managed to make her feet move, but her legs had little starch.

He headed for a stand of trees clustered around some rocks and set her on the ground. Kneeling in front of her, he touched her cheek. "Still with me?"

"Yeah." She looked at him through hooded eyes, then coughed. "Ugh. Coughing makes my head hurt."

"Have the pain meds helped at all?"

"A little. My thigh doesn't ache as much. And the pain in my head only comes when I cough."

"Good. I need to go back and get our stuff. Do you need anything?"

She shook her head. "I'm fine. Go."

"Okay. I won't be long."

At her nod, he turned and jogged away.

True to his word, it only took him about ten minutes to go down the hill and collect their things. He was pleased to see she was still awake when he returned. And she looked perkier.

"Are you feeling better?"

She lifted a hand and waved it side to side. "Sort of. My body still feels heavy, but I don't feel so sleepy."

"That's great." He knelt beside her and opened her pack, finding the food she carried. "Here. Eat." He held out a protein bar.

Amy wrinkled her nose and waved it away.

"Please? Just a couple bites. It'll give you some energy."

Face still scrunched, she took the bar. The wrapper crinkled as she opened it. Ezra dug one out of his own pack and bit into it.

"God, it's beautiful here."

He glanced over to see her staring out at the expanse before them. Shifting, he sat down beside her. "Agreed." With the waning light from the setting sun, the rusted earth glowed bright orange, contrasting beautifully with the deep blue sky and golden clouds on the horizon. The areas of scrub grass dotting the landscape shimmered a silvery green in the breeze. Even the air itself had color, a shining gold that would rival any treasure. Ezra didn't think he had ever seen a more beautiful sunset. If their circumstances were different, he'd truly be enjoying this adventure. The landscape, though sparse because of the semi-arid climate, was still lush. Stands of trees dotted the earth while flocks of birds flew along the river, black silhouettes in the growing darkness. The slight wind brought the scent of damp earth and the newness of spring with it. Ezra briefly closed his eyes and let the peace of this beautiful location wash over him.

"Do you think anyone realizes we're missing yet?"

Ezra opened his eyes and turned to her. "Probably. We should have landed at Dalton Creek a few hours ago. Anna would have contacted the authorities."

"Should we have stayed with the plane?"

"No. We needed water, and at least some shelter." He gestured to the trees overhead.

"How far do we have to go, still?"

"I'm guessing thirty miles. The cattle station was about forty miles northwest from the crash site. We went about eight today, I think."

She groaned. "Even if we put in a full day, we're looking at what—two more days? Three?"

Expression grim, he nodded. "We don't have any other choice. It could be even longer if we stay put and wait for someone to find us. That fuel leak couldn't have happened in a worse location. We were over one of the most remote spots in Queensland. I doubt anyone noticed the crash. And there wasn't much left to burn when we went down, so the fire didn't last long." He looked off in the distance from the way they'd come. Smoke no longer rose into the air, and what had was dispersing into the clouds.

"When I get home, it will be a very long time before I venture anywhere again."

He nudged her leg and smiled. "Nah. You'll be back out exploring again in no time."

Her lips tilted in a smile, making his widen.

"There's that pretty smile."

Color bloomed on her cheeks. "You don't need to flatter me. I know I look like garbage."

Ezra chuckled. "You're beautiful. Even covered in river scum."

She wrinkled her nose. "Thanks. I want a shower to be the first thing I do when we reach civilization."

"Me too. Well, maybe after a giant cheeseburger."

Amy's stomach growled, and she laughed.

"Finish your protein bar." He pointed at the partially eaten bar in her hand, smiling broadly.

Dutifully, she lifted it and took a bite.

Ezra nodded in approval and took another bite of his, finishing it off. Stowing the wrapper in the bottom of his bag, he got to his feet. "I'm going to collect some firewood. Drink the rest of the water in that bottle you opened earlier. I'll fill it and any others we have empty so they can sit with the purification tablets overnight."

Head bobbing, she chewed.

Satisfied she was okay for now, he walked off, making a circuit around the tree to gather fallen limbs and twigs. Dumping his armload near where she sat, he wandered away to another copse of trees. Soon, he had a nice pile of dry wood to burn.

With the wood gathered, he emptied Amy's backpack into his, then put all the water bottles that needed filled into hers and went down to the river. So long as they could stay near a water source, they would be okay. The map showed this river meandering north, toward the cattle station noted on the map.

They would follow the river as far as possible before they had to turn west to find help.

Darkness gathered as Ezra returned to camp with his load of water. He dug out the purification tablets and added them to the water bottles. The only thing they couldn't get rid of was the sediment. He'd tried pouring the water over the bottom of his t-shirt, but it was a haphazard solution. Tomorrow, he'd come up with something better.

Water issues taken care of, he cleared an area in front of them of debris, then arranged some of the wood into a small stack and stuffed dry grass into the cracks. With the flint from the survival bag, he lit it. Fire crackled to life, casting shadows over the campsite. Stowing the flint, he dug a long-sleeved shirt out of his backpack and put it on. It was wet, but it would dry faster on him than it would balled up in his bag, and he would need the layer later. Amy was wearing her long-sleeved shirt, but it had already dried some since he pulled her from the water. With the fire going, her thin clothing would dry out quickly. He wished he had something other than the jeans he wore. The heavy denim held water, but he didn't dare take them off and expose his legs to the nighttime insects of the Australian desert. He did not need bug bites in unmentionable places.

Night fell, and the landscape came to life. Insects chirped and whirred and dingoes howled in the distance. A breeze blew over Ezra's face, bringing the fresh scent of nature with it. Fatigue pulled at his mind. He glanced at Amy. "You ready to get some sleep?"

"Yeah. I need to use the facilities again, though." Her face scrunched in that adorable way once more.

Ezra grabbed the survival bag and pulled out the flashlight, handing it to her. "Do you want help?"

She shook her head, getting to her feet. Her legs shook, but held.

"Don't wander far."

"I won't." She laid a hand on his shoulder and squeezed lightly, then wandered behind their tree stand.

He tried not to listen, but he wanted to be alert to any problems, like if she fell. Getting up, he picked up a long branch and poked the fire. With one ear behind him, he stared straight ahead into the dark, muscles tense. When she reappeared a few minutes later, the tension eased from his shoulders. "Feel better?"

She nodded and took her seat near their bags again. "I'm definitely ready for bed now, though."

"Give me just a couple minutes and I'll join you." He wandered behind the trees, relieving himself. Tomorrow, they needed to drink more. As much as they could stomach. They were both dehydrated.

Dirt crunched under his shoes as he returned to camp. Amy had laid down and tucked the backpack full of clothes and gear under her head. Ezra sat down beside her and rolled her toward him. "Use me as your pillow."

Without a word, she snuggled into his side, laying her head on his chest. He moved the pack and scooted down, propping it under his head and shoulder. Closing his eyes, he let out a long breath, relaxing into the ground. Wind gusted over them, sending a chill down his neck, and he tucked Amy a little closer to keep her warm. He wished they had a blanket. There was a foil one in the survival bag, but he didn't want to dig it out unless he had to. Those things made him sweat, which would just make him colder once they got up.

"Ezra."

Amy's soft voice made his eyes open. "Hmm?"

"We're going to be okay, right?" She didn't raise her head to look at him, but he could still sense her fear. It colored her voice.

He gave her a quick squeeze. "Yeah, Tinkerbell. We'll be fine."

She looked up. "Why do you call me that?"

A corner of his mouth rose. "Because you're small and beautiful, like a fairy, but feisty." He lifted and curled the arm under her to brush a strand of hair away from her face. "You just remind me of her, I guess."

"Oh."

"I won't call you that anymore if you don't want me to."

"No. It's fine. I just wondered."

"Well, now you know."

She nodded, laying her head against his chest, and hugged him a little harder.

"Warm enough?"

"Sort of. I'll be okay."

"If that changes, let me know. I'll do what I can to warm you up."

Again, she nodded. "Thank you, Ezra." Her voice floated to him on a whisper. Sleep was taking hold.

"Anytime, Tinkerbell." He pressed a kiss to her head. "Get some sleep." Closing his eyes, he rested his cheek on top of her head. He prayed they both could get some rest. Tomorrow would be another long day.

Fourteen

Amy felt like death. Actually, she felt worse than death. If she were dead, nothing would hurt, because she'd be dead. No, this must be what purgatory felt like. Or hell. Probably hell. Everything hurt. Every joint, muscle, *hair*—it all hurt. Especially her thigh and the top of her head. Oh, and her chest. That felt like she had an elephant sitting on it.

Cracking an eye open, she attempted to swallow, but her dry, tacky mouth wouldn't let her. She raised her head, noting that her warm Ezra pillow was gone, and she was resting on the backpack.

With a groan that turned into a crackly cough, she sat up.

A water bottle appeared in front of her face. She glanced up into Ezra's sky-blue eyes.

"Drink."

She took the bottle and unscrewed the cap, putting it to her lips. Cool water hit her tongue. It tasted like dirt, but it wet her mouth. She drank several mouthfuls before recapping the bottle.

"Better?"

Amy nodded, then coughed again.

"You sound terrible. How do you feel?"

"Terrible." Another cough wracked her body. She curled inward as her muscles seized, holding her breath hostage.

"Okay. That doesn't sound good."

"You"—she coughed—"think?" She rolled her eyes. God, this was bad. How was she supposed to walk today? She couldn't even get off the ground.

Ezra dragged the survival bag over and pulled out the first-aid kit. He took out the digital thermometer and held it out. "Put that under your tongue."

She took it, pushing the button to turn it on, then did as he asked. Clamping her lips together, she tried to keep her mouth shut as she continued to cough. The thermometer beeped, and she pulled it out, frowning as she looked at the number. It was in Celsius. "Do you know the conversion rate?"

He looked at the readout, nodding. Eyes lifting skyward, she could tell he was doing calculations in his head. When he sighed, she knew it wasn't good.

"Crap. What is it?"

"About a hundred and one." He got up. "We need to get moving. You need a doctor."

"We're still—" She broke off, coughing again.

"I know we still have a ways to go, but the sooner we get moving, the sooner we reach civilization." He picked up the first-aid kit, using an alcohol swab to clean the thermometer, then put it back in the box and stowed it in the survival bag. The used wipe went in his pocket. "Drink more while I pack up."

Amy uncapped the bottle and took another swig of water, watching him stuff the survival pack into his backpack. He kicked dirt over the remnants of their fire, then did a quick look around their area to make sure he had everything picked up.

"Are you going to be able to walk?"

"I can try." Her head pounded, and she still coughed, but what choice did she have?

He held out a hand and helped her to her feet. The world tilted for a quick moment, then righted itself.

"You good?" Ezra held on while she got her legs under her.

"Yeah. I'm okay."

"Do you need to pee?"

She shook her head.

He frowned, then pointed to the water bottle in her hand. "Drink."

"You're a bloody broken record." But she raised the bottle and took another sip.

"Get used to it." He picked up his bag and hefted it onto his back, then grabbed hers, putting it over one shoulder.

"I can carry that." She reached for it.

He turned, moving it out of her reach. "Your job is to put one foot in front of the other and carry that water bottle." He pointed to the bottle in her hands.

"Ezra—"

"Nope. You're sick. I'm not. Let's go." He circled a finger, then pointed north.

Her mouth flattened. "Fine."

"Good girl."

She glared at him, and he flashed her a grin.

"You set the pace." He motioned her forward. "I don't want to out-walk you."

Amy snorted. They'd be lucky to do two miles if she led. But she had to try.

They set off. Amy concentrated on her footing and tried not to think about how awful she felt. Every so often, she took a drink of her water. Mostly, she kept her head down and forged ahead. She meant what she said yesterday. It would be a very long time before she went on vacation again. This one sucked.

Fifteen

Ezra glanced at Amy. Her pace had slowed even more than when they started an hour ago. She wasn't going to last much longer. But they needed to find help. She needed help. He couldn't leave her, though. For one, he wasn't sure he could find her again if he did. And two, she'd be defenseless once night fell. Easy pickings for a pack of dingoes.

But she couldn't continue like this.

Mentally, he went over the items they had, trying to come up with something that could help. There was rope in the survival bag. If he could fashion some sort of sled, he could pull her behind him as he walked. But the ground would tear up fabric. He'd have to make a platform out of wood first, and he didn't think he had enough rope for that. Plus, it would cost precious time she didn't have.

Amy stumbled, her foot catching on a rock. She pitched forward, landing on her hands and knees before Ezra could reach for her. He rushed the few steps to her side and crouched beside her.

"Are you okay?"

She shifted, sitting down in the dirt. "Yeah. My knees hurt now, but I'm fine."

"I think it's time we change things up."

She sent him a frown. "What do you mean?"

"I'm going to carry you."

Her eyes widened. "What? How? I mean, I get you're big and strong, but we have a long way to go."

"I know." Ezra swung the packs off his back and dug into the one with the survival bag. He pulled out a bundle of rope. "I'll use this."

Amy gave it a skeptical look. "That sounds terribly uncomfortable."

He couldn't help but smile at her proper tone. "It won't be that bad." For her, anyway. His shoulders would be dead by the time the day was over.

Unfurling the rope, he cut off two lengths, about two feet each, then another length about six feet long. The rest he coiled.

"How does this work? Do you know what you're doing?"

"Yes, I know what I'm doing. It's an improvised harness. We learn it as part of our search and rescue training. I thought about making you a stretcher, but I think the terrain's too rough for that." He separated the coils as he talked and tied one of the shorter rope lengths around the spot where the strands met.

"Okay. But how are you going to carry me and all our gear?"

"You can wear one of the backpacks. The other, I'll put on my chest." He tied a modified handcuff knot in the longer rope, pulling the loops wide. He stood up, holding out a hand to help her to her feet. "Before I strap you on, you need to drink some water." He bent, opening a bag to take out a bottle.

Amy took it and downed half. She handed it back, and he

drank the rest.

"Are you hungry?"

She shook her head.

"How about the restroom? Do you need to go?"

Again, she shook her head.

"Okay." He arranged the rope on the ground. "Step into the coils. The bound part will sit against your chest between us."

She grimaced, but did as he asked. "Yep. Majorly uncomfortable. But that's the last you'll hear me complain. I understand the stakes here."

It was Ezra's turn to grimace. This had to work, or they could have worse problems than they did now. Walking up behind her, he held up the shorter, knotted rope. "Put your arms through this. Like backpack straps."

She slid her arms in, and he pulled the ropes up over her shoulders. They sagged, but they wouldn't once they went around his arms too. It was more to secure her to his back so she wouldn't have to hold on so tight than anything else. Most of her weight would sit on the coiled rope.

He picked up her pack and put it on her back. "Comfortable?"

"Yes."

"Okay. Pull that up and hold it in front of you." He pointed to the rope at her feet.

She picked it up and held the coils open. He snatched the last length of cut rope off the ground and walked in front of her. Bending at the knee, he slipped one arm through it and the single strand rope harness she wore.

"Can you hop up and wrap your legs around me?"

Amy put her hands on his shoulders and jumped, encircling his waist with her legs. Ezra caught her right thigh and reached back with his left arm, threading it through the ropes. After adjusting her so the ropes didn't bite into her thighs, he took the length of cut rope and tied it around the coils on his chest, holding the harness in place.

"I don't know how you're going to manage this all day." Her breath whispered over his ear as she spoke beside it.

"I'll be fine. You don't weigh much more than a full gear pack." He walked around, testing the weight and making sure they were both as comfortable as possible. Satisfied it was as good as it would get, he squatted and picked up his backpack. Putting it on backward, he passed the waist strap behind his back. "Can you fasten that?"

She reached between them and grabbed the straps, clicking the buckle into place.

"All right. Hold on."

Amy locked her ankles around his waist. Ezra took off at a fast walk.

This was much better. They should be able to cover some decent ground like this.

Ezra's long legs ate up the rusty ground. Sweat soon coated him, but he felt good with the load. Half an hour into their trek, he felt her legs trembling.

"You can let go." He tapped her ankles. "The rope will hold you."

"Are you sure? I don't want to make things harder on you."

"It's fine. Sit however is comfortable."

She unlocked her legs, and her weight sagged lower on his back. It pulled on the ropes over his shoulders, but the strap on his chest held, keeping her from sliding too low.

"How're you feeling?"

"Miserable. Hot."

Ezra agreed. The sun was ruthless, but he knew her fever factored into how she felt. "Just hang in there, Tinkerbell. I'll get us as far as I can."

She hummed a non-answer. Ezra picked up his pace.

Sixteen

His shoulders were on fire, and his spine ached something fierce. Darkness crept closer, but he didn't want to stop yet. He'd covered fifteen to twenty miles today, he thought, but every foot he walked put them closer to help. So, he kept walking until he strained to see through the gathering twilight.

Spotting a copse of trees near some rocks, he walked over, turning his back to set Amy down on a boulder. It would be easier than trying to slide her to the ground.

Her butt hit the rock, and she groaned. "My legs are dead."

Ezra untied the rope on his chest and slid his arms free of the harness with a wince. "Yeah. Sorry."

"It's okay. It's better than having to try to stay upright. Or only walking a couple of miles." She coughed hard, illustrating why they wouldn't make it far with her on foot.

He rolled his shoulders and arched his back. "Yeah. We made good progress. Are you okay here for a few minutes while I fill our water bottles? I want to get down to the river before it's fully dark."

She nodded, shrugging out of the ropes and her backpack. Ezra picked up the bag and jogged away. They were closer to the river than he'd like, but the trees had thinned out, and he wanted the cover.

Reaching the water, he refilled the empty bottles, then went back to Amy. She hadn't moved except to lean back against the rocks.

"How're you feeling now? Worse than the last time we stopped?"

Her eyes glittered, feverish in the low light. "About the same. The medicine helped."

"Good." He'd given her some ibuprofen when they stopped a few hours ago. Her fever had climbed even higher, and she'd been lethargic. She still looked awful, but her eyes weren't so hooded now.

"Do you think you can eat?"

"I'll try."

That was all he asked. She'd refused food most of the day. But she'd done well drinking, so he hadn't pushed.

Digging in his bag, he put purification tablets in the water, then found their food stash and passed her some trail mix. He took a protein bar for himself. It wouldn't come close to filling him up, but it was better than nothing. Peeling off the wrapper, he took a bite. The chalky texture and bittersweet taste of the chocolate caked in his mouth. He chewed and swallowed, reaching for the last of his clean water. That cheeseburger sounded better all the time.

"How are your shoulders?" she asked, her voice quiet.

"They hurt. But I'll be fine." He put the rest of the bar in his mouth, chewing quickly, then washed it down. "I need to gather some firewood. Do you need to use the restroom?"

"No."

"You're sure?" He frowned. "You haven't gone since lunch."

"I'm sure." She closed the trail mix bag and handed it back.

Ezra took it, then passed her the remnants of her water. "Drink that." He wished he had more to give her. Her fever was burning off more than he could get into her.

She took the bottle, unscrewing the cap.

He stood. "I'll be back." Walking away, he scrounged for enough wood to get them through the next few hours. Once he had a pile, he cleared the ground and lit a fire. The warm glow illuminated the area, warding off the heavy darkness.

Ezra sat down next to Amy, studying her face in the firelight. She didn't look good. He lifted his wrist and set an alarm on his watch. They were setting off at first light.

"Have you ever seen anything so beautiful?" Amy pointed up, then coughed again.

He followed her gaze, looking to the heavens. Stars covered the sky, bright even in the last moments of sunset. "Yeah, it's pretty awesome." Soon, the Milky Way would appear and lend another breathtaking aspect to the night sky.

"I can't regret what's happened. I mean, this trip has sucked, but being here—seeing this—" She broke off and gestured to the sky. "It's incredible."

Ezra turned away from the vista to look at her.

"Despite all the trouble, this has been the adventure of a lifetime. If I make it through this, I'll never forget the last couple of days."

A fierce frown drew his eyebrows down. "What do you mean, if? I'm not letting you die. You're getting out of here even if I have to run the rest of the way." His fingers toyed with a rock in the dirt. Agitated, he got up and paced away. Thinking about what could happen—he couldn't.

Amy's phlegmy cough drowned out the Outback's nocturnal sounds. Ezra clenched his teeth and closed his eyes, sending up a prayer he could keep his word and get her to help.

"It's not your fault, you know. Stop blaming yourself."

He spun back to look at her. "How do you figure that? I crashed the plane." He'd been trying not to think about how things would be different if they hadn't crashed. Or if he'd flown just a little further.

She rolled her eyes. "Which had a failure no one foresaw. Your skills kept us alive. And have continued to keep me alive." Another cough cut off her words. Groaning, she seemed to sink into the rock at her back. "I'm grateful I'm with you, Ezra. No matter what happens, I know you tried."

Getting angry at her refusal to stop talking like she might die, he stomped back to her and dropped to his knees at her side. "You are not going to die. We are getting out of here. Tomorrow. You're going to go to the hospital, get pumped full of whatever the doctors think you need, then spend the rest of your vacation soaking up as much Australian culture as possible. Understand?"

Her lips twitched, amusement shining in her eyes. "Yes, sir."

Ezra huffed and sank to his butt, leaning on the rock beside her. "Sorry. But I can't think like you're going to—" He broke off and swallowed hard. "That you won't—" He couldn't make the words come.

Amy's hand covered his. He turned his hand over and threaded his fingers through hers.

"Fine. No more 'what if' scenarios. Tell me a story." She tipped her head, resting it against his shoulder.

"A story?"

She nodded.

"What kind of story?"

"I don't know. What were you like as a kid? Where's the

most exciting or interesting place you've ever been? Tell me more about you." Her body wiggled as a quick cough erupted.

"I was your typical country boy, I guess. My sister and I spent a lot of time outside. We played and hunted and fished. I did normal things at school too. Played sports. Did well in school. I was boring."

She let out a soft chuckle. "You are far from boring."

"Well, I was definitely not the kind of kid who stood out. Yeah, I was a good athlete and got decent grades, but am I the kid all the teachers remember? No."

"I'd remember you."

He'd remember her too. Not because she was beautiful or smart—though she was those things, and he did notice. No, he'd remember her because her soul spoke to his. She made him smile. It made him happy just to see her face. To watch her expressive chocolate eyes tell him exactly what was on her mind. He loved her enthusiasm for life. And her willingness to try things that terrified her—like coming on this vacation. It humbled him to know that she trusted him.

Ezra kissed her forehead, the heat from her fevered body searing his lips. "I'm glad."

"Do you talk to many of your classmates?"

"Not really. I have a couple friends I'll grab a beer with when I go back home. After graduation, I went off to college, and it was hard to maintain those long-distance ties, you know?"

She nodded.

"Then, once I joined the Army, I was too busy to foster any friendships I had left."

"I understand that. Where life leads us turns out to be nowhere near what we thought we wanted."

"Have you given any more thought to what you want?"

She let out a snort, then coughed, shaking her head. "No.

It's all swirling up there, a jumbled mess. Right now, I'm just focusing on surviving."

"Yeah." Ezra stared off into the distance. Fierce determination filled his gut. He would get her out of here. Even if he had to fight and claw to the last inch. She wouldn't die on his watch.

Seventeen

The high-pitched beeping of Ezra's watch woke him. Coming awake, he silenced the alarm and blinked. It was still dark, but the eastern sky had the first vestiges of color rising above the horizon.

Glancing at Amy, he saw she still slept peacefully, for which he was glad. When they finally stopped talking and laid down, she'd spent some time coughing as her body adjusted to the nighttime air and the change in position. He'd worried she wouldn't sleep much.

Disentangling himself from her, he got up, taking care of his morning routine—survival mode-style—then ate a handful of trail mix and drank some water. He wanted to fill the bottle again before they set off, so the purification tablets had time to work. After checking on Amy again, he went down to the water's edge and filled the bottle.

With the sky lightening, he kicked dirt over the remnants of their fire, then shook Amy awake. "Tink. Time to get up."

She kept sleeping. He put a hand behind her neck, turning her head. She moaned, her head lolling to the side, but she didn't open her eyes. Ezra's heart rate quickened. He tapped her face. "Amy. Honey, wake up."

Moaning again, her eyelids fluttered. Ezra sat her up. "Amy." She opened her eyes and looked at him. He pressed his lips to her forehead. She was even hotter than last night. "Damn."

He propped her against the rock and reached for his bag, digging for the first-aid kit. Finding it, he found a packet of paracetamol, grimacing as he realized they only had one more packet of that and one more dose of ibuprofen left. He needed to get her out of here and to safety today.

"Okay, Tink. You need to take these pills." Grabbing some water, he tore open the medicine package and tried to hand her the pills. She looked at them, but made no move to take them. Ezra cursed under his breath. Somehow, he needed to get the medicine into her.

"Baby, can you take a sip of water for me?" If he could get her to drink, maybe it would wake her up a little more. He put the water bottle to her mouth and tipped it. Weakly, she moved her lips as he dribbled water into her mouth.

"That's good, honey. Let's try some meds now, all right?" He put one of the tablets to her mouth, and she parted her lips. Pushing the pill inside, he put the water back to her mouth and tipped the bottle.

She sputtered, but after a moment, came around enough to swallow the tablet. Ezra slid the other one into her mouth and repeated the process. Once he had the medicine in her, as well as a few more sips of water, he made sure she could sit up on her own, then grabbed the rope sling.

"Do you need to pee before I put you on my back?"

"No."

Ezra's frown grew deeper. It had been close to twenty-four hours since she went. "Are you sure?"

"Yeah. I just want to go back to sleep," she mumbled.

Alarmed even more by her words and her weak voice, Ezra didn't waste any time fitting her into the ropes and getting her onto his back. Wincing as the sling dug into his bruised shoulders when he took her weight, he adjusted her as best he could, then picked up their gear. It was time to hoof it.

Keeping a close eye on the ground, Ezra moved as fast as he dared in the growing daylight. The sun still hadn't come over the horizon, but he could see well enough not to step in a hole. And it was cooler.

He turned his head, glancing at Amy from the corner of his eye. "I'm going to jog. If you feel like you're bouncing too much, tell me, and I'll slow down."

"Okay."

Ezra's heart skipped at the weakness in her voice. She was barely awake. Even her coughs now were weak. Like she couldn't muster the energy to push the air out of her lungs.

He took off, running as fast as he dared. They needed to go as far as possible before it got too hot. The sun would force him to slow down. But he could run a mile in full gear in ten minutes. She weighed more, so he was guessing it would take him about twelve. The sun wouldn't bake him for another couple of hours, so he could go eight to ten miles before he had to slow down. He hoped.

Pain hammered his shoulders with each step, but he blocked it out. Amy needed help. He didn't care what the pace did to his body if it got her to a doctor.

Eighteen

The sun rose as Ezra ran, bathing the world in an orange glow as it hit the rusty dirt. Sweat trickled down his brow as the temperature climbed. He'd have to slow soon, but not yet. Concentrating on every step, it took a moment for the thumping noise to register. He'd thought it was his heartbeat in his ears, but as it got louder, he realized it was a helicopter.

Slowing, he glanced at the sky, shielding his eyes from the sun with his hand. He scanned the area, looking for the source. In the distance, a black speck scuttled across the sky. He watched it for a moment to see where it was headed. It grew larger.

Yes! It was coming at them. With a mental fist pump, he took off in its direction, hoping whoever was in the aircraft looked down and noticed him. Getting closer, he waved his arms. The chopper started to turn away, and Ezra cursed. He should have put the flare gun somewhere accessible; it was buried in the survival bag. Running forward, he continued to wave his arms, praying someone looked back.

The helicopter flew to his right. Ezra followed it and saw a herd of cattle. The chopper was herding them. He dashed toward the herd. One cow turned its head and looked at him, then mooed. Ezra yelled and waved his arms, running right at it. The animal gave a little hop and ran forward, away from him and the rest of the herd. He chased after it, hoping the chopper would go looking for strays.

A moment later, the helicopter swooped around. Ezra looked up and waved his arms high, making eye contact with the pilot. The chopper turned, moving away to an open area fifty yards away. It hovered for a few seconds before setting down.

Adrenaline pushed him to hurry toward it once it landed. The door opened, and a man climbed out. Ezra met him halfway.

"Oh, you don't know how happy I am to see you." Ezra paused in front of the man, relief making him dizzy.

"Are you all right? What are you doing out here?"

"Our plane crashed." Ezra gestured in the general direction from which they came, swallowing hard as he tried to catch his breath. "Two days ago. We've been walking to find help. My friend"—he motioned to Amy—"nearly drowned when we crossed the river. She needs a doctor badly."

The man's light blue eyes went to Amy, who still rested her head on Ezra's shoulder. Ezra couldn't tell if she was awake.

"Okay. Get in." The man tipped his head toward the chopper.

Ezra followed him to the aircraft. The man opened the side door, and Ezra walked closer, turning to set Amy on the floor. He swiftly untied the rope holding the sling together over his chest and shrugged his arms out. She tipped backward, but the man caught her, holding on while Ezra got the rest of the ropes off. Once she was free, Ezra climbed in and pulled her onto the seat with him. The man closed the door, then got in the pilot's seat and passed him a set of headphones. Ezra put them on.

"My name's Steve. What's yours?"

"Ezra. This is Amy." He pointed at the woman in his arms. She wasn't coherent. Her eyes were open, but she was extremely dazed.

"Where were you headed?"

"When we crashed?" Ezra felt the chopper lift, and the ground receded out the window.

"Yeah."

"Dalton Creek. My sister is married to Wayne Dalton."

"Damn. I heard about his accident."

"Is he okay? That's why we were going. To pick up Anna and take her to Darwin." He hoped Anna made it to the city to be with him.

"He's alive. I don't know much more than that. No one mentioned you two, though."

"We just arrived from the U.S. Wayne had a plane in Brisbane for maintenance. The plan was for me to fly it back the same day I arrived, but our plans changed. Then Anna called about Wayne, and we headed out."

"Do you know what happened? Why you crashed?"

"We were losing fuel. I tried to send a mayday, but the radio glitched too. I set down without a problem, but we hit a deep crack as we rolled to a stop. The friction of the fuselage skidding along the ground lit the plane on fire. I think we'd have been fine walking to help—we had water and some food—but then Amy got clocked by a log in the river and inhaled a bunch of water. She's been running a fever since yesterday morning. It's just getting worse." He glanced down at her, brushing her hair back from her face. She was pale, despite the red tinge to her cheeks.

"We get back to the homestead, I'll call for a medical airlift."

"How much further did we have to go? The homestead is on my chart; it's where we were headed."

"You weren't too far. Another ten kilometers or so. I'm impressed you made it this far. Did you carry her the whole way?"

"Mostly." Ezra looked out the window, seeing buildings come into view. In moments, Steve touched down behind the house. As the rotors spun down, Ezra opened the door. Sliding out of the helicopter, he pulled Amy to the doorway and gathered her into his arms.

Steve got out and pointed toward the house. "Let's go in there."

Ezra turned, seeing a woman standing on the back porch, arms crossed as she stared at them with concern etched on her face.

"That's my wife, Jillian." Steve started toward the house, gesturing to the woman.

Following, Ezra mounted the steps.

"What happened?" Jillian looked at Steve, then to Ezra and Amy.

"I found them wandering about ten kilometers to the south. Their plane crashed. The woman needs medical attention."

Jillian's eyes widened. "Call for help. I'll get them settled." She looked at Ezra. "Follow me." She pulled open the screen door and went inside.

Steve held it open for Ezra to pass through. Jillian led him into the white and gray kitchen, then through a dining room decorated in similar tones to a living room. Tan couches sat clustered around an area rug in shades of blue. From a doorway across the room to his left, he saw two small faces watching. The children were young, but not toddlers. Maybe five and seven.

"Mitchell, go get some water from the kitchen. Sarah, can

you fetch me a wet washcloth and the first-aid kit from the bathroom?" Jillian glanced at the kids.

The two scampered in different directions to do as their mother asked.

"What's your name?" Jillian motioned for Ezra to sit.

He grimaced, perching on the edge. He didn't want to dirty her nice couch. "Ezra. Are you sure you want me to sit here? I'm filthy."

"I've got two kids." She waved a hand. "It washes. Sit back and get comfortable. Is this your wife?"

"Friend. Her name is Amy. She inhaled river water Monday afternoon and is running a fever."

The older of the kids, Sarah, returned with the items Jillian requested.

"Thank you, sweetie. Go sit down, now, please."

The girl went to the other couch and hopped up, dark eyes focused on them. She brushed her blonde hair back from her face.

Jillian sat on the couch next to Ezra and opened the first-aid kit. "When was the last time you checked her temperature?"

"Last night. I didn't need a thermometer this morning to know she was warmer than before. I got her to take some paracetamol to bring it down, then just put her on my back and ran."

The woman blinked. "You ran with her on your back?"

He nodded. "I made a rope sling with the rope from the plane's survival bag and walked with her in that all day yesterday. Today, I ran." He touched Amy's hair again. "She's not doing well."

Jillian turned on the thermometer and slid it into Amy's mouth. "No. I can see that." She laid the wet rag over Amy's forehead.

Mitchell returned with several water bottles. Jillian took them. "Thank you. Go sit by your sister."

Obeying his mom, the boy climbed onto the couch, giving Ezra a look similar to the one his sister still sported.

The thermometer beeped, drawing Ezra's attention.

Jillian took it, looking at the readout. "Oh my."

"What is it?"

"Forty-point-two."

Ezra did the math, then cursed under his breath, conscious of little ears listening. Amy's temperature was over a hundred and four.

"I'm going to get some more cold rags. We'll put them under her arms and on her groin." Jillian stood, hurrying out of the room.

"Medical flight is on the way. It'll be over an hour. Their base is almost five hundred kilometers away," Steve said, coming back into the room.

"There's nothing closer?" Ezra grimaced, looking down at Amy. She'd passed out again. Her breathing was quick. And crackly. He could hear it rattle in her chest.

"We have a clinic in Boulia, but it's nearly two hundred kilometers away. The plane will get here in about the same amount of time it would take me to fly her there in the chopper, and it will have a doctor onboard. They'll probably take her to a larger hospital. The one in Boulia is small."

Jillian returned with the wet wash cloths. "Let's lay her flat on the floor. It'll be easier to keep the rags where they need to be. And it's cooler than the sofa."

Ezra gathered Amy into his arms and stood, walking a few feet away to spread her out on the wood floor. She moaned at the change in position, but didn't wake.

"Steve, could you take the kids into another room? I want to remove some of her clothing to cool her down."

"Of course. Come on, guys. How about you show me what you've been working on for school?"

Ezra sent them a quick glance as they left the room, then turned to Jillian. "How can I help?"

"Start taking clothes off of her. Leave just her underwear on. We need to bring her temperature down. Or at least keep it from going higher." She laid the wash cloths on the floor, then grasped the waistband of Amy's leggings and pulled.

He took hold of her jacket sleeve at her wrist and tugged her arm free, whisking it under her body and off her other arm. Getting behind her, he sat her up enough to take off her t-shirt.

Jillian sucked in a breath, making Ezra pause.

"Those are quite the bruises." Jillian pointed to Amy's legs.

Ezra's jaw worked as he saw what the rope harness had done to her legs. "Yeah. My shoulders probably look the same. The ropes dug in, even coiled to take some of the pressure off. That, though"—he pointed at the outside of her leg—"is from the log that knocked her down in the river. It hit there first, then clipped her in the head."

"Her lethargy isn't from the head wound, is it?"

"No. She was coherent until the fever took hold."

"Okay." Jillian picked up the rags and passed him several. "Put those at her pulse points." She tucked two on either side of her groin, then moved to Amy's knees. Ezra put one under each of her arms and around her neck. Jillian spread another one over her abdomen.

"We'll need to change them out several times before the flying doctor service arrives, but hopefully, this helps." Jillian stood and went back to the couch, picking up a bottle of water. "Here." She handed it to him.

"Thank you." Ezra took it and unscrewed the cap, gulping down the cool contents.

"Would you like something to eat?"

He shook his head. He'd eat later. After Amy was in the right hands. Right now, he just wanted to watch over her.

"How about clean up? The bathroom's down the hall." She pointed to her right.

"I'm fine. But thank you. The water is plenty." He swiped the side of his face on his shoulder, getting rid of some of the sweat, then grimaced again. It probably just put a dirt streak on his face. Another one. He sighed, mind spinning as it tried to process that they were safe—if not out of the woods yet.

One thought stuck, though, and he glanced at Jillian. "Could I use your phone? I want to call my sister. She's probably worried sick."

"Of course." She got up and walked into the room where the children had been and came back a moment later with a cellphone. "Here you go." She unlocked it, then held it out.

"Thanks." He took the device and stared at it for a long moment. His mind didn't want to conjure Anna's phone number.

"Here." Jillian crouched in front of him and laid a hand over the phone. "Can you tell me what town she lives in? I can call their local government offices and try to get a number. Everyone knows everyone in the Outback towns."

Ezra closed his eyes and nodded. He was so tired. "Yeah." He cleared his throat. "That's a good idea." Letting his head hang, he spanned his hand across his forehead and rubbed his temples. "Um, she's probably not home, though. Her husband was injured in an accident on their cattle station and was taken to Darwin. We were on our way to pick her up and fly her there when we crashed."

"Are you serious?"

He glanced up to see her wide eyes and incredulous expression. "Yes."

"Oh my goodness. That's terrible." She looked down at

her phone. "I'll try the hospital in Darwin first. What's her name?"

"Anna Dalton."

Jillian's hand paused over the phone. "Is her husband Wayne?"

He nodded. "Your husband mentioned he'd heard about Wayne's accident."

"We all have. News like that travels fast through the ranching community."

"What happened?"

"He was in a pasture and got trampled. That's all anyone knows right now." She shook her head. "And now you crash on your way to help. What else could befall your family?" She turned her attention to the phone, clicking through screens before lifting it to her ear. A moment later, her expression brightened. "Hello, yes. My name is Jillian Thompson. I'm trying to find the wife of one of your patients. The circumstances are a little wild and unusual. I have her brother at my house. He was in a plane crash on his way to see her." Jillian paused, listening. "The patient's name is Wayne Dalton. His wife is Anna." She paused again, then tilted the phone away from her mouth and looked at Ezra. "They're connecting me to the nurse's station in the ICU."

Ezra bit back a curse. Wayne's injuries must be grave.

Jillian went through her spiel again about who she was and why she was calling. A smile brightened her face, and she pulled the phone back again. "She's going to get her."

He sat up and held out a hand for the phone. Putting it to his ear, he waited. A minute later, his sister's voice came over the line.

"Ezra?"

"Hey, Annie." His voice grew thick.

"Oh my God! I thought you were dead! Your plane never arrived, and when I called the airport, they said you took off around nine. They set up a search, but your transponder wasn't working. What happened?"

He swallowed around the lump in his throat and blinked back the moisture in his eyes. "We had a fuel leak. Like, rapid. I had to set down pretty quick. I tried radioing in our position, but the radio was dead."

Anna gasped. "Did it work when you took off?"

"Yeah. It had some static, but it was clear enough. It's not the first aircraft I've flown with a sketchy radio, so I didn't think anything of it."

"Where are you now?"

"Thompson Downs, southeast of Diamantina National Park."

"Oh, they're good people. I think they have an airstrip too. I'll tell Wayne's brother, Jericho, and he can come get you."

"Don't. Not yet, anyway. Amy's sick. She nearly drowned Monday, and now she's battling a lung infection. There's a medical flight on the way to pick her up. I don't know where they're taking her or if I'll be able to go along. I should probably get checked out too." His shoulders ached. So did his head. He knew he was dehydrated. And sunburned.

"God, Ezra."

He could hear the wobble in her voice.

She sniffed. "This is a nightmare. Why is this all happening at once?"

"I don't know, Annie. How's Wayne? Is he going to be all right?"

"Eventually, yeah. He has a bunch of busted ribs, a broken arm and leg, and there are two fractures in one of his cheekbones. He's in ICU because they had to put in a chest tube. His lung collapsed because of the rib injuries. It'll be a long road, but he'll be okay."

"And what about you? How are you holding up? How's the baby?"

"She's fine. With her being so little, I can just strap her to my chest and off we go. And I'm okay. Better, now that I know you're safe. And your friend. I called Jericho after you didn't come, and he detoured on his way to Darwin and picked us up. Their parents are on their way home now, and should be here tonight."

"Good. I'm glad you aren't alone. I'll be there as soon as I can. I just need to make sure Amy's okay." He looked at her. "She's in rough shape."

"You stay with her. Then bring her with you when you come. We'll get her healthy. Her and Wayne. They can recuperate together."

Ezra smiled. "Yeah." His expression sobered. "I'm sorry, Anna. I never meant for this to happen."

"It's not your fault, E-Z."

His smile returned at the use of the nickname she gave him when they were kids.

"You take care of yourself and your friend. Get both of you healthy. I want to meet her."

"Yeah. I want you to meet her too. I think you'll like her."

"Good." She paused, drawing in a breath. "I better go. Maylee's getting hungry."

Ezra could hear the baby cooing in the background. "Okay. Can you give me your cellphone number before you go? My phone went up in flames with the plane." And her number still escaped him. "I'll call you later with an update." He glanced at Jillian, who was getting up and going into the schoolroom.

"Sure."

"Hang on, I need something to write with."

Jillian came back with a sheet of paper and a pencil. He smiled at her in thanks, then spoke into the phone. "Okay, go ahead."

Anna rattled off the number.

"Great." Ezra glanced up after writing it down. "I'll talk to you soon."

"You better. I love you, big brother."

"I love you too. Bye."

"Bye."

He pulled the phone away from his ear and clicked the icon to end the call, handing the device back to Jillian. "Thank you. It was nice to talk to her."

"You're welcome. Is Wayne doing okay?"

"Yeah. He should be fine after some time. He's pretty banged up."

"Cows will do that." She offered him an encouraging smile, then reached out to touch the rag on Amy's stomach. "We should probably change these. They're warm."

"Oh. Right." He pushed himself up off the floor, wincing as his shoulders protested the movement.

"Sit." Jillian waved him back down. "I'll do it. You rest."

"It's okay. I can—"

"Sit, Ezra." Her voice took on a firmer tone. "You've done your part to save her. Let someone else do theirs."

He pressed his lips together, studying her for a moment, then nodded. "Okay. Thank you."

"No worries. I'll be right back." She gathered all the rags and left the room.

Ezra sank back down to the floor. He laid a hand on Amy's head and stroked her soft skin. She was still so warm.

Her eyelids fluttered open. "Ezra?"

"I'm here, Tinkerbell. You're safe. The doctor will be here soon."

"Mmm."

His stomach clenched, and his heart ached at her quiet moan. Bending forward, he pressed a kiss to her forehead. "It'll be okay, Amelia. I promise."

Nineteen

The buzz of the airplane flying low as it approached the station's runway made Ezra sit up. Wincing, he pushed to his feet from the plush sofa. He'd moved off the floor half an hour ago to give his aching back and shoulders a break and let Jillian take over Amy's care until help arrived. With the adrenaline gone, he was beginning to feel the effects of their trek through the Outback.

"I'll go get the team and bring them up." Steve headed for the door.

Ezra followed, but didn't go outside. He stood in the doorway and waited, urging them to hurry. His pain receded as adrenaline spiked again. Amy would finally get the help she needed.

In minutes, Steve returned in a utility vehicle with a man and a woman in blue flight suits. Ezra held the door for them, then followed them to the living room.

"What have we got?" The woman, who had the word doctor emblazoned on her back, looked at Jillian, then at Ezra and Steve. "The report said something about a plane crash?"

Ezra nodded. "We had a hard landing about thirty miles south of here early Monday afternoon. We were fine—no injuries from the crash—but when we crossed the river on our way to help, she got knocked down and basically drowned. She's had a fever since yesterday morning. I've tried medications to keep it down, but it's just rising. She has a cough too."

The doctor nodded. "What's her name?"

"Amy."

"And yours?"

"Ezra."

"I'm Dr. Raymond. Emma. This is Bruce." She motioned to the man who came in with her as she crouched next to Amy. "Amy?" She touched her shoulder. "My name's Emma. I'm a doctor. Can you open your eyes for me?"

Amy's brow wrinkled with a frown, and she moved her head, but didn't open her eyes. The woman looked up at her companion. "Bruce, can you start a line on her?" She unzipped her bag and took out a stethoscope. "Amy, I'm just going to listen to your chest." Emma popped the stethoscope into her ears and placed the bell on Amy's chest.

Ezra didn't like the frown that darkened the doctor's face.

Sitting back, Emma looped the stethoscope around her neck and reached for another pack. "I'm going to pop some oxygen on her. Her lungs are congested. She's likely developed aspiration pneumonia. River water is disgusting."

That was no lie. Ezra smelled terrible, and not just because he'd been lost in the Outback for two days. The river left a stench on them both, and their clothes were stiff.

"These bruises—what are they from?"

"One's from the log that knocked her down. The others are from the ropes I used to hold her on my back."

The woman paused and turned to stare at him. "You tied her to your back?"

He nodded. "She couldn't walk far without needing to stop. I knew she needed help, so I used a rope to make a harness and carried her piggyback-style."

The doctor blinked. "That's—impressive."

He shrugged. "I did what I had to do."

Emma nodded. "It's a good thing. She's very sick." She turned back to her patient.

Arms crossed, Ezra watched the medical team work. They started an IV and checked Amy over well, before putting her on a stretcher. With her ready to go, the doctor approached him.

"How about you? I can see you're sunburned. Do you have any injuries?" She looked him over with a critical eye. "Your posture is off."

"My shoulders are sore from carrying her."

"Let me see."

"I'm fine. I can get checked out at the hospital."

"You can, but I need to let them know what I'm bringing to them. Now let me see."

Lips pursed, Ezra pulled an arm free of his t-shirt. He winced as he lifted his arms to pull it over his head.

Jillian gasped. He looked down, then closed his eyes and took a breath. He knew they were bruised, but they were also raw. No wonder they burned so much.

Cool, gloved-covered hands probed the tops of his shoulders. "Does it hurt when I push here?" She tested the joint at his collarbone.

He winced. "Yeah. But only on the surface. It's all muscle and skin."

A corner of her mouth lifted. "You sound like you speak from experience."

"I'm a special forces chopper pilot. You get banged around in my line of work."

Surprise rounded her eyes. "Wow. Yeah, I guess you would." She shook her head. "I'd say it's a good thing you do what you do. It probably saved both your lives. Okay. You can put your shirt back on." She glanced back at her partner. "Let's get them loaded."

"I need to get our gear. It's still in the chopper." Ezra motioned to Steve.

Emma nodded. "Go ahead. We'll meet you outside."

"Do you need me to help you carry her?" Steve motioned to Amy.

"No. Bruce and I can handle her."

"All right, then." Steve glanced at Ezra. "Come on."

The two men left the house and jogged toward the helicopter resting on the lawn. Steve opened the rear door and reached inside, passing a bag to Ezra, then shouldered the other.

"Thank you again for all you've done." Ezra looked at him as they headed back to the house.

"Of course. I'm just glad I found you out there and saved you several kilometers of hiking."

"Me too."

They reached the utility vehicle, where Bruce and Emma were situating the stretcher over the back. With ratchet straps, they secured Amy to the vehicle, then climbed into the rear seats, turning sideways to hold on to the stretcher. Ezra got in the front next to Steve, holding the bags on his lap. Once they were all settled, Steve started the vehicle and headed for the landing strip. In minutes, Ezra was strapped into a seat, and Amy was loaded in on the stretcher.

"You let us know how things turn out." Steve lifted a hand in farewell.

"I will. Thank you again." Ezra nodded.

"You're most welcome. Take care." He stepped back, and Bruce closed the door.

Ezra leaned his head back against the seat and closed his eyes. He was so tired now. All the ups and downs were finally taking their toll. As the plane's engines revved and they took off, he let himself fully relax for the first time since they crashed. He knew the respite wouldn't last long, but an hour of sleep was better than nothing.

When the plane touched down, he jerked awake and sat up, rubbing his eyes. Glancing through the window, he saw civilization. It was a welcome sight. The aircraft slowed and taxied toward a building, coming to a halt.

Bruce got up and opened the door, lowering the stairs. He motioned Ezra toward the exit. Gathering his things, Ezra left his seat and went down the steps and waited for the others. An ambulance pulled up as they unloaded Amy. Once they had her transferred to the ambulance, Ezra got in. They said goodbye to the flying doctor and paramedic, then made the short journey from the airport to the hospital.

The stretcher wheels clacked as they bumped over the threshold to the emergency department. Cool air blasted him, chilling his sunburned skin. He ignored the goosebumps that popped up and followed the paramedics. Controlled chaos greeted them as they made the turn into the treatment area. He stopped at the edge of the curtained cubicle they wheeled Amy into.

"Sir, why don't you come with me?" A nurse approached him, gesturing down the hall.

"He needs looked at," one of the paramedics said.

The young woman nodded and motioned for Ezra to follow her. With one last look at Amy, he did.

She led him down the corridor to another curtained cubicle. "Have a seat on the bed."

Ezra dropped his bags in the corner, then sat on the thin mattress.

"I need to take some vitals and get some information from you."

He nodded. Sitting back, he let her do what she needed and answered her questions. In five minutes, he was alone.

Letting out a soft groan, he scrubbed his dirty hands over his dirtier face. He didn't want to be in here. He wanted to be down the hall with Amy. He was fine. They were wasting resources on him. Some painkillers and some burn cream and he'd be peachy.

Ezra got up and walked to the edge of the curtain, staring out toward Amy's cubicle. People went in and out; some carrying things, others entering to help. He wanted to know what they were doing. If she was going to be okay.

"Are you the man from the plane crash?"

With a start, Ezra turned. A plain-clothes police officer stood a few feet away, holding up his badge.

"Sorry. Didn't mean to startle you. I'm Detective Larson. I just have some questions for you."

"Sure." Ezra stepped back into his cubicle and sat down.

"First off, I'm glad you and your lady friend are all right. That must have been quite a harrowing ordeal."

"Yeah." It wasn't the first hard landing he'd ever had, but the journey to safety was definitely the worst.

"So, tell me what happened. Start at the very beginning. Before you even took off."

Ezra blew out a breath and thought back. Forehead wrinkled in concentration, he told the detective everything he remembered, answering a few questions along the way. When he finished, the man stared at him for several seconds and shook his head.

"It's a damn good thing you were the one with her. Most pilots, even experienced bush pilots, would have trouble hiking out of the Outback. Especially with an ill partner."

Everyone kept saying that, but Ezra didn't see it. She

wouldn't have been in the situation if it weren't for him. She'd be safe in Brisbane, or somewhere along the coast. Probably enjoying a cocktail on the beach. Instead, she was in a remote hospital, fighting for her life. He pressed his lips into a flatline and held the man's gaze.

A light of understanding entered the man's eyes. He tapped his notepad against his hand. "Do you know where you went down?"

Glad the detective changed the subject, Ezra got up and dug into one of the backpacks to get the map. "Roughly. I marked where I thought we were based on the last coordinates I saw on the flight computer before it died." He spread the map out on the bed and showed the detective.

The man let out a low whistle. "It's a good thing it's not the rainy season. That area around the river is usually flooded. You never would have made it across."

"Amy almost didn't, anyway."

Detective Larson patted the back of his shoulder. "Don't dwell on it. You got her to safety. The doctors here are topnotch. She'll be fine."

Ezra chewed on the corner of his lip. Easier said than done.

The curtain rattled, and another man in green scrubs stepped in. "Hi. I'm Dr. Fitzgerald. Ezra?"

"Yes." Ezra nodded.

The detective held out a business card. "If you think of anything more, call. I'll get your contact info from the staff here. I'm sure we'll talk again."

"Okay, thank you."

"Yep. Best of luck to you and your lady." The detective brushed past the doctor and pulled the curtain closed.

Ezra gathered up his map and faced the doctor. "I'm fine. Really. Just give me some ibuprofen, and I'll be right as rain."

A smile kicked up one side of the man's face. "All things

considered, I'd say you're doing mighty well. But you're not fine, Mr. Chastain. Have a seat."

Grimacing, Ezra dropped the map on top of his bags and did as the doctor asked. If it weren't for Amy being down the hall, he'd pick up his stuff and leave. "Fine. Just make it quick."

TWENTY

A loud beep in the hallway, pulled Ezra from his restless slumber on the vinyl couch in Amy's hospital room. Yawning, he tucked an arm under his side and pushed, wincing as pain shot through his bruised shoulder. With a groan, he made it upright.

Rubbing the sleep from his eyes, he glanced at the bed. Amy still slept, an oxygen cannula tucked into her nose and wires snaking out from beneath her hospital gown. Her color was better, which he was glad to see. Last night, she'd been so pale. He hoped she'd wake up a little more today. So far, she'd only winced away from light when the nurses checked her pupils, but otherwise stayed unconscious. He hadn't really expected much else, though. They'd only been here less than a day, so far. He just hoped the medications being pumped into her veins did their job and her condition improved.

Noise from the hallway intruded again as the door opened. Ezra looked over to see one of the attending physicians walk in with his entourage of nurses and junior doctors. A young dark-haired woman smiled at him and walked closer.

"Hello. I'm Lanie. I'll be Amy's nurse today."

He offered her a small nod. "Ezra. Nice to meet you." Another yawn cracked his jaw, and he covered his mouth. "Oh, sorry."

Lanie's smile turned knowing. "We won't be long."

Ezra waved a hand. "Take your time. I'm awake." Barely. But he didn't want to go back to sleep. He was stiff from lying on the uncomfortable couch and wanted to move around.

She nodded, then turned away to focus on the doctor and Amy.

"Good morning." The doctor lifted a hand. "I'm Dr. Armand."

Ezra waved back.

Dr. Armand glanced at Lanie. "Any problems overnight?"

Lanie shook her head. "No. She's been stable, and her temperature's dropped. The medications seem to be working."

"Good." The doctor unwound his stethoscope from around his neck and put the ends in his ears. Placing the bell on Amy's chest, he listened for several long moments. "She still sounds congested." He glanced at the monitor. "But her oxygen levels are good."

"When I took over for Debbie this morning, she said the congestion was improving," Lanie replied.

"That's what I like to hear." Dr. Armand put his stethoscope back around his neck, then did several other checks before stepping back. He looked at Ezra. "She's improving steadily, so I think we hit on the right antibiotics. Cultures on the fluid we took from her lungs yesterday should come back either tonight or tomorrow morning. We'll change up medications as necessary then. For now, though, I'm going to leave everything alone. She's doing well for what she's been through."

Ezra's head bobbed. "Good." A measure of relief went through him. It made all his aches and pains worth it to know he'd gotten Amy to help in time to give her the best shot at a quick recovery.

Dr. Armand tipped his head. "How about you? How are you doing? Talk of what happened to you two is all over the hospital. The E.D. cleared you, right?"

"Yes. I'm fine. Just sore. Nothing's broken. Just strained and bruised."

The doctor offered him a soft smile. "I'm glad. What you did was nothing short of heroic. She wouldn't have lasted more than another day without medical intervention."

Again, Ezra nodded. He swallowed around the lump in his throat. "I couldn't let her die."

Dr. Armand tipped his head in acknowledgement. "With some time, I think she'll make a full recovery."

"When do you think she'll wake up?"

The doctor glanced at Amy, then turned back. "Hopefully soon. It just depends on how much rest her body thinks it needs. I'd say probably within the next twenty-four to forty-eight hours. If she's still unconscious past that, then we'll need to do some more tests. See if there's something else going on. But all signs point to her moving in the right direction."

"Okay." Ezra stared at Amy, a little of the worry creeping back in at the doctor's words. He hoped she woke up soon.

"Do you have any other questions?"

Ezra looked at the doctor. "No. I'm good for now."

"All right. If you think of anything, please don't hesitate to ask."

"Thank you."

With a nod and a smile, Dr. Armand motioned for everyone to exit. Only Lanie hung back, standing in the doorway after everyone else left.

"The cafeteria makes some strong coffee. And a hearty breakfast."

He tossed her a grateful smile. "Thank you. I'll wander down there soon."

"You're welcome." With another smile, she stepped into the hall and closed the door.

Ezra blew out a breath and swiped his hands over his face, then stood. He walked to Amy's bedside to stare down at her. She looked peaceful, even attached to all the wires and tubes. He was happy she was resting comfortably now. When she did eventually wake up, he knew that would change. She'd feel the consequences of their ordeal, then.

Reaching out a hand to brush back a tendril of her hair from her cheek, he was surprised to see a tremor in his fingers. It wasn't from the pain in his shoulder. The lump in his throat reappeared. He swallowed hard, but it refused to leave, growing larger instead. Touching her soft skin, he felt the first tear trickle down his face. All the emotions he'd been holding back hit him. He'd come so close to losing her.

His fingers curled into a fist, and he withdrew his hand, stepping away from the bed to stand by the window. Staring outside, he tried to corral his thoughts and make sense of them. They were a jumbled mess. Images and feelings from the last several days warred with the doctor's words and his own guilt about what happened.

How could he have let this happen? Could he have done anything to prevent it? He hoped the detective he talked to yesterday was able to find the plane. He'd like to know what they found in the wreckage—what caused the crash. Until he knew, he wouldn't be satisfied that he couldn't have done something to prevent it.

He glanced at Amy's sleeping form again. The doctor was wrong. What Ezra did wasn't heroic. It was just necessary. He meant what he'd said—he couldn't lose her. Somehow, over the last six days, she'd gotten under his skin and was rapidly making her way toward his heart. Forget the thought of what could have been. He didn't want to think about what would happen at the end of their vacation and they had to go their separate ways. One thing he knew, he couldn't let her walk out of his life. But he wasn't sure how to stop it.

Twenty-One

It took everything Amy had to open her eyes. Her eyelids felt glued shut and like they weighed a hundred pounds each. She managed to get them cracked open, only to squeeze them shut as bright light pierced her brain. Moaning, she lifted a hand, blocking the light, and blinked.

"Amy?"

She turned toward the deep voice that had been her constant companion for days. "Ezra?"

A warm hand landed on her head and stroked her hair. "Hey, Tinkerbell. Welcome back."

"What?" A frown pinched her brow. What was he talking about? She blinked, trying to bring the room into focus. Slowly, she noticed the acoustic tile ceiling. And the tube blowing air into her nose. "Where am I?"

"Mount Isa Hospital. You developed aspiration pneumonia from your dip in the river. You've been unconscious here for a couple of days." His other hand covered hers and wrapped around her fingers.

Amy closed her eyes and tried to swallow. Her mouth was tacky. "Can I have some water?"

Ezra's hand left hers and reached for something lying on the bed. "Let's call the nurse and find out. They'll want to know you're awake." He raised a tan remote and pushed a button.

"May I help you?" The tinny voice came through the remote speaker.

"Yes. Amy's awake."

"Oh, wonderful. I'll be down in a moment."

"Thank you."

"You're welcome."

Ezra set the remote down, then sat on the edge of her bed. "How're you feeling?"

"Yucky. But better than the other day. What happened? The last I remember, you were forcing me to drink water, then hoisting me onto your back."

"Yeah. You pretty much passed out after that. I ran several miles, then came upon a rancher out herding cattle with a helicopter. He picked us up and took us to his house. He and his wife looked after us and called for help. A medical flight brought you here. Brought both of us here."

Amy rubbed at her forehead, processing that. She'd missed a lot. "Are you okay?"

"I'm fine. Some bruises and a wicked sunburn. Nothing that won't heal."

She closed her eyes and let her head fall back against the pillow. "Good." She knew she should say more, but words wouldn't form in her brain to exit her mouth.

The door swung open. "Well, hello. Welcome to the land of the living."

Amy opened her eyes to look at the nurse. "Hi."

"Hi. I'm Lanie. How're you feeling?" The dark-haired woman smiled, her hazel eyes crinkling at the corners.

"Crummy."

The nurse's smile broadened. "That's to be expected. I've called your doctor. He's on his way down to look at you."

"Can I have a drink?"

"A couple sips of water won't hurt, sure. Give me just a couple minutes. I want to run some obs on you first, then I'll go grab a pitcher." She reached for the blood pressure cuff hanging from a hook on the monitor.

Amy closed her eyes and gritted her teeth. She didn't want her blood pressure taken. She just wanted a damn drink. When she passed out, she was thirsty. Now she'd awakened thirsty. She was tired of being thirsty.

"Um, are you feeling okay?" Lanie asked.

"Why?" Amy opened her eyes, pinning the nurse with an annoyed glare.

"Your heart rate picked up."

"I'm thirsty." Her raspy voice reflected that fact. "I just want some water. You'll get better numbers if you get me a drink first."

Lanie pressed her lips together and studied Amy. She nodded. "I can see that. Okay." She hung up the cuff. "I'll be right back." Spinning on her heel, she walked out.

Amy blew out a breath, then coughed. "Damn." She winced, putting a hand over her chest. "Ow." Her ribs ached. Her entire body hurt, but her chest hurt the most.

"Take it easy, Tinkerbell. Don't make the staff wish you were still asleep."

She aimed a glare at Ezra. "I'll remind you of this the next time your mouth feels like you ate the Sahara and something crawled in and died."

Ezra's lips twitched. "Noted."

The door swished open. "Okay. Let's get you hydrated, so the doctor doesn't think you're dying." The nurse smiled, holding up a pitcher and a plastic cup.

Amy sat up, wincing as the muscles in her legs

complained. She hadn't seen them yet, but she imagined she had some nice bruises from the ropes and from the log that smacked into her.

Lanie poured water into the cup, then took a paper-wrapped straw from her scrubs pocket and handed it over. "Sip slowly. You don't want your stomach to rebel."

Nodding, Amy tore the paper off the straw and put it in the water. Her hand shook as she tried to take the cup from the nurse.

"Let me." Ezra took it and held it close enough for her to get the straw between her lips.

She closed her mouth around the straw and sipped. Cool liquid hit her tongue, and she nearly swooned with relief. It slid down her throat, wetting her dry vocal chords, then hit her stomach, sending a chill through her body. After she sucked down several mouthfuls, she didn't feel like the desert lived in her mouth anymore and released the straw.

"Better?" Ezra set the cup on the nightstand.

Amy nodded.

"Great." Lanie stepped closer. "Let's try this again." She lifted the blood pressure cuff from the hook and wrapped it around Amy's arm. Pushing a button on the monitor, the cuff inflated. While the machine worked, she took a digital thermometer from her pocket and ran it over Amy's forehead and behind her ear. It beeped and she looked at it.

"What is it?" Ezra asked.

"Thirty-seven-point-four. Doing much better."

"Was my fever really high?" Amy looked between Ezra and the nurse.

"It was one-oh-four-point-two when the medics loaded you on the plane. And that was after Jillian and I tried cooling you down," Ezra said.

Briefly, Amy wondered who Jillian was. But the nurse spoke before she could ask.

"I think it was right around that when you got up here from the emergency room too." The monitor made a noise, and Lanie took the blood pressure cuff off Amy's arm. "You look much better now. The antibiotics did the trick. I imagine the doctor will move you to a regular room in the morning."

Amy wrinkled her nose. "How long do I have to stay?"

"That would be a question for the doctor. He'll be able to tell you more." She took a pen from her pocket and wrote a few things in a small notebook, then clicked the pen closed. "Can I get you anything else?"

"A toothbrush, maybe? The desert is gone, but the dead animal is still there."

The woman grinned. "I'll bring some things in to you. You can't get out of bed just yet, but your boyfriend can help you. You're a lucky lady, you know? He's been here the whole time. Only left long enough to clean up, then came right back."

Boyfriend? Amy looked at Ezra, raising an eyebrow. He gave her a small half-smile and shrugged one shoulder.

She turned back to Lanie. "I'm very aware of how lucky I am. He saved my life. More than once." Her voice grew thick. Ezra's hand covered hers. Amy turned her palm up and clutched his fingers.

The nurse offered them both a smile and backed toward the door. "I'll give you two a few minutes. You need anything besides the toothbrush?"

Amy shook her head. "No. Thank you for the water."

"You're welcome." With a bright smile, Lanie left.

The door barely closed when Amy spoke. "Thank you, Ezra. I didn't say that when I woke up, but I should have. Thank you for everything you did. I'm not sure—" Her voice broke and tears welled in her eyes. Her mind had cleared some, and she was acutely aware of how close she came to dying.

Ezra squeezed her hand. "You don't need to thank me,

Amy. I wasn't about to let you die. Not when I could do something to prevent that."

"I know, but still... Are you really okay?"

He rolled his shoulders; the tightening of his expression told her they hurt. "I'm all right. My shoulders are strained, a little raw, and badly bruised. Like you, I just need some time."

"You're sure that's all?"

"Yes." His tone took on a note of exasperation. "Stop worrying about me. Worry about getting better. My sister wants to meet you."

Amy's face brightened. "You talked to her? How's your brother-in-law?"

"He's doing okay. Battered and broken, but he'll heal. You get out of here and we'll go to Darwin. Have a big convalescing party at the house Anna rented there."

Amy chuckled. "That's exactly what I envisioned for my vacation."

Ezra's smile faded. "I'm sorry to have ruined it."

"You didn't. All this was an accident."

"Right, but I made you come with me."

"You did no such thing." She narrowed her eyes, the strength returning to her voice. "I joined you of my own free will. None of this is your fault."

He rubbed his forehead with his free hand. "How about we agree to disagree?"

"Ezra—"

The door opened again. Amy bit back a growl.

"Well, hello there, young lady. It's good to see you awake." A man in his fifties entered, a smile on his tanned face. "I'm Dr. Armand. How are you feeling?"

Didn't these people ever talk to each other? "Better than when I came in."

"Good." He took a stethoscope from his pocket. "May I have a listen to your lungs?"

Amy nodded. The doctor pressed the stethoscope to her chest and asked her to take several deep breaths, sitting her up to listen to other spots.

"You sound better." He removed the stethoscope from his ears, letting it sit around his neck. "Less crackly. You're a lucky woman. A few more hours and we might not be having this conversation. At least not yet. We were on the fence about intubating you Wednesday, but you responded well to the antibiotics we pumped into you."

"I'm glad. How soon can I get out of here?"

"A few more days, I'd say. I know you're on holiday, but I don't want to send you off before the medicine's done its job. The IV stuff is stronger—and faster acting—than the pills."

Amy wrinkled her nose. "Okay."

He smiled. "I'm glad you're feeling well enough to protest. That's a good sign."

"Sorry. I'm just—" She waved a hand, unable to put into words how she felt. Annoyed. Upset. Angry. Sad. All those emotions were there, and for multiple reasons.

"I understand. I'll release you just as soon as it's safe. Doctors aren't right around the corner in this part of Australia. I don't want to let you go too soon and then you get sicker."

He made a good point, which helped temper some of what she felt. She nodded. "Okay. Thank you."

"Of course. Can I get you anything?"

"No. I think I'm all right for now."

"Good. I'm going to start you on some liquids—other than the water you have." He gestured to the cup on the table. "Maybe tonight you can bump up to solids."

"Sounds good." Now that he mentioned food, her hunger kicked in. She doubted she'd have any trouble eating.

"All right. I'll go get the orders entered. What would you like to start with? Broth or jelly?"

"Jelly?" Amy frowned. That wasn't liquid.

"Sorry. Gelatin. We call it jelly."

"Oh. Right. Can I have both? I'm actually pretty hungry." She laid a hand over her stomach.

"Sure. Red, blue, orange, or green?"

"Red."

He nodded and backed toward the door. "I'll put in the order. Call the nurse if you need anything."

"I will. Thanks."

With another nod, he turned and left.

Amy looked at Ezra. Really looked. Dark purple circles cast shadows under his eyes. Stubble lined his jaw, black against the reddened skin on his face. She saw a few blisters near his hairline and on his nose and cheeks. Her face stung, but she didn't think it was as bad as his. She'd buried it in his back for most of their trek. Mostly, though, he looked tired.

"You still look exhausted."

"I am. I haven't slept much. That couch isn't the most comfortable thing." He gestured to the opposite wall.

Amy glanced over at the blue vinyl sofa under the window. It looked much too short for his tall frame. And like it would be hot. Plastic didn't breathe. "You've been sleeping in here?"

He nodded. "They didn't admit me, and I wasn't about to leave you alone and check into a hotel, so they let me stay with you. Our foreign status has some perks, I guess. So does their assumption that we're dating. I didn't bother to correct them. But the staff were in and out all the time during the night. Your IV pump beeps for random reasons. It's not been restful."

"I'm sorry. You can go find a hotel now if you want. I'm awake and aware of what's happening." A thought hit her, and she gasped. "Wait. If I was unconscious, who made decisions for me? I know they wouldn't let you do it, even if you were actually my boyfriend. You're not my next-of-kin."

"I got a hold of your parents."

Her eyes widened. "Oh, man. I bet that went well. How?" Her phone took a dunk in the river. She doubted it still worked. Their number was in it, and she hadn't been awake to tell him what it was. Unless she did so and didn't remember.

"You told me where you lived and what you did for a living. I have some friends who can do some freaky things with very little information, and they found them for me." He held up a hand. "And no, your parents aren't on their way here. I promised them you were mostly out of danger and to give them regular updates."

Amy's eyebrows lifted. "And they believed you? I never mentioned you."

"One of the nurses let me borrow her phone, and I sent them a picture of you lying in the hospital bed. Once they saw that, they talked to your doctors and were able to say, yes, you'd want everything possible done." His mouth flattened. "They weren't too happy when the doctor mentioned intubation. But they understood it might be necessary."

"I'm glad it wasn't."

"Me too." He leaned down and pressed a kiss to the top of her head. "I'm really glad you're okay."

Amy closed her eyes, letting his low voice wash over her. She shouldn't want him—a man she met a week ago—holding her hand in her hospital room, kissing her. But she did. And she didn't want him to leave.

Her fingers tightened around his, and she echoed his words back to him. "Me too."

Twenty-Two

Bright sunshine hit Amy's face as the nurse wheeled her out of the hospital toward the waiting cab. She took a deep breath, filling her lungs with the hot Outback air. It felt good to be out of the hospital. And on her birthday, no less. She was happy she wouldn't have to spend it as a patient. Though still weak, she was well enough to leave, thanks to a steady diet of supplemental oxygen and the strong antibiotics they'd fed her this past week.

But she wasn't too happy about their method of transportation out of town. The first leg of their journey was a short car ride to the airport. After that, she had to get on another small plane. This one flown by the brother of Ezra's brother-in-law, Jericho.

"Ready?" Ezra held a hand out to her.

"As I'll ever be." She took it and let him pull her to her feet. With a hand under her elbow, he helped her into the car.

Smiling her thanks, she settled into the seat. After a week in the hospital, she felt much stronger, but still tired quickly. She was glad the nurses made her ride down to the car in a wheelchair. She'd have been huffing and puffing by now.

Ezra got in beside her with the backpack containing her meager belongings. He'd gone shopping to get them a few things. Mostly clothes for himself. But he'd bought her some slippers and a couple of pajama sets so she could get out of the hospital gowns. And the leggings and t-shirt she now wore, along with her undergarments. That had been embarrassing. She'd never had a man buy her underwear. At least, not the mundane, everyday stuff. Andy bought her lingerie on occasion, but it was always for the bedroom. Never for her to just wear. She was grateful, though. He'd done so much for her. She didn't know how she'd ever repay him.

The car pulled away from the curb. Ezra's hand landed on her knee, and she glanced at him.

"Doing okay?"

She nodded. "I'm fine. Glad to be out of there."

"I bet. That's not a fun way to spend vacation."

No, it was not. She planned to do nothing risky for the next two and a half weeks.

Amy bit back a sigh. Was that really all she had left? It seemed like it should be more. She wished it were more. She'd have to make the best of the time. But safely.

They wound through the city, headed for the small regional airport where Jericho waited for them. He was taking them to Darwin, where Wayne was still in the hospital. Ezra said Anna had rented a house near the hospital; they were all staying there for now. Amy was still too tired to argue. She needed time to recuperate and knew if she was on her own, it would be much harder for her to rest. It felt weird to stay at a house with people she didn't know, but knowing Ezra would be there helped.

He'd been a godsend. She couldn't imagine muddling through the last week without him. He kept her occupied, talked to her family, made sure she had clothes, and even handled the investigators who showed up to ask about the crash. They'd pressed her for details, but her addled brain couldn't remember much at the time. He'd kicked them out, telling them to come back another day when she felt better. That day had been yesterday. She told them what she could, which was very little. They'd looked disappointed, but she couldn't help it if all she knew was the engine sputtered and the fuel gauge dipped. What else was she supposed to say?

The airport came into view. Amy's stomach rolled. She did not want to get on that plane. But Darwin by road would take too long, and there was more risk in driving the isolated road than flying. She still didn't like it.

Turning into the airport, Ezra directed the driver where to go. The man took them as far as he was allowed, then parked. Ezra paid him, then helped Amy out while the driver retrieved Ezra's bags from the trunk.

"You all have a good trip." The driver waved and got back in his taxi.

Amy tried to smile, but knew it came out as more of a grimace.

"Are you okay to walk to the hangar?" He gestured to the building in front of them.

"I'll be fine. It's not that far." For which she was glad. The heat here was something. She could already feel it weighing her down.

Giving her a critical once-over, he grabbed his bags from the sidewalk and looped them over his shoulder, then reached for her elbow. Amy let him steady her. His touch helped her nerves.

The doors swished open, admitting them to the small office. A man looked over from staring at the map on the wall.

"Hello. Can I help you folks?"

"We're here to meet Jericho Dalton."

"Ah. He mentioned he had passengers today." The man walked forward. "Graeme Tennyson. Nice to meet you."

Ezra took his hand. "Ezra Chastain. This is Amy Preston."

Graeme tipped his hat to Amy. "Ma'am." He backed toward the door. "I'll go get him. It'll be just a moment."

"Thank you." Ezra nodded.

Sweat popped out on Amy's brow. It was warm in here. Not as hot as outside, but still warm. She fanned her face.

"You all right?"

"Yeah. Just hot."

"It'll be cooler in the plane once we take off."

She hummed. That didn't help her now. Her ears were ringing. Walking away from him, she sat down in the chair along the side wall. At least if she passed out, she wouldn't slam her head on the floor now.

The door to the back opened again and a man with light brown hair stepped through. "Ezra." A wide smile covered his handsome face.

"Hey, Jericho." Ezra held out a hand. "Good to see you again."

"You too. Though I wish the circumstances were different. I'm glad you're both safe."

"Us too." Ezra glanced at Amy. "This is Amy. Amy, Jericho Dalton."

She lifted a hand and waved.

Jericho's smile faded and a frown took it's place. "You doing okay, ma'am? You don't look so great."

"I'm fine. Just hot. After being ill, the heat is taking its toll."

"Well, let's get loaded up and get going." He motioned for them to precede him through the door.

Amy pushed to her feet. Ezra wrapped an arm around her waist, and she clung to him. "Thank you," she whispered.

He bent his head close to her ear. "I've got you, Tinkerbell."

Oh, he sure did. In more ways than one.

They moved through the door and into a large hangar. Jericho led them to a small white plane that looked a lot like the one they'd crashed. Amy's anxiety ratcheted up another notch.

"Relax," Ezra whispered in her ear. "Same model, different plane. We'll be fine."

"You're sure?"

His mouth flattened, and he didn't answer. Amy's heart skipped. His hesitation didn't help her nerves.

"You two can climb onboard. I just need to finish my final checks."

Ezra headed for the plane's door, towing Amy along. "Check the fuel line well."

"Oh, trust me." Jericho leaned around the front of the plane to look at them. "I've checked and rechecked every system. I did it when I took off from Dalton Creek this morning, and I'm doing it again now. We're not crashing. Not from mechanical failure."

His confidence buoyed Amy's spirits a little. Heart rate slightly slower, she climbed the stairs and sat down. Ezra sank into the seat beside her.

"You can sit up front, if you want." She motioned toward the cockpit.

He glanced at the pilot's seat, then at her. "I'm good back here."

She frowned. "No you're not. Don't lie. You want to be up there, so you know what's going on."

He lifted a shoulder. "I'll be fine back here."

Amy huffed. "Ezra—"

"I'm staying with you. Stop arguing."

Peeved he put her feelings above his, she crossed her arms and glared. She appreciated the sentiment, but she was a big girl and could handle sitting by herself.

"What? Why are you looking at me like that?"

"I'm not a child."

"Didn't say you were."

She huffed again. "I'll probably sleep through the flight. You don't need to babysit me."

"Didn't I ask you to stop arguing?"

"Yep. Doesn't mean I'm going to listen."

He eyed her, pursing his lips. "If I stay back here, you're going to stay pissed at me, aren't you?"

"Probably." For a little while, anyway. Until she fell asleep and forgot all about it.

"I know you're nervous. I am too, to be honest. I don't want to leave you back here by yourself."

She laid a hand over his arm. "I promise not to freak out and try to jump from the plane, okay?"

His mouth twitched. "Wasn't really worried you would." His amusement faded, and those brilliant blue eyes pierced hers. "Are you sure you'll be all right back here alone?"

"Yes. One hundred percent." That was a lie. She'd be nervous as hell. But his presence next to her would only alleviate it a little. And he was still nearby. "Sit up front. I'm going to buckle in here and snooze. The heat really is doing me in." That part was not a lie. Her body felt heavier with every passing minute.

He stared at her for a long moment. "If you're sure..."

"Yes!" She shoved at his arm. "Go."

"Fine. When Jericho is ready, I'll go up there. Right now, though, you need some water." He opened his backpack and pulled out a refillable bottle and handed it to her. "That's yours, so keep it with you."

"Oh." She looked at the purple bottle in her hand. "Thank you."

His head bobbed once.

Moisture gathered in her eyes. She opened the bottle and took a drink, hiding her face.

"What's wrong?"

Dammit. She wasn't fast enough. Lowering the bottle, she put the cap on and sniffed. "Nothing. I'm fine."

He just arched an eyebrow.

Amy blew out a quick breath. He wouldn't drop it until she explained. One thing she'd learned in the last ten days was that Ezra could read her like a book. There was no hiding when she was upset. And he refused to let her stay that way. It was both nice and maddening. Sometimes, a woman just wanted to wallow in her sadness and get over it in her own way.

Ignoring him now, though, wasn't an option. If she did, he'd stay back here with her for the flight. She wanted him to be where he was comfortable. "You're a good man."

That eyebrow rose again. "That makes you sad?"

"No. It makes me overwhelmed. You've been so good to me. It's nice." Her voice ended on a whisper.

Ezra took her hand. "I'm glad I've made you happy. It makes sleeping on that hospital couch worth it." One side of his mouth lifted.

Amy chuckled. "You could have gone to a hotel. Or on to Darwin without me. But I appreciate that you stayed." She drew in a shaky breath and sniffed. "It's been nice not being alone." She would never admit that to anyone but him, though. She did not need her family and friends telling her I told you so.

He squeezed her hand, then brought it to his lips and pressed a kiss to the back. "You're very welcome."

Amy offered him a tremulous smile, then turned to the door at the commotion on the ground. Jericho was coming up the stairs. She withdrew her hand from Ezra's and dashed away the wetness on her cheeks, grateful for the reprieve. The man was getting under her skin. And in her weakened state, she was powerless to resist. Not that she really wanted to. Ezra was nice. But she still needed to figure out her life first.

"Are we all ready?" Jericho entered the cabin, hunched over in deference to the ceiling height.

"Yes." Ezra shifted. "Do you mind if I sit up front with you?"

Jericho's brows dipped a fraction, and his gaze went to Amy. "You sure you don't want to stay back here?"

"She's kicking me out. Said she just wants to sleep."

A smile slashed over Jericho's face. "Sounds like a plan. I'll try to give you a smooth flight."

"That would be great. My last pilot sucked." She grinned as she looked at Ezra.

He flattened his mouth and rolled his eyes, then smiled. "Yeah, yeah. Whatever."

Chuckling, Jericho walked between the seats and sat down.

Ezra rose and turned to look at her. "If you need anything—"

She waved a hand. "You're only a few feet away. I'll be okay. Go. Be a less nervous flyer. I really am going to try to sleep."

"Okay." With one last, long look, he joined Jericho up front.

Amy fastened her seatbelt and sank against the back of the seat. Sleep sounded wonderful. Moving from the car to the plane zapped all her energy. Nerves still fluttered in her belly, though, keeping her awake.

Closing her eyes, she tried to tune everything out and reminded herself that if she dozed off, the nerves would go away. If she was lucky, she might even sleep through a plane crash and never know what happened until she woke up in heaven.

Amy rolled her eyes and looked out the window. She'd be

lucky if her dreams didn't terrify her. There had been some doozies since the crash.

The engine whirred to life, filling the plane with a buzzing whoosh. Amy closed her eyes again and let the sound drown out everything else. It made for good white noise.

With a soft jolt, the brakes released, and the plane rolled forward. She cracked an eye open as the sunlight hit her in the face, then closed it again, sleep weighing on her mind. A minute later, she felt the aircraft speed up, then they were lifting off the ground. As they leveled out, her brain finally gave up, and she fell asleep.

Twenty-Three

The touch of the plane's wheels on the ground jolted Amy awake. She sat up, heart thundering, and looked out the window. Black tarmac raced by along with a line of buildings. They'd landed safely at the airport in Darwin.

She blew out a breath and rubbed the sleep from her eyes, yawning. The aircraft slowed and turned. Amy watched the terminal go by. She leaned forward to look out the front and saw more buildings looming.

Bumping along the tarmac, they soon reached the hangars, where Jericho parked the aircraft. Ezra unfastened his seatbelt and got up. Amy unbuckled and slid toward the edge of her seat.

"Did you have a good nap? I looked back and you were out."

"Yeah." She offered him a tired smile. "I'm still sleepy, but not dead-tired like I was when I sat down." Though she'd probably need another one when they reached their destination.

"Good." He reached for the door handle and opened the door, lowering the stairs. Holding out a hand, he motioned her forward. "Jericho gave me the keys to the four-by-four. We'll go get it started and get the air-conditioning running while he finishes up here."

Amy picked up their backpacks and handed him his. He took them both, giving her a look, which made an amused smile flit over her face. She'd offended his sensibilities by only offering him his backpack.

Still grinning, she descended the stairs to the pavement. Heat radiated from the surface, making sweat pop out on her face. How was it hotter here than in Mount Isa? Fanning herself, she glanced back to see Ezra coming down the steps.

He took her hand. "Come on. Let's go cool off. This is nuts."

She agreed.

Together, they walked the short distance to the parking area on the side of the hangar and found the car. Ezra unlocked it and got in, starting the engine. Amy went around to the passenger side and sat down, leaving the door open until the A/C had a chance to turn cool. The car was new, so it only took a minute for the hot air coming from the vents to turn icy. Swinging her legs in, she shut the door and pointed the vents at her face.

"Oh, that feels nice." She leaned back and savored the cool air blowing over her.

"Yeah." Ezra shut his door. "How're you doing?"

"I'm okay. Stop worrying about me. How are your shoulders?" She knew they still hurt. Every once in a while, she caught him lifting an arm and rolling his shoulder. She hadn't seen the bruises, but if they looked anything like her thighs, it would be another week before the pain faded. Amy was just happy he hadn't done any serious damage—like separating his shoulders—by carrying her the way he did.

"They're fine. And I will worry about you if I want." The upward slant to his mouth softened his words.

An answering tilt lifted hers. She closed her eyes and stayed silent. His hand closed over hers. Her heart skipped at the tender gesture, and she turned her hand over, twining their fingers together.

They sat in silence for several minutes, not feeling the need to talk while they waited on Jericho. When he arrived, Amy wished he hadn't. She was enjoying the moment. But they couldn't stay in the car at the airport forever.

Getting out, she moved to the backseat while Ezra came around and took her spot. Jericho climbed into the driver's seat.

"All ready?" Jericho glanced at her, then at Ezra.

Amy nodded.

"Yep," Ezra said.

"Awesome. Let's go." Jericho put the car in gear and drove away from the hangar.

Once outside the airport gate, he wove through the city streets until they reached a two-story house with towering palm trees in the yard.

Amy stared at the white and gray house. It looked like a stripped-down, modern version of the cookie-cutter houses in many American suburbs. It was all clean lines and no adornments. The property was well kept, though. Flowering bushes bloomed under the front window and the grass had been recently mowed.

"Everybody out." Jericho opened his door.

Amy followed suit, stepping out of the car. Ezra waited for her, then put a hand on her back as they walked toward the front door. It opened before they reached it to reveal a dark-haired woman. A bright smile wreathed her face.

Ezra dropped his hand, walking toward the woman. A wide smile brought out his dimples and transformed his face. He held out his arms and embraced the woman.

"They look nothing alike, right?" Jericho sent a wry smile at Amy.

She glanced up at him with a chuckle. The two were obviously related. They had the same nose and coal black hair. Amy couldn't see the color of Anna's eyes yet, but she was sure they were the same electric blue as her brother. And she was tall, like Ezra.

"Amy." Ezra stepped back from his sister's embrace and beckoned her forward. "This is my sister. Anna, this is Amy."

Amy held out a hand. "It's nice to meet you."

Anna smiled, but instead of taking Amy's hand, she gave her a hug.

"Oh." Surprised, Amy glanced at Ezra as she hugged the woman back. He smiled.

"I'm so glad you're okay." Anna pulled back to look at her.

"Thank you. How's your husband?"

Some of the joy in Anna's gaze faded. "Holding his own. It's going to be a long road to recovery, but he'll get there. Let's go inside, shall we? It's hot out here."

Amy followed her into the house. It was blessedly cool.

"Have his doctors given you an idea of when they'll release him?" Ezra asked.

Anna shook her head. "Another week, probably. Part of the problem is we live in the sticks. They want to be sure he won't regress if they send him home. They took the chest drain out the other day, and they've set all his broken bones. His arm might require another surgery. He tore some ligaments in his wrist. But that will be down the line another month or so. I think they want to see how it heals up from what they've already done."

"It's all just insane," Jericho said. "None of it should have happened."

"What did happen?" Ezra asked.

"Someone let the bull into the wrong pen. Wayne said he

remembers putting him in the far pasture, but the accident happened in the one by the barn. When Wayne went in to refill the hay feeder, he didn't see the bull until it was too late. Luckily, he had Max with him. The dog ran the bull off and kept the other cows away." Jericho shook his head. "We don't know how the bull got into the wrong pen."

"It was the dog barking that brought me outside. He normally barks some when they go out, but not like that. It had an edge to it." Anna's mouth pulled down. "I could see him running back and forth behind the barn and just knew something was wrong. That dog saved Wayne's life." She rolled her lips in and pressed them together, blinking hard.

Amy's stomach clenched at their tale. Wayne Dalton was a lucky man. And she was glad, for Anna's sake, that she wasn't a widow with a newborn.

Ezra put a hand on Anna's shoulder and squeezed, offering silent comfort. Anna nodded, then sucked in a breath. "Do you want to meet your niece?"

The mood in the room shifted. Ezra smiled. "Yes. Definitely."

Anna tipped her head. "She's in the living room." Turning on her heel, she walked through a doorway toward a playpen near the window.

Through the mesh, Amy could see a tiny infant lying on the bottom. Anna bent and scooped the baby up, cradling her close. The baby cooed and stretched, waving one small fist.

Smiling, Anna looked at her brother, turning the baby in her arms so she faced Ezra. "This is Maylee." She gripped the baby's tiny wrist and waved it at Ezra. "Say hi to your Uncle Ezra, baby girl."

"She's beautiful, Annie." Ezra's deep voice held a wealth of emotion in that short sentence.

Amy clasped her hands tight and blinked, watching the exchange. Awe and love were evident in every line of his face.

"Here." Anna stepped closer to him, holding the baby out.

Ezra's big hands closed around Maylee, and he tucked her into his chest. "Hi there, sweet girl." He stroked the baby's face with one finger in a tender touch.

Oh, sweet Jesus. Amy pressed her lips together and fought to keep her knees locked. She'd thought Ezra gorgeous before. But holding a baby with a look of pure love on his face? How could any woman resist that? She couldn't. Especially not in her weakened state.

Ezra glanced up with a smile. "It always amazes me how tiny they are when they're new. She's light as a feather."

Anna laughed. "She didn't feel that way coming out. And she's grown. She's out of newborn sizes now."

His nose wrinkled. "TMI, Annie. Didn't need that image."

She laughed again. "Sorry."

He grinned. "Did you get that thing I asked you for?"

Anna's smile broadened. "I did. It's in the kitchen."

"Perfect. Why don't you lead the way?"

"Sure." Anna walked past him.

Amy frowned. What thing? She glanced at Jericho to see if he knew what they were talking about. A knowing smile hovered on his chiseled face. It seemed she was the only one in the dark.

Ezra looked at her. "Come on." He tipped his head toward Anna's retreating figure.

"What are we doing?" She walked toward him.

"You'll see." He led her from the room and down the short hallway. It opened into a bright, airy kitchen.

She barely had a chance to take in the space when Ezra moved to the side, giving her a clear view of the island. On it was a round cake covered in purple flowers and the words "Happy Birthday" written on it.

Amy gasped and covered her mouth. Her gaze went to

Ezra. "How—" She never told him her birthday. Just that it was this month.

"You repeated it to the hospital staff often enough, there was no way I'd forget it." His eyes crinkled at the corners as he smiled.

That was true. She hadn't thought of that. "Thank you. This is very thoughtful." Moisture gathered in her eyes again. *Dammit.* Since when had she become one of those women who cried over everything? Sniffing, she blinked and battled back the tears, refusing to cry. She could let him know she was touched by the gesture without looking like some simpering female. "This has been my most interesting birthday yet." Amy walked forward to get a closer look at the cake. It looked like it came from a bakery and not a supermarket. The rosettes swirled up the sides in an ombre pattern. And in her favorite color. Deep royal purple on the bottom and a lighter lilac toward the top.

"At least you're out of the hospital." Anna gave her a bright smile.

Amy's mouth turned up. "That's true."

"Let's cut this thing, shall we?" Ezra handed the baby back to his sister, then walked toward the bank of cupboards to his right. "Annie, where's the silverware?"

Anna pointed. Ezra opened the drawer and found a knife.

"What flavor is it?" Amy hoped it was chocolate, but she'd eat any kind. She loved cake.

"Red velvet. I wanted chocolate, but this was all she had left. She added the rosettes for me." Anna glanced over her shoulder as she took plates from a cabinet.

Red velvet was close enough to full chocolate. Amy's smile grew. "I love red velvet."

"All right." Ezra held the knife over the cake. "Let's slice this bad boy."

"Wait." Jericho held up a hand. "Shouldn't we sing?"

Amy groaned. "Please don't."

He chuckled.

Anna set the plates down next to Ezra, then waved her hand. "She's not a little kid." A devilish smile crossed her face. "Besides, I didn't buy any candles."

"That's all that's saving me? I'll take it." Amy laughed.

"Fine. No song." Ezra lowered the knife. "How big of a slice do you want, birthday girl?"

Amy's mouth watered. "Not tiny." After their ordeal and her illness, she'd lost weight. A giant slice of cake wouldn't hurt a bit. Not that she cared, anyway. She worked out, but not religiously. Her routine was more to stay strong than anything else.

Ezra sliced through the cake and cut off a piece, laying it on the plate Anna held up.

"Yum." Amy took the dish, fetching a fork from the drawer.

"Dig in." Ezra nodded to her plate. "Don't wait for us."

He didn't have to tell her twice. She cut off a chunk and slipped it between her lips, having to bite back a moan as she got her first taste. It was like a cloud. A rich, chocolatey cloud. Her eyelids fluttered as her eyes rolled up. "Oh, that's good."

Anna smiled. "I'm glad you like it. One of the nurses recommended the place."

"She knows her cake." Amy took another bite. It was delicious. Spearing another piece, Amy looked at Ezra as he dished out the last slice. This might not be the trip—or the birthday —she envisioned for herself, but she didn't mind how things had turned out. Okay, she could have done without the plane crash and the pneumonia. But getting to know Ezra wasn't something she would change. He'd been so kind and considerate. It boggled her mind the man was still single.

Ezra made a face of pure ecstasy as he took his first bite of cake. "Oh, man."

Goosebumps erupted on Amy's skin at his moan. Her mind went to places it had no business going. Ezra was a friend. That was all. And he couldn't be more. Not until she figured out her life. No matter how much she wanted to wrap herself around him and make him make that sound herself.

TWENTY-FOUR

Amy stared at herself in the mirror with a sigh. The soft grayish-green t-shirt and charcoal cotton shorts were comfortable, but she really needed some new clothes. Maybe she could talk Ezra into going shopping today. She much felt better. So long as they took breaks and stayed hydrated, she could handle a couple hours browsing through stores for clothing.

With a determined nod, she spun around and exited her room to head downstairs for breakfast. Descending the stairs, she saw Anna in the living room with Maylee. The other woman nursed the infant while she sipped on a mug of tea.

Anna glanced up and smiled. "Good morning."

Amy smiled back. "Morning." She stepped off the last stair and glanced around. "Are we the only ones up?"

"No. Ezra went for a run, and Jericho already left for the hospital."

Amy paused at the corner of the couch with a frown. "Without you?" The two of them had been going together, often leaving in the morning and not coming back until much later in the day.

Anna nodded, turning a bright smile on Amy. "I'll go up later. I have other plans for this morning."

"Oh?"

"Yep. We're going shopping."

Amy's eyes widened. "Okay, did you read my mind?"

Anna laughed. "No. But I figured you were probably getting tired of recycling the same two outfits. And since my brother is blind when it comes to such things, I figured it was up to me to take you. So, go eat some breakfast. As soon as Maylee finishes hers, I'll be ready." She gestured to the baby nestled to her chest.

Clapping her hands, Amy smiled. "You don't have to tell me twice." With a couple of quick steps, she rounded the couch and headed for the kitchen, hearing Anna chuckle behind her.

Amy made herself an omelet and a cup of tea, finishing up as Anna changed Maylee's diaper. She stowed her dishes in the dishwasher, then headed for the stairs. "I'm going to grab my purse and shoes."

Anna nodded, putting the baby's shorts back on. "Sounds good. I just need to grab the diaper bag and we can go."

Bounding up the steps with more energy than she'd had in days, Amy found her shoes and purse and went back downstairs. Anna was tucking her wallet into the diaper bag as Amy stepped into the living room.

"Ready?" Anna looked over with a questioning lift of her eyebrows.

Amy nodded. "Yep. Should we wait for Ezra? To tell him where we're going?"

Anna shook her head and headed for the door. "I told him my plans before he left."

"Oh. Okay, good." Amy was glad. She honestly didn't want to wait. She was ready to shop—and to get her body moving.

They left the house, going to the small car parked at the curb. Anna slipped the baby into the infant seat in the back, then got in the driver's seat. Amy climbed in beside her.

"This is so weird." Amy stared out the windshield, feeling strange without a steering wheel in front of her.

Anna grinned as she buckled up. "It certainly takes some getting used to. I found it harder to be a passenger than the driver when I first moved here. Especially at night."

"How so?" Amy buckled up.

"The headlights." Anna started the car. Hot air blasted from the vents, quickly turning cool. "They come at you from the wrong side of the road. It's one of those things you don't think about, but your mind registers. In the U.S., when the headlights come at you from that side, you better say a prayer, because you're about to be in a head-on collision."

Amy's eyes widened. "Oh my. I guess that's true."

"Yeah." Anna pulled away from the curb with a chuckle. "I had a few mini heart attacks until I got used to it."

"I bet." Amy laughed. "So, where are we going?" She knew absolutely nothing about Darwin's shopping scene.

"There's a mall nearby I thought we'd go to. It'll keep us out of the heat."

"Sounds good to me." She'd had enough heat to last her a while.

Watching the scenery, the drive to the mall was short. Anna pulled into the parking garage.

"Oh, this place has parent parking. Yes!" Anna turned, following the signs. "There are benefits to shopping with a baby. Most notably, the wider spaces." She turned into a parking space and put the car in park, then glanced at Amy. "I don't know if you noticed all the spots I drove past, but they're tiny. Even for a car this size."

"I did. I'm glad—for your sake—we get to park in a bigger spot. Reversing in a parking garage is no fun."

"No." Anna shook her head, unbuckling. "It's not." She opened her door and got out.

Amy followed suit. Once they had Maylee and her gear loaded into the stroller, they headed inside.

"So, what do you want to look for first? Shorts? Dresses?"

"Underwear."

Anna laughed. "Sorry, I should have thought of that." She sent Amy a quick glance. "Did my brother do okay picking things out for you?"

Amy's cheeks flamed. It still embarrassed her to think Ezra had bought her bras and panties. "For the most part. But I want a real bra. He took the easy route and bought a two-pack of sports bras. The underwear are okay, though. Simple, but they fit well."

"Good. He's pretty practical, so I figured he'd just grab the basics."

"I'm glad he did. I don't know about you, but I'm pretty particular about my undies."

Anna chuckled. "Yeah. Wayne only buys me the sexy stuff. He knows I like to be comfortable and doesn't have a clue what brands I like or which styles." She stopped in front of a tall directory board. "All right, let's see here." She tapped the screen several times until it brought up a list of stores that sold lingerie.

"There's one that's close." Amy pointed.

"Works for me." Anna cleared the screen. "Let's go."

They meandered down the concourse, getting lost in the crowd. The mall was huge, boasting two floors of shops. They passed several specialty stores before reaching the large department store anchoring this end of the mall. Anna steered the stroller inside and headed for women's lingerie.

Amy loaded her arms with bras and panties in all the styles and colors she liked. Frowning as they left the lingerie section, she glanced around. "I might need a cart. Do they have them here?"

Anna extended the visor on the stroller. "Yep. Right here." She patted the top.

Grinning, Amy deposited her load on top of the canopy. "That works for that stuff."

"Let's look through their clothes and see what we can find. There's quite a bit of room at the bottom of the stroller to hold anything you buy. We can always take a load back to the car, too, if need be. You have a lot of clothes to buy."

"I also don't need to replace it all today. A few outfits and a couple of dresses is plenty. Just enough to add some variation." She glanced down at herself. "And maybe a little more —formality?" She chuckled. "Like denim."

With a smile, Anna walked forward. "Well, then, let's find you some jean shorts."

Wandering through the store, Amy found a couple pairs of shorts and some plain t-shirts and added them to her pile. She saw more that interested her, but she also wanted to look at some of the other stores. There were things here she couldn't buy in the U.S. If she had to replace her summer wardrobe, it might as well be unique. Bypassing the plain tank tops that were normally a staple for her, she led the way to the register and checked out.

They left the department store and picked out some smaller shops. Amy found several tops and a dress before she felt her energy levels flag.

"Do you mind if we get a drink and sit for a bit?" She fanned her face as she looked at Anna.

"Of course not. I could use something cool to drink, anyway." Anna turned around and led them back to the center of the mall and the food court. There they got smoothies, then found a seat that gave them some extra space for the stroller.

"So, how are you feeling?" Anna asked. She slid her straw into her mouth and took a sip, looking at Amy over her cup.

Amy swallowed the mouthful of strawberry-banana-mango smoothie she just took and nodded. "Pretty good. A little weak, but not bad. I think I only have one more day of antibiotics left. And I didn't need my inhaler at all yesterday. That was a first."

"Good. Ezra told me how sick you were. I'm impressed at how fast you've recovered."

"Me too. But I'm not complaining. I think it's been all the rest. I haven't had to worry about getting back to work, or making sure I have food. You and Ezra and Jericho have done all that. I'm so grateful." Amy stuffed her smoothie straw back into her mouth and blinked back the moisture gathering in her eyes.

"Don't do that." Anna pointed at her. "You'll make me cry too."

A wrinkle formed between Amy's eyebrows. "Why?" she asked, genuinely curious. "You barely know me. And only because your brother dragged me here to recuperate."

"Because you're important to him. And because I've gotten to know you this past week. I like you, and you're good for him."

"You've got that backwards. He's been good for me." She couldn't imagine these last couple of weeks without him. He'd provided company and a safety net when she'd needed it most.

"You've been good for each other, I think." Anna took another drink, canting her head thoughtfully. "I don't mean to pry, but what's going on with you two? The attraction between you is obvious to anyone with eyes."

Amy chewed on her straw and took a drink as she thought about that. She'd been trying not to think about her feelings for Ezra. It was just too much for her to cope with at the moment on top of everything else. But she needed to deal with it. The feelings were there, and they weren't going away.

She eyed Anna over the top of her cup. "You're brother's a nice man. I like him a lot. But I'm not sure where anything is headed. My life is a mess. Did he tell you why I came on this trip?"

Anna nodded. "Something about you contemplating a career change."

"Yeah. On top of ending a committed relationship. My fiancé cheated on me. That was kind of the last straw." Amy lifted a shoulder. "I needed time and space to think. I've had space, but no time, thanks to everything that's happened. I'm still very confused about what I want." And she hadn't given it much thought since she left the hospital—not in-depth, anyway—preferring to focus on healing her body. She knew she needed to be physically strong enough to deal with the emotions she'd locked away. So, she'd just let the thoughts swirl, not ignoring them, but not focusing on them much, either.

"And Ezra's a part of that confusion." Anna's expression cleared.

"Yeah. I don't know where he fits in. Or if he even does. I think I'd like him to, but—" She broke off and shrugged again. "There's just a lot to work out."

"Well, I have faith it will all work out the way it's supposed to." Anna smiled and took another drink.

"You think?" Amy flicked her thumbnail on the edge of her cup lid and stared at her hands. She just didn't know how she was going to sort everything out. It was all such a jumble in her head.

"Of course. Make a list of what you want, then another list of how to get each one. You don't have to write it down; it can be in your head. The idea is to see which paths lead you to the most things. And then what you'd need to do to get the rest. Or to get an arrangement that makes you happy."

"I thought about making a pros and cons list." She just hadn't done it.

"That's what I did. When I decided to move here for good. I listed out all the things I wanted and what it would take to get them. And what it would cost me for each thing. Not just financially, but emotionally. In the end, Wayne won. When it came down to it, I couldn't imagine my future without him in it. I won't sit here and tell you it was easy. But it was very much worth it." She peeked into the stroller to look at a snoozing Maylee; a soft smile crossed her face.

Amy's heart squeezed as she looked at the baby. She wanted that. A child of her own. There was no doubt about that now. Being around Maylee this last week had solidified that desire. It was about the only thing she knew for sure.

She looked at Anna. "You've definitely given me something to think about."

"Can I offer one last piece of advice?"

"Sure."

"Don't think too hard. Let your heart help."

Amy straightened in her chair, those words hitting heavy.

"Your brain will try to keep you safe. But sometimes, the safest option isn't the best."

True. Amy raised her cup, taking another sip of her drink as she stared out over the mall and the people walking by. Thoughts churned in her head. Ezra featured prominently. But she just didn't know if trying to start something with him was the best thing for her. She needed to do as Anna suggested and write things down—or at least make a mental list. That wouldn't happen here, though. And she didn't want it to, anyway. Today was supposed to be about having fun. Not the heavy stuff.

Blinking, she turned back to Anna and smiled. "I'll give all that some thought later. Right now, though, I'm ready to shop some more. Are you?"

Understanding lit Anna's bright blue eyes. "Yes, I am. I saw a fantastic baby store just before we turned around to get these." She waved her smoothie cup.

"Well, then, let's go find it again." Amy stood up, feeling lighter. She might not have things figured out yet, but she was on the right path. That was enough for now.

Twenty-Five

Ezra glanced up from his seat on the deck and smiled at his sister as she came out the back door. "Hey."

"Hey, yourself." Wrinkling her nose, she sat down beside him. "Why are you out here? It's over a hundred degrees. Didn't you get enough of the heat already?"

He lifted a shoulder, putting a finger in the book he was reading to mark his place. "I don't mind it. And I wanted some air." Truthfully, he'd needed to get away from Amy. It had been a week now since they arrived in Darwin, and he was finding it harder all the time to resist the urge to wrap her in his arms and kiss her senseless. Tonight, she'd been holding his niece, swaying with her to the music playing through the speaker hooked to Anna's phone. She'd looked so beautiful, holding the baby. And happy. It put ideas in his head. Ones he knew he shouldn't be entertaining. Amy didn't come here to start a relationship. She came for herself. He refused to stand in the way of that. But it was damn hard to remember that sometimes.

Anna stared at him for several long moments. "Why are you fighting it?"

"Fighting what?"

"What you feel for Amy? A blind man could see you two fancy each other. Why haven't you taken her on a date?"

A muscle in Ezra's jaw worked. Anna always could read his mind. No matter how much he tried to keep his expression blank, she always figured him out. "She doesn't want a relationship. Not now."

"No." Anna held up a finger. "She doesn't know what she wants out of life. And before you argue, she told me that herself."

"What else has she told you?" He knew Amy and Anna talked. The two women had been getting along swimmingly since they met. It was a bit scary how quickly they became friends.

"It's not what she's said, but more what I see when she looks at you. Or at Maylee. Or at you holding Maylee. I think she wants that. The connection of a husband and children." She shrugged. "Why shouldn't she have that with you?"

"Hold up." Ezra held up a hand. "It's not even been three weeks since we met. We've only got another nine days before she heads back to the U.S. I'm not interested in a long-distance relationship, and I doubt she is, either."

"You don't know if you don't ask. And she's already contemplating a move. Why can't that move be to Clarksville with you?"

"It's not like curator jobs are prevalent near my base. And even if she went the route of opening an antiques store there, I can't guarantee the Army won't move me elsewhere." He didn't want to make Amy choose between her dreams and him.

"E-Z, if it's meant to be, it'll all work out." She leaned forward and patted his knee. "But you have to take the first step."

"What if taking that first step causes pain? For both of us?"

Anna sat back and pinned him with a look. "What if it ends up being the best thing you've ever done?"

Dammit. Why did she do this to him? He was the older sibling. Wasn't he the one supposed to give out sage advice?

Mouth turned down, he stared out at the yard. "Fine."

She laughed. "Don't sound so enthused."

His expression smoothed out, and he sighed. "Sorry. She's just got me all tied up in knots."

"That's good."

"Maybe."

"No. No maybe. Yes." She made a shooing motion. "Go. The outdoor market at Mindil Beach is open tonight. Take her there. Enjoy the sunset while you eat some yummy local treats. Be a tourist, for God's sake."

A grin slashed over his mouth. "What? You want me to be normal?"

She chuckled. "For once, yes."

His smile turned soft. "Thanks, Anna. I know this isn't the visit we planned, but I'm still glad to be here."

"Planning is overrated." She waved a hand. "Things never go the way we want. It's how we respond and make the best of shitty situations that defines us. I think we're doing pretty well."

"Me too." Ezra stood, feeling more buoyant. "I'll see you in a few hours, I guess."

"You have fun. Bring me back something sweet."

"I will." Bending down, he kissed the top of her head. "Love you, Annie."

She sent a bright smile up at him. "You too."

With a wave, Ezra went inside. He blinked, letting his eyes adjust to the darkness as he looked around the room. Amy turned from standing by the front window with Maylee in her arms. His heart clenched in his chest.

"Hi." She smiled.

"Hey." He walked closer, keeping his eyes on the baby as he approached. If he looked at Amy, he'd end up tongue-tied and unable to ask her anything. Lifting a hand, he touched the baby's tiny fingers. Maylee latched on, making his heart squeeze for another reason.

"Do you want to hold her?"

Ezra shook his head. "Actually, I wanted to ask you something."

"Oh?"

He chanced a look at her. Curious brown eyes met his gaze. The dark pools sucked him in. He looked at Maylee again and cleared his throat. "Yeah. Would you like to go out this evening?"

"Out? Why? To do what?"

"On a—a date." He cast a quick glance at her again.

"Oh." She nibbled on her bottom lip and dropped her gaze to the baby, saying nothing.

Ezra's heart sank. "Never mind. Forget I said anything." He pulled his hand away from Maylee and took a step back.

Amy's hand landed on his arm. "Wait. Actually, that sounds nice."

He blinked twice as his brain caught up. Once it did, his heart skipped a beat, then raced. "Great. Anna mentioned there's some outdoor market at Mindil Beach. Does that sound good?"

"Sure." She brought her hand back to tuck under the baby and readjust her as the infant moved. "I need to change and find my shoes."

"You look fine." And she did. He liked her shorts and t-shirt. Though she could wear pretty much anything and he wouldn't mind.

She wrinkled her nose. "There's baby puke on my top."

Ezra chuckled. "Well, if you insist on cleaning up…"

Amy laughed. "Give me just a few minutes. Here." She lifted the baby to pass her over.

"Oh." Ezra took Maylee, cradling her close. "How you doing, munchkin?"

The baby protested her change in position. Ezra jostled her, making a shushing noise.

"Do you want me to get Anna?"

He sent a quick narrow-eyed look her way. "I can handle a baby. Go change." Maylee squalled again, and he looked down at her. "Hey, now. Don't make a liar out of me, darlin'. Give Uncle Ezra a break."

Amy laughed. "I'll be right back."

Smiling, Ezra nodded. "Take your time. Miss Maylee and I are going to dance." He swayed with the baby, humming a soft song. That feeling in his heart exploded, and he clenched his teeth. If Anna was right about what Amy wanted, she wasn't the only one.

TWENTY-SIX

Amy hurried away, clamping mental hands over her ears to drown out the smooth tones of Ezra's singing voice. It threatened to light her up and leave her simmering on high all night. That was the last thing she needed if she was to spend the next few hours alone with him. But seriously, was there anything the man couldn't do?

She hurried through changing, donning a lightweight summer dress in tones of white and purple that she found while out shopping with Anna yesterday. Putting on her new sandals, she grabbed the small purse she also bought on her shopping trip and made sure she had some cash and her ID inside. Not bothering with makeup—she'd just sweat it all off—she went downstairs again.

Ezra's deep voice drew her toward the patio doors. He still sang, but she couldn't make out the words. Reaching for the handle, she drew the door open and stepped out. He held Maylee out, away from his body, singing to her as he waltzed around the patio. The two-month-old baby watched his face, transfixed.

She wasn't the only one. Amy couldn't take her eyes off of them.

Changing direction as he spotted her, Ezra twirled and sidestepped toward his sister. He ended his song and handed the baby over with a flourish.

Anna laughed as she took her daughter. The baby turned her head to look at Ezra as her mother snuggled her close. "You have a fan."

He bowed low. "I am her humble servant." Leaning in, he kissed the baby's head. "Until next time, my love."

Amy curled her fists and put those mental earmuffs back on. She couldn't handle the cuteness. It made her ovaries ache.

Still laughing, Anna gave her brother's shoulder a shove. "Go. Have fun."

"We will." Ezra turned to Amy. "Ready?"

Her heart pounded, locking the words in her throat. She nodded.

"Then let's go." He motioned toward the door.

Spinning around, she went inside, pausing to wait for him. He walked past her and headed for the front door.

"How are we getting there?"

"I called a taxi. It should be here soon."

Through the window, as they approached the door, Amy saw a car pull up out front.

"Well, that was good timing." Ezra smiled and opened the door. He motioned for her to go ahead of him, then shut the door as he stepped out behind her.

The driver waved at them through the window. Ezra opened the back passenger door, and Amy climbed inside, sliding across the seat.

"Good evening." The driver looked between the seats. "Where to?"

"Mindil Beach." Ezra closed the door and buckled up.

The driver frowned, a curious glint in his eyes. "Americans?"

Amy and Ezra nodded.

"Are you enjoying your trip?" The driver turned around and put the car in gear, pulling away from the curb.

Rolling her lips in, Amy looked at Ezra, amusement in her eyes.

"It's been interesting," Ezra replied.

Amy saw the driver's reflection in the rearview mirror. His eyebrows dipped at the tone of Ezra's voice, but he didn't comment.

They zipped through the city to the western side. Amy admired the scenery as they went, catching glimpses of the ocean just beyond the houses. She'd yet to make it to the beaches of northern Australia. This week, she'd spent her time recuperating; resting when she needed to, and just generally being lazy. Apart from her outing with Anna, she'd done very little. She felt much better and was looking forward to sinking her toes into the sand.

The driver pulled up to a drop-off point at Mindil Beach. Ezra paid the driver, and they got out. Music and the sound of people greeted them. It smelled like a fair, but with a hint of ocean under it all. Excitement put some spring in her step.

"Where to first?" Ezra took her hand, pulling her out of the way of a group of teens coming down the path.

Amy shrugged. "How about we just start walking?"

"Works for me." Not letting go, he turned toward the market, leading her toward the stalls.

Hand-in-hand, they strolled through the booths, stopping to look at all the brightly colored wares. Amy bought a handbag and a dress—both in shades of purple. She also bought dresses for her sisters and a bag for her friend Kasey. Ezra bought a belt made of crocodile leather and a picture book for Maylee. At one stand, Amy admired the opal jewelry.

"That's pretty." Ezra pointed to a pendant.

Amy agreed, but the price tag made her hesitate. She hadn't spent much on room and board this trip. She'd offered to help with the rental cost of the house, but Anna just gave her a look like she was nuts and said no. But that necklace would take up a chunk of her funds. And she had medical expenses to take into account. Her travel insurance covered some of her hospital stay, but not all. Mouth twisting, she turned to the rack next to it that had similar necklaces, but at a lower price point.

"We'll take that one." Ezra pointed to the one she'd previously admired and looked at the shopkeeper expectantly.

"What?" Amy turned to him.

The woman smiled and picked it up.

"Ezra!" Amy hissed, turning to face him. "I didn't want to spend that much."

"You're not. I am."

She frowned, then it dawned on her it was probably a gift for Anna or his mom. "Oh."

He looked over her head at the woman. "You don't need to wrap it. She's going to wear it."

Amy did a double-take. "Huh?"

Ezra smiled, then handed the woman his credit card.

"Do you want a bag for the box?"

"No. We'll put it in one we have. Thank you."

"Of course." She slid his card into a portable machine, then handed it back, along with a receipt.

"Thank you." He put his card away and stuffed the receipt in his pocket.

Amy stared at him, confused.

The woman passed Ezra the jewelry box. "Thank you. Enjoy the rest of your evening."

"Yes, ma'am." He smiled. "Thank you." Ezra put a hand on Amy's arm and nudged her out of the stall.

"Ezra—"

"Let's go over there." He gestured to a bench across the path from where they stood.

Frowning, she moved toward it and sat down. He sat beside her and took the necklace from the box.

"What are you doing? Did you really buy that for me? It's too—"

"If you say it's too expensive, I'm going back and buying the matching earrings."

Amy clamped her lips together and stared.

His mouth twitched. "No comment? Damn. The earrings would look good on you."

She rolled her eyes. "Why are you buying me expensive jewelry?"

"Because it'll look pretty on you." His blue eyes glittered in the dying sunlight.

"Ezra." Amy held his gaze, and he chuckled.

"Don't look at me like that. I wasn't trying to take the decision away from you or imply that you can't buy your own jewelry. I bought it because I wanted to. Let me spoil you."

"I don't mean to sound ungrateful, but why?" She tipped her head, genuinely curious why he would buy her such an expensive gift.

"It's simple." He opened the clasp. "I'm with the prettiest woman at the market, and she should have the prettiest necklace." His eyes took on a liquid look, the colors shifting in the light. "I want to be the one to put it on her. To let everyone know she's with me."

The breath caught in Amy's throat at the look in his eyes. It was different from any she'd seen yet. It was intense and hot. And possessive.

A shiver went down her spine. Her body screamed, "Yes! Possess me!" She swallowed, trying to bring back some of the moisture to her mouth that had fled south. It was decision time. They'd danced around the topic of what they were to each other since they met. In the last week, it hadn't come up. There had been heated looks and some lingering touches, but not once had they talked about what those things meant. If she accepted the necklace, she not only acknowledged the fire burning between them, but told him she wanted to see where it led.

Amy searched his eyes, trying to decipher the emotions burning in their depths. What pulled at her most, though, wasn't the passion or the desire, but the earnestness. That this man wanted her—*her*—floored her; and suddenly, some clarity came over her mind.

She wrapped her hands over his. "I've done nothing but think this week. About what I left behind. What happened before I left. What that all means for me, and what I want when I go home. Even when I tried to avoid the thoughts— and there were many of those times—they were still there. I'm still not sure, but I know one thing. I want whatever that is to include you." Seeing just how much he wanted her solidified what had been percolating for a while. She didn't want to go back to a life without him in it.

The light in his eyes burned brighter. His lips parted. Amy laid a finger over them. "Let me finish."

He nodded, and she dropped her hand.

"I don't know what's happening between us or where it will lead. But I've never met a man like you. It doesn't seem fair that someone so kind and smart and brave could be wrapped in such a—well—" She held her hand up, moving it up and down as she gestured to him. "You're beautiful, but you know that." She sighed, letting her hand drop back to his. "I guess what I'm saying is you don't feel real. None of this does. It's like we're in a bubble that will pop when our vacation ends."

"I understand that. But this isn't a vacation romance,

Amy. I don't want it to be that. I want us to try to make this work when we go home. Will it be messy and complicated? Probably. We live in different states. But it'll all work out the way it's supposed to. I think we need to give it a chance." He raised his hands a fraction, nodding toward the necklace. "What do you say?"

The earnestness in his eyes did her in again. She couldn't say no. Not when the feelings in her heart echoed the ones she could see in his eyes. She nodded. "I say thank you. It's beautiful."

A bright smile curved his lips. He motioned for her to turn around. Amy swiveled, pulling her hair to the side. Cool metal touched her skin, and his fingers brushed the back of her neck as he fastened the necklace. Goosebumps erupted as his warm breath fanned over her ear. When he kissed her exposed shoulder, her belly clenched and all the moisture in her mouth fled south again. She clamped her lips together to hold back a soft moan.

Abruptly, Ezra stood. "Come on. Let's keep walking."

Amy looked up, confused at the rapid shift. He stuffed his hands in his pockets and stepped back, so she could get up. Rising, she touched his arm. The muscles shifted beneath her touch. His jaw looked like carved granite, and he stared straight ahead.

"Are you okay?"

He looked at her then. Fire blazed in his eyes. "I'm fine. But we need to keep moving. You're testing my control. It's on a thin wire."

"Oh." Amy dropped her hand. Well, crap. Now she was afraid to touch him. But part of her—that feminine part that took delight in driving a man wild—stood up and rejoiced. It also fanned the flames of her libido.

She walked around him, a little extra sway in her hips. "Sounds like a good idea. Let's go."

TWENTY-SEVEN

Electrified. That's how Amy felt. Every nerve-ending in her body was on alert as she strolled through the sand with Ezra. Since he put the necklace on her, electricity sparked between them. The tension only grew as they walked through the market. Once they'd seen most everything, they wandered into the food area again and got some treats, then headed for the beach. Amy had since polished off her snack. Without something to keep her hands occupied, she only grew more aware of his presence next to her. All she wanted to do was stop and run her hands through his short, dark hair while he kissed her senseless.

Water lapped at her feet, startling her. She sidestepped. The tide was coming in.

"Whoa, there." Ezra's arm wrapped around her waist.

Amy stilled. She pressed a hand to his chest for balance and looked up. His face loomed in the low light, eyes glittering like stars in the sky. He was so damn pretty.

Ezra's hand came up. He cradled her chin, touching her bottom lip with his thumb. Amy parted her lips, wanting him to kiss her. With agonizing slowness, his head lowered. Impatient, she rose on her toes and met him halfway.

Rays of light burst through her brain, sending spikes of euphoria down her limbs. They ricocheted, coming together in her belly to create a delicious heat.

Amy turned. She heard their bags hit the sand, then his arms were around her. His broad hands spanned her back. He made her feel tiny, but cherished. His embrace created a cocoon, shutting out the world. She could live right here, never needing anything else.

A larger wave hit them, splashing their legs. Amy jumped back with a yelp, then laughed. Ezra took her hand, then snagged their bags and hauled her higher up the beach, away from the water.

"Maybe we should head back. Especially now that these are wet." He lifted the bags with a grimace. "I'm not sure how much longer they'll hold."

"Yeah. And it's getting late." Despite the time, she didn't want the evening to end. She'd been enjoying their date.

He tugged on her hand and led the way back up the beach toward the market entrance. Leaving the beach, they strolled along the path in the now thinner crowd. The market was winding down.

At the transit stop, they waited for a taxi to pull up. Amy wrapped her hands around Ezra's arm and snuggled into his side. He dropped a kiss on top of her head.

"Warm enough?"

She nodded. The evening was a warm one, and the heat hadn't died much with the setting sun.

A taxi pulled up with a soft squeal of its brakes. Ezra opened the door for her, and she slid inside. He got in next to her, stuffing their purchases between his feet, then gave the driver the address to the house Anna rented. Leaning into Ezra, Amy settled in for the ride. Her body still hummed with desire. She was probably setting herself up for a long night of tossing and turning, but she needed to be near him. He made her feel a myriad of emotions; all of them pleasant. She wasn't ready to give up those feelings just yet.

By the time they reached the house, every brush of his body, every whisper of wind on her heated skin, inched her need closer to the top. When she stepped out of the cab, she clenched her fists, glad Ezra had their soggy bags to carry so they couldn't hold hands. If he touched her now, she'd go off like a rocket.

He paid the driver, then they walked up the path to the front door.

"I hope Anna left this unlocked."

Amy did too. The house was dark. She didn't want to wake anyone to let them in. Grasping the doorknob, it turned easily in her hand. She pushed the door open and stepped inside. Ezra followed, turning the locks as he closed it. On light feet, they went upstairs, stopping in front of her door.

She turned, one hand on the knob, and looked at him. "Thank you for a lovely evening."

"You're welcome." His whisper-quiet voice matched hers. He nodded toward her room. "Open the door. I'll put your bags inside." He lifted the shopping bags in his hands.

"Oh, right." She twisted the knob and pushed, flipping on the light switch as she entered.

"Where do you want them?"

"Anywhere."

He set the bags in the corner behind the door, where they were out of the way. "There you go."

"Thank you." Amy crossed her arms, hugging herself so she wouldn't reach out to him. She really wanted him to stay, but was unsure if that was a wise decision.

Ezra stared at her. Amy could see the heat in his eyes. It ratcheted up the fire lighting up her insides.

"I should go." He hooked a thumb toward the door.

Amy nodded. "Yes." *Please don't.* Her traitorous body tingled at the blatant desire in her subconscious voice. She ground her teeth, holding on to her willpower by a thread.

"It's late, and we both need some sleep."

"We do." She held back the snort. Like she'd be able to sleep.

"Though I'm not particularly tired. Are you?"

"No." The word was out before she could stop it.

A new light entered his eyes. The predatory look made her core clench. She pressed her lips together, holding back the moan that wanted to escape. That look threatened to eat her up, and she was here for it.

He took a step closer. "If I'm not tired, and you're not tired, what could we do about that?"

Amy lifted a shoulder. "I don't know. Read, maybe?"

Ezra hummed, taking another step. "I like to read. I doubt I could concentrate well enough right now, though. You?"

"Probably not." Her voice came out breathy with the desire steadily building in her veins. She dropped her arms, pulled toward him like a magnet. "There's a TV downstairs. We could watch something."

He took another step. "We could. But if I'm going to watch something, I can think of other things I'd rather watch than television."

Amy swallowed, moistening her dry mouth. "Oh?"

One more step brought him within touching distance. "Yeah. Things far more interesting than what's on TV."

She sucked in a sharp breath. "Like what?"

He raised a hand, stroking her cheek. Heat suffused Amy's face.

"Like the pretty blush that steals over your skin when I touch you. Or the goosebumps that pop up along your arms when I do this." He skimmed his hand along her jawline to cup the side of her head, his fingers threading into her hair.

Goosebumps did indeed erupt down her arms—and everywhere else.

"I'd love to watch your body tremble as I kiss every inch. I want to see the expression on your face as I strip you bare and touch the most intimate parts of you. As I drive you to the height of bliss."

Sweet baby Jesus. Amy's knees threatened to give out. She locked them, but not before he noticed her slight sag and stepped close enough to wrap an arm around her waist. Her belly collided with his hips, and she felt the unmistakable ridge growing thicker behind his fly.

"How does that sound? Do you think that would help us sleep?"

"No," she whispered. "Not at all."

"Yeah. Me, either." He swooped in and kissed her.

The crackles of electricity making the goosebumps erupt on Amy's body solidified into a steady stream, lighting her up like a million Christmas lights. Any reservations she had about whether this was a good idea got buried beneath a mountain of sensation. She no longer cared about the consequences. All that mattered was getting him naked—and herself—and seeing how hot he could make her burn.

Ezra sidestepped backward, toward the door, and closed it. Once he'd shut out the world, Amy went to work on her mission. She tunneled her hands beneath his t-shirt, feeling the smooth skin and its light dusting of hair over hard, powerful muscles. Muscles he'd used to protect her and keep her safe. She wanted him to know how much she appreciated them.

His mouth traveled away from hers and along her jaw. He rained kisses along her neck and onto the top of her shoulder. Amy tipped her head, giving him better access. She raked her nails over the firm muscles of his back when he nipped at her collarbone.

He let out a low groan and stepped back, taking off his shirt. Every ounce of moisture in Amy's body fled south to pool in her core as she got an eyeful of his perfect chest and abs.

A modicum of reality intruded as she saw the fading bruises on his shoulders. The skin was a dappled yellow and green around several scabs, where the ropes rubbed his skin raw.

"None of that." He hauled her into his body. "I'm fine. We both are." He kissed her again, and Amy forgot all about the scars they both still bore.

The straps of her dress sagged down her arms as he worked his way over her neck and shoulders again. He hooked a hand around her thigh, drawing her leg up, hooking it over his hip. His fingers gathered the fabric of her dress until he could reach the smooth skin of her thigh. The ache in her core intensified.

Amy bowed her back, creating some space between them, and reached for the front of his shorts. She unfastened the button and lowered the zipper, letting him fall into her hand. Through the fabric of his underwear, she squeezed. His low moan sent a jolt of pleasure through her body, and she sucked in a quick breath.

Hands circled her waist and thrust her back. Amy's gaze flew to his, widening when she saw the intensity in his eyes. He picked her up, marching to the bed and laid her down, covering her body with his as he kissed her again; this time with an urgency that sent her need flying higher.

Cool air whispered over her lower body as he pushed up her skirt, exposing her. His fingers trailed fire up her thighs, stopping at the barrier of her panties, but only long enough to slip beneath. She let out a sharp shout that he swallowed with another kiss as he touched her center. He swirled his fingers, coating them with the moisture flooding her core. Without warning, he slid them inside.

Amy couldn't breathe. Stars sparkled in her vision, then exploded in a flash of light when he curled his fingers and stroked her walls.

"So much better than any TV show."

She opened her eyes to see him staring down at her. "I agree."

"Good. Because we're gonna do that again."

He grasped handfuls of her skirt and drew her dress up. Amy raised her arms, letting him take it off of her. It fluttered to the floor, leaving her in the scrap of mint-green cotton she called underwear.

Ezra looked at her with hooded eyes, reaching out to stroke her breasts. "You have no idea how hard I had to resist touching these all night. I knew you weren't wearing a bra."

Amy bit her lip, then released it on a gasp as he tweaked her nipple. She was glad he liked her breasts. She wasn't a buxom lady by any means. The cut of her sundress had been sufficient to keep her girls in check all night.

He leaned in and sucked the tip of one breast into his mouth. Amy bucked her hips and whimpered. Ezra sat back, pushing his shorts and boxer-briefs down, lifting one leg, then the other, until his clothes joined her dress on the floor.

She hummed, propping herself up on her elbows to stare at the sight before her. A bead of liquid gathered on the tip of his shaft, glistening in the overhead light. She wanted to lick it off.

But he didn't give her the chance. He hooked his fingers in her panties and yanked them down her legs, then pushed her thighs wide, settling between them. His shaft bumped her entrance, and she moaned, her eyes rolling back and her eyelids fluttering as pleasure threatened to overwhelm her again.

Ezra sat up with a curse. Amy's eyes flew open. "What?"

"I need my wallet." He got off the bed, picking up his shorts from the floor and digging into the pocket. Finding his leather billfold, he opened it and withdrew a foil packet. "I only have the one, so we need to make this count." He climbed back onto the bed. "I'll get more tomorrow."

Amy blushed. She was naked and ready for the man to take her, but she was embarrassed talking about condoms? A giggle bubbled up, but it quickly died when he opened the condom and rolled it over himself. Suddenly, what they were about to do was all too real.

"Remember what I said about watching as I drove you to the heavens?"

She gave a shaky nod.

"I'm going to do that now. More than once."

A quick thought of how he would do that with only one condom crossed her mind for a split second before he pushed her legs wide and lowered his head. He slid his tongue through her folds, drinking her in and obliterating any rational thought. Her hips jerked, lifting off the bed. She clenched her teeth, holding in the shout of pleasure.

He continued to lap at her center, driving her mad. When he added those talented fingers to the mix again, she flew apart into a million tiny fragments of light.

Vaguely, she was aware of him shifting. She opened her eyes when the bright light overhead dimmed and saw him hovering above her. A fierce desire burned in his eyes, and he held her gaze.

"Time to touch the stars, baby."

"I already—oh!" Her words ended on a breathy moan as he impaled her in one long stroke. The stars in her vision appeared again, growing brighter with each thrust. She lifted her legs, anchoring herself to him and drawing him closer. The shift in position was enough to touch all the right places, and her climax rocketed through her body. Floating in space on a wave of light, she felt Ezra stiffen in her arms. He buried his face in her neck, muffling his harsh groan.

Amy went boneless, sagging into the mattress. Ezra pushed up, then rolled to the side. She wanted to curl into him, but couldn't make her muscles work.

A low chuckle emanated from his chest.

She turned her head. "What?"

"I was wrong about it not making us sleepy."

She let out a soft laugh. He was right. Already, she could feel sleep pulling at the edges of her mind.

He hooked an arm around her waist and tugged. She rolled into him.

Ezra pressed a kiss to the top of her head. "Goodnight, Tinkerbell."

Amy sighed a response and let her eyelids slide closed.

Twenty-Eight

Ezra nudged his sunglasses higher up his nose to block out the bright sunshine. He stared out over the yard, watching Amy as she carried Maylee from bush to bush, pointing out the blossoms and the insects she found as she went. A fierce longing punched him in the sternum as he watched the pair. The desire to have what his sister had had only grown stronger since he spent the night in Amy's bed three days ago. In fact, he hadn't returned to his room. And if it weren't for his sense of morality, he'd have forgone the condoms and done his best to plant his seed in Amy's womb. The feeling was driving him crazy. He'd never had such an urge with any other woman. He wanted to chalk it up to his age and the circumstances, but he knew that wasn't it—or at least not all of it. The woman had a lot to do with how he felt. Ezra couldn't imagine any other woman in the role of mother to his children. Not even his ex-girlfriend, whom he'd contemplated asking to marry him before she dumped him and left for her next assignment.

"So, you really met that girl on the plane over here?"

At his brother-in-law's question, Ezra glanced at Wayne,

who sat beside him on the patio after being discharged only hours ago. The man hadn't made it in the door before he demanded to sit outside. Said he was tired of being cooped up, and that he could sit on a patio chair just as easily as the couch. So, they'd all traipsed out back so Wayne could enjoy the sunshine.

"Yep."

"Funny how fate works, isn't it? Opposite side of the world and you still find *the one*." He huffed a soft laugh. "And apparently Australia is lucky for your family." With a wide smile, he glanced at Anna, who sat on his other side, holding his hand.

"Wayne, leave him alone. They're not putting labels on anything." Anna leaned forward to look at Ezra. "Even though he's suddenly stopped sleeping in his bedroom."

A flush crept up Ezra's neck. He was glad for his mirrored aviators. They kept Anna from reading his expression. "I don't know what you're talking about."

She hummed. "Sure."

He didn't want to talk about his relationship with Amy. Anna was right; they weren't labeling anything yet. Just enjoying their last few days together before life forced them to deal with it. He changed the subject. "So, what's the timeline on your recovery?" He glanced at Wayne.

"Too long." Wayne's face turned down with a deep frown. "It'll be another three weeks, minimum, before they let me walk unaided. Even though this brace does a fabulous job of providing support." He tapped the black brace encircling his leg from hip to ankle. "I still have to use crutches or a cane."

"For good reason." Anna turned narrowed blue eyes on her husband. "You broke a lot of bones. And not just in your leg. Your balance is terrible."

He waved a hand. "It's not that bad."

"Until you catch your toe on something. Or turn too fast."

"Stop worrying about me, woman."

Anna huffed, making Ezra grin.

"Do you remember what happened?" Ezra had gotten a quick rundown from Anna, but he hadn't actually talked to Wayne about it.

"Not entirely. Once I got knocked out, things are fuzzy. But before that, I remember going into the pen to put hay into the feeder, then suddenly our bull was there. And he shouldn't have been." He looked at Anna. "Did Jericho check the gate between the pastures?"

She nodded. "There was no sign it was broken."

"Then either I didn't latch the gate or someone let him out."

"You were the only one out there."

"I know. And I know I latched that gate. I always double check and make sure it's latched. I don't need the damn beast going after the bull calves to get to their mamas. But I can't fathom who would have opened it."

Something that had been brewing in Ezra's mind over the last couple of weeks solidified at Wayne's words. There were just too many coincidences. He sat forward. "Wayne, does anyone have it out for you or for your family?"

Anna's soft surprised intake of air matched the surprise on Wayne's face. "Like a grudge?" he asked.

Ezra nodded. "Or another reason to want to harm you or your family?"

Wayne started to shake his head, then paused, a deep frown forming between his eyebrows. He glanced at Anna. "We had a man come to the station a couple months ago. Offered to buy the place. And he offered a shit-ton of money too. But I told him it wasn't for sale. It's our home, you know? And even if it was for sale, I wouldn't have sold it to him."

"Why not?"

"He had this air about him that was just—"

"Smarmy," Anna interjected.

Wayne nodded. "Yeah. That's a good word. He was a slick character. Bright white teeth, perfect hair. Fake tan. He looked like a salesman who would say and do anything to convince you to buy. Except he was the one buying."

"Did he give you a name?"

"Landon Hemingway. Said he was a land agent from Perth."

"Perth?" That was thousands of miles away.

Again, Wayne nodded. "When I asked him what he was doing in the Northern Territory, he said he was looking to branch out his business."

Ezra's eyebrow shot up. "By buying a multi-million-dollar cattle station?"

"Exactly." Wayne tipped a finger at him. "Anyway, after I told him no, he left a business card with me and said to call him if I changed my mind. I didn't. He called me, though, checking in. Several times, in fact. After the third call, I told him to stop calling and blocked his number."

"Did that work?"

"For the phone calls. Then he started with the emails. I just marked them as spam and deleted them."

"We got several hang-up calls in the last few weeks," Anna said.

"We did?" Wayne looked at her. "You didn't mention that."

She lifted a shoulder. "I didn't think too much of it. Phone service can be spotty. The calls don't always go through. I figured it was someone trying to call, but the call dropped."

Ezra's internal warning system blared. Something wasn't right. "The plane that I flew—who knew about that?"

"I'm not sure. It wasn't a secret. Plane maintenance is part of life. Though we don't fly too many to Brisbane very often. The Piper was special."

"How so?"

"My normal mechanic was booked up. He's the one who referred me to Brisbane. Said his friend there did good work. I didn't have any reason not to believe him."

Ezra gave a soft huff. He did now.

"Do you really think this all has something to do with that guy?" Wayne asked.

"I'm not sure." Ezra stared out into the yard, his gaze landing on Amy but not really seeing her. His mind whirled. "I know a guy who might be able to help us figure it out, though."

"How?"

"Is this illegal?" Anna speared her brother with a look.

Ezra smiled. "Only if he gets caught. Which he won't."

She groaned.

"But I think we need to do it anyway. It's too much of a coincidence." He looked at Wayne over the rim of his sunglasses.

The man's mouth flattened, but he nodded. "Do it."

Ezra turned to Anna. "Annie, can I borrow your phone?" He held out his hand.

Her eyebrows shot up. "You want to do it now?"

He shrugged. "Why not?"

"Maybe because it's the middle of the night in the U.S.?"

"He's not in the U.S."

"Where is he?"

"Costa Rica."

Anna rolled her eyes. "It's still the middle of the night there."

"So? He won't care."

She blinked. "Your friend won't care if you call him in the middle of the night?"

"No. He owes me."

"Of course he does." She sighed and lifted her hip, taking her phone from her back pocket.

Ezra smiled and took the device. "Thanks. I'll be right back." He got up and walked into the house. No one needed to overhear the conversation he was about to have with Asher.

Recalling the man's number from memory, Ezra entered it into the phone, then listened to it ring. Despite what he said to Anna, he wasn't sure Asher would pick up. The call wouldn't come back to Ezra. Though knowing Asher Horn, he knew everything about Ezra, including his sister's name and where she lived.

The line rang several times, then, a gruff voice answered. "Horn."

"Asher, it's Ezra Chastain. I need that big brain of yours."

A long pause came over the line, then a yawn. "What's up?"

Ezra outlined the situation, starting from Wayne's accident and the plane crash to what Anna and Wayne told him about Landon Hemingway.

Rustling on the other end told Ezra Asher was on the move. "You're right. Something does sound off. Where was the plane stored in Brisbane?"

Ezra named the maintenance company at the airport.

"You have any other details on Hemingway? Like a company name or an address?"

"Hang on." Ezra hurried to the sliding doors and poked his head outside. "Wayne?"

Wayne and Anna turned.

"You still have Hemingway's business card?"

"No. I tossed it. Why?"

Ezra's mouth twisted. "Do you remember the name of his company or its address?"

"It was called Bell Properties."

Pieces of the puzzle clicked in Ezra's mind. "Seriously? Bell Properties?" He arched an eyebrow and gave a soft snort. "What are the chances he gave you a fake name?"

Wayne frowned. "What do you mean?"

Anna groaned. "I get it. *For Whom the Bell Tolls*, written by Ernest Hemingway."

"Yep." Ezra frowned and looked at Wayne. "Do you remember the address?"

"No. Just that it was in Perth. You could try looking it up online."

"Okay. Thanks." With a nod, Ezra stepped inside. "He said it's in Perth, but can't remember the address."

"I'm already looking." There was a short pause. "I found the company website. Hang on."

Ezra paced while Asher did his thing. The man was a computer genius. Or, as he preferred to say, a hacker. If it lived online, Asher could find it, no matter what you hid it behind. Ezra was counting on that now.

"Okay, so the address listed on site is linked to a building in downtown Perth. It's an office high-rise. I'm checking their directory..." His voice trailed off. "I don't see a Bell Properties on it."

"Are there any real estate firms?"

"Several. Getting a list of employees now."

"I'm not sure what good that will do us. I doubt Landon Hemingway is his real name."

"No, but I can gather images of employees that fit the age range and see if your brother-in-law recognizes anyone."

"Oh. I guess that's true." Ezra braced a hand on his hip and looked around the room as he listened.

"How old was this guy?"

"No idea. Hang on." He should just stay outside at this rate. Walking to the door, he opened it and stuck his head out again. "How old was Hemingway?"

"Thirties."

Ezra relayed that to Asher.

"Perfect. Give me twelve hours or so. I'll get back to you." Asher clicked off before Ezra could say goodbye.

Turning off the screen, Ezra stepped outside. He held the phone out to Anna. "Hopefully, he'll come up with something."

"What is he going to do?" She took the phone, then waved her free hand. "Never mind. Probably the less we know, the better."

"The less we know what?" Amy asked, walking up.

"Ezra's suspicious about my accident and the plane crash. He called a friend," Wayne said.

Amy sent a curious look at Ezra. "Oh?"

"Just a hunch. We'll see what pans out. I could be wrong, and it could all be a terrible coincidence."

She stared at him; the look in her eyes told him she knew he didn't believe that. He didn't deny it. Ezra had an awful feeling everything was connected.

His gaze landed on the baby in Amy's arms. His family was in grave danger. He just hoped he could figure out why and from whom before someone died.

Twenty-Nine

Ezra stared at the email on the laptop screen. Asher must never sleep. Or eat. There was a book here, and it was full of nothing but names. He clicked on the attached file folder, which contained images of every person on the list. Each one had a number in the corner that corresponded to a name on the list.

Picking up the computer, he walked outside. Wayne was once again on the patio. At least it was a little cooler since it was morning. Ezra glanced at the time Asher sent the email. Two-thirty a.m.—Australia time. He shook his head. It hadn't even taken him the twelve hours he requested to gather all the material. Ezra didn't know how he did it.

Wayne looked up as Ezra stepped outside. "Morning." He raised his coffee cup in greeting.

"Hey." He sat down next to Wayne. "I hate to intrude on your solitude, but I have some pictures for you to look at."

"From your friend?"

Ezra nodded. He held out the laptop. "He sent a file of images. Look through them and see if you can identify Hemingway."

"Sure." Wayne set his mug on the ground, then took the computer. His eyes widened. "That's a lot of people."

"Yeah. Fifty some, from the looks of it."

"Your friend works fast." Wayne clicked on the first image, then used the arrow that popped up on the side of the screen to scroll through the rest. A third of the way through, he stopped. "That's him."

Ezra studied the man smiling back at them. He was in his early thirties. With his dark hair perfectly combed and teeth so white they gleamed neon, Ezra understood why Wayne didn't trust him. Everything about the man screamed fake. He glanced at the number on the picture. "Minimize that and go to the email."

Wayne clicked away from the pictures.

Ezra followed the list down until he got to number seventeen. "William Ernest. Well, now we know at least part of the reason he chose Hemingway as his fake name. Do you have your phone? I want to call Asher."

"It's in the house." Wayne hooked a thumb toward the door. "On the kitchen counter. We need to get you a new cell, mate."

A corner of Ezra's mouth kicked up. "Yeah. It's number one on my list when I get back to the U.S." He stood. "I'll let you know what Asher says."

Wayne nodded and picked up his coffee and held up the laptop with his other hand. "Sounds good."

Ezra took the computer and retreated inside. He found Wayne's phone and called Asher. The man picked up on the second ring.

"You realize I was up the rest of the night finding information for you, then had to work the rest of the day, right?" Asher's voice was thick with sleep. "I just went to bed an hour ago."

"Sorry. It's morning here."

Asher's loud yawn came over the line. "Don't worry about it. I'm used to little sleep. Ford likes to send me down rabbit holes too," he said, mentioning their mutual friend, Ford Wagner, for whom Asher now worked. "Did your brother-in-law recognize anyone?"

"Actually, yes. Number seventeen. William Ernest."

"Ah. He was my pick for this. Ford's too. I told him about what's going on, and he helped me compile the list. Glad to know our instincts are still good. Let's see what we can dig up."

Ezra heard movement, then the click-clack of Asher typing.

"So, how are things going there? Is business good?" Their friend Ford had opened a fishing charter service after he left the military. Several of their friends had followed him to Costa Rica, seeking a life away from the hustle and bustle of the U.S. Asher had moved down this past year, needing an escape after spending years as an intelligence analyst.

"Can't complain. We have charters every day. Actually, yes, I can complain. I don't get enough time out of the office. But I don't know much about boats, so Ford stuck me on the front desk at the office. I'm about ready to put up an awning and set up a desk outside."

Ezra chuckled. "At least your new office has windows."

Asher barked out a laugh. "That's the truth. No more basement dungeon for me. Oh, what do we have here?"

"What? Did you find something?"

"Yes. Mr. Ernest has an off-shore bank account under the Bell Properties name. He thought he was being smart; he nestled it under his real estate company's holdings. But he's not smarter than me. I wonder if his bosses know about this?"

So did Ezra. "How did he do that? Wouldn't he need documentation to set up an account under a legit business? Especially one he doesn't own?"

"Would you care to guess what Mr. Ernest does for said real estate company?"

"What?"

"He's their CFO."

"Seriously? That guy is their chief financial officer? He's a baby."

"Yep. He's older than he looks. Probably thanks to some plastic surgery. His driver's license file says he's thirty-nine."

Damn. Ezra wouldn't have guessed more than thirty-two. "What else did you find out about him?"

"He's single."

Shocker. Ezra rolled his eyes.

"Originally from Alice Springs."

Ezra sat up. Dalton Creek was close to there. "Oh?"

"Yeah. He moved to Perth for college and never left."

More typing sounded in the background.

"I'm looking up his bosses. And to see if there's anyone else attached to that bank account or to Bell Properties. So far, it looks like it's just Ernest."

"You know, I don't think you'll find anyone. You said he's from Alice Springs. My brother-in-law's cattle station isn't too far from there. Maybe a few hundred miles at most. This might be personal."

"Hmm. I'll call you back." The line clicked.

Ezra pulled the phone away from his ear and stared at it, then chuckled. Good ol' Asher.

He set the phone down and wandered to the fridge. He hadn't eaten breakfast yet. Instead, he went straight to Anna's laptop and logged into his email when he got up, hoping he'd gotten something from Asher.

Finding a yogurt, he shut the fridge door, then popped some toast in the toaster. He grabbed an orange from the bowl on the counter and started peeling it while he waited on the toast.

"Hey, you."

Ezra looked up at the sound of Amy's voice. He smiled. "Hey."

She walked up and stood on her toes to give him a kiss. "You snuck out on me."

"I didn't want to wake you. You were zonked."

She hummed. "For good reason." A hot gleam entered her eyes.

His blood heated. "Don't plan on sleeping much tonight, either." He leaned in to kiss her.

The phone rang.

Cursing Asher's timing, Ezra stepped away from Amy and picked it up, answering the call. "That was quick."

"Ford's getting on a plane this afternoon. He should be there tomorrow. Early."

"What?" Ezra frowned. "Why? I can take what you give me to the authorities."

"You can take his identity to the authorities. All the rest of this I didn't obtain through legal means. They'd have to rediscover it all."

Ezra let out a sigh. "So what's Ford's purpose here? He's not exactly an investigator-type. He's more of a protect and shoot type."

Asher chuckled. "Exactly. If this is personal, your family needs someone like that watching their backs. And I know you have to come home soon."

A lump formed in Ezra's throat. He cleared it. "I appreciate that, Asher. Thank you."

"You'd do the same for any of us. Hopefully, he'll be blessedly bored, and the anonymous tip I'm about to send to the Australian authorities will land Ernest's ass in jail and eliminate the problem."

Smiling, Ezra glanced at Amy, who looked on, curious. "Sounds good. Email me his flight information."

"Will do." The line clicked again.

"You look happy." Amy tipped her head.

Ezra set the phone down. "It pays to have friends in the right places. That was Asher. He's dug up some interesting information on Landon Hemingway, a.k.a. William Ernest. Another of our friends will be here tomorrow to provide a little extra protection for Wayne and Anna."

"Protection? There's that much danger?"

"Not sure. But it's looking like this might be personal. I'll know more once Ford gets here and Asher does some more digging into Ernest."

She frowned. "We were supposed to leave for Brisbane tomorrow."

Some of his euphoria at making headway into Wayne's accident and their plane crash died. They were spending the night in Brisbane before her flight left Friday. His wasn't scheduled until Sunday. But he couldn't leave until he got everything settled here.

"It's fine." She waved a hand, reading his thoughts. "I understand. I can go alone."

"Now, hold up. I can still go. Asher said Ford's coming in early, so I should be able to go with you. The flight doesn't leave until two."

She raised an eyebrow. "So, you're going to brief him, then leave a total stranger here with Wayne and Anna? And then come back? Or are you going to stay in Brisbane like you planned? Either one is ridiculous. Just stay here. I'm a big girl, Ezra. I can handle flying to Brisbane by myself."

"I never said you couldn't, Tinkerbell. And you know that's not why I wanted to go with you." His voice took on a hard note. She was putting words in his mouth, and he didn't like it.

She crossed her arms and looked away. He walked closer and wrapped his hands around her biceps. Bending at the knee, he tipped his head to look her in the eye. "Hey. I know you're upset. I am too. But I can't just leave my family hanging. Not with something like this."

"I know. But hey, maybe it's for the best. This way, there will be no looking back or searching for one last glimpse when I board the plane in Brisbane."

Ezra's heart clenched so hard it hurt. He did not want her to leave. Not tomorrow. And certainly not without him. "It will only be temporary."

"Will it?" Her gaze met his. "We live in different states. And even if we weren't, you said yourself you're gone a lot because of your job. I just—"

Footsteps on the stairs cut her off. She pressed her lips together and looked away again.

Ezra said a silent curse and turned, forcing a smile onto his face as Anna entered the kitchen, carrying Maylee.

"Good morning." The smile that accompanied her greeting slowly faded as she took in their expressions. "Oh, sorry. I didn't mean to interrupt."

"You didn't." Amy stepped around Ezra. She held out her arms, pointing to the baby. "Here, let me take her so you can eat." Her hands closed around the infant, and Anna relinquished her with a look of surprise.

"Oh, well, thank you."

Amy nodded. "You're welcome. We're going to go for a little stroll before it gets too hot. Enjoy your breakfast." She offered Anna a smile, then walked out, not looking at Ezra.

He watched her go, his muscles tight. Dammit.

"Okay. What's going on? You two have been the most sickening lovebirds for the last few days, and now she won't even look at you. What did you say?" Anna crossed her arms and arched a brow.

"Why would you assume I said something?"

"Did you?"

"No." He sighed and rubbed his forehead. "It's more the circumstances." He quickly explained what he found out this morning as well as Asher's plan.

Anna's expression turned pensive. "I appreciate that you and your friends are so willing to help. But I don't want it to come between you and Amy. Maybe you should go to Brisbane. Ford's your friend, so I'm okay with him being here without you. I know you wouldn't let a psycho stay with us."

"It won't matter if I go with her. She's not upset about me staying behind. It's more what's going to happen once we're both stateside. She's scared. And I don't blame her. So am I. I don't want to lose her, but I don't know how we're going to make this work."

"Ezra, I moved across the world for Wayne. Gave up everything I thought I wanted because I wanted him more. If that's the kind of love you two share, then it will all work out. Have some faith."

Anna's words gave him pause. Would it? Were they meant to be? He didn't know. But he did know he loved her. It hadn't truly hit him until now. But it had been there, in the back of his mind, for days. He didn't want to imagine life without her. If she didn't feel the same way, though, he'd have to.

"You two need to talk. Take her to dinner tonight and figure it out."

That wasn't a bad idea. They definitely needed to talk. A soft smile crossed his face. "You're still as bossy as ever. Age and motherhood haven't changed that."

She slapped at his chest. "Shut up. You're still older than me."

Chuckling, he pulled her into a hug. "I love you, Annie. Thank you for being a fount of sage advice."

She hugged him back. "You're welcome. I love you too."

THIRTY

Amy stared at the suitcase open on the bed. Unsure if she was doing the right thing. She didn't want to leave, but if she stayed, she'd be rotten company. Not to mention a basket case. The anticipation of leaving tomorrow—leaving Ezra behind—would be torture. Especially since she'd have to act like it didn't bother her. That she wasn't upset about not knowing what the future would bring. She couldn't stay here. Couldn't fake it.

It was too late to change her mind, anyway. She'd already made arrangements to leave. Reaching out, she flipped the suitcase lid shut and zipped it closed. Grasping the handle, she lifted it off the bed. Her cab would be here any minute.

When she got back from her walk with the baby, Ezra had been buried in Anna's laptop screen, digging into that man he and his friend had fingered as responsible for the issues here. Realizing she couldn't pretend she wasn't upset and worried about the future, she'd borrowed Wayne's phone—he liked to leave it lying around—and called the airline to change her ticket, then a cab company to come get her. She'd been lucky. A flight left for Brisbane in two hours. Just enough time for her to pack and get to the airport. And no time for her to linger and pretend she wasn't falling apart inside.

Picking up her backpack, she slung it over her shoulder, then hefted the small suitcase and left the bedroom. Her heart thundered in her ears as she descended the stairs. She thought about making a beeline for the front door and hoping no one saw her, but knew she couldn't do that. Ezra at least deserved a goodbye.

It wouldn't have mattered, anyway. He was in the living room. There was no sneaky escape when he was right there.

He glanced up. "Hey." His gaze returned to the screen, only to shoot back to her when he saw her suitcase. A deep frown wrinkled his forehead. "What are you doing? Why do you have your suitcase?"

"I'm leaving."

Every muscle in his body froze. He didn't even blink as he stared at her. "What?"

"There's no point in me lingering, pretending like everything is fine. I'm going to spend my last day in Brisbane. Alone."

"You changed your flight?" He got up, moving closer.

Amy stiffened her spine. *Don't lean into him. Keep your hands at your sides, sister.* She clenched and unclenched her hand around the handle of her suitcase. "Yes."

He blinked several times. "I don't understand. I mean, I knew you were upset about me staying behind—"

She held up her free hand. "It's not about that. I just—" She broke off and bit the corner of her mouth, glancing away. "I can't pretend."

"Pretend? Baby, what are we pretending about?" He took her hand.

Amy clenched her teeth, steeling herself against the feelings he provoked. "That we're going to continue this when we get home. I've decided not to quit my job. Opening an antiques store is just too risky. I've had enough risk this past month to last me a lifetime." She'd never said anything more true. And as she'd packed she'd gone over that mental list she made and realized that she'd failed to consider risk in and of itself, as well as safety. Staying in D.C. was safe and risk-free. Both two things she appreciated now more than ever.

Ezra swallowed and stared at her for a long moment. "Okay. So, we'll do the long-distance thing for a while. I can probably get a transfer—"

"No." She pulled her hand away. "I'm not letting you give up a job—a career—you love for me. I don't want that on my conscience." And she didn't. She knew she was consigning herself to some heartache—okay, a lot of heartache, considering what he meant to her—but in the long-run, she felt her plan was best. Neither of them had to put their lives on the line for something that had so many insurmountable obstacles in the way.

"Amy—"

She shook her head and backed toward the door. "This month has been amazing." A car horn beeped outside. "That's my ride."

He grabbed her hand and pulled her into his body. "Wait. Tinkerbell, you can't leave." His voice was gruff.

"Ezra, please. I have to go." She blinked, fighting back tears. She couldn't cry. Not yet.

"No. You don't. Honey, we can make this work."

He cupped her jaw, the warmth of his skin seeping into her face. She stared at his Adam's apple. If she looked him in the eye, she'd lose it.

"I love you."

Amy's breath caught, and her gaze flew to his. "What?" she breathed.

"I love you. We will make this work. It might not be easy, but we'll figure it out."

Her lower lip trembled. She sucked it between her teeth and looked away. He loved her? She loved him too. Which was why she was walking away. This last month had been a fairytale. But it was just that. When they got home and reality intruded, everything would be different. They'd be hundreds of miles apart with little chance of bringing their lives together. Love wasn't enough.

A tear rolled down her cheek. "I love you too. But it's not enough. We're too different. Our lives too far apart." She pulled out of his arms, turning her gaze away from his. The pain in his eyes made her feel two inches tall. She hadn't wanted to hurt him. Hurt either of them. But this was for the best. It would save them from more pain in the future.

Another tear escaped. She blinked, holding the rest back. When she was alone, she could break down. "Thank you for the memories," she said, forcing the words around the lump in her throat. Spinning on her heel, she pulled her suitcase behind her and made a hasty exit, not looking back.

THIRTY-ONE

Arms crossed, Ezra stood in the main lobby of the Darwin airport, waiting for Ford. His plane had landed not long ago, so he should be coming out soon.

He didn't want to be here. He wanted to be on a plane back to the U.S., going after Amy. Somehow, he needed to convince her they were worth fighting for. That they could mesh their lives and make things work. But he had to make sure his sister and her family were safe first.

So, he stared at the crowd, waiting for a man he hadn't seen in years.

It didn't take long for Ezra to spot him. There was no mistaking Ford Wagner. Nearly Ezra's height, the man oozed confidence and carried a deadly air. People gave him space without realizing it. He was like oil to water, repelling everyone around him. Ezra didn't really understand why. He looked a bit like a surfer. Since he left the military, he'd let his hair grow out. His wavy, light brown locks were sun-bleached. But even before that, he looked like a surfer. Lean, but strong, he favored shorts and flip-flops over anything else when he wasn't in uniform. But there was something about the way he carried himself that made strangers wary, and it undercut his approachable appearance.

Ford spotted him and smiled, lifting his fingers from around his backpack strap in a wave. Ezra walked forward.

"Ezra. Good to see you." Ford held out a hand.

Ezra shook it. "You too. Thanks for coming."

"Of course. But why was Asher the one to ask and not you? You know I'd have come. Even without details."

Mouth flattening, Ezra tipped his head toward the door, indicating they should walk and talk. "One, he didn't mention he was calling you until he'd already called you. And two, Australia's a long way for you to come to keep an eye on my sister. Asher was making good headway on gathering evidence against Ernest. I'm not sure your presence is necessary."

Ford lifted a shoulder. "Eh, I needed a vacation, anyway."

Ezra let out a soft huff. "You live in Costa Rica. Every day is a vacation for you."

"Nah. That's just home."

They stepped through the sliding doors into the heat.

"Sweet mother of God. Is it always this hot? I live in the jungle and it's not this warm."

"You get used to it, I guess."

Ford arched an eyebrow before pulling a pair of sunglasses from his pocket and sliding them on his face. "You've been here a month. Are you telling me you're already used to it?"

Mouth twisting, Ezra paused at the edge of the road, waiting for a car to go by. "No. I've just learned to ignore it. Spending days in the heat with no shelter or sunscreen will do that."

"What?" Ford glanced at him, brows dipping.

"Asher didn't tell you?"

"Tell me what? All he said was there was a threat against your family and you needed my help. He said you'd give me the details."

"I was in a plane crash last month."

"What!" Ford stopped and pulled off his glasses to look Ezra up and down. "You look okay. Was it bad?"

"Bad enough. We went down in the middle of nowhere. Made it out of the aircraft all right, but we had to walk a long way to help."

"We?"

"Yeah." Ezra's mouth flattened as thoughts of Amy intruded. He'd tried to keep her off his mind as much as possible so he could focus. There would come a time to figure out things with her, but it wasn't now. "I met a woman on the flight over from the States. Long story short, we ended up traveling together, and the plane we were in went down. It was one owned by my brother-in-law's cattle station. All the trouble is surrounding them. From what Asher's pieced together, it looks personal. Like this William Ernest guy has it out for the Daltons. But we don't know why."

"What else has happened?"

Ezra started walking again, giving Ford the details as they made their way to the taxi stand.

Ford let out a low whistle when Ezra finished his story. "I'm glad your brother-in-law is okay. Tell me about Ernest."

"He's a real estate agent in Perth, but he's originally from Alice Springs. Dalton Creek is only a few hundred miles from there. We think he has a personal reason for the things that have happened. Asher's still digging into his background, but he's not turning up much from when he lived there. Just some high school stuff. Sports teams he was on, yearbook photo— that sort of thing."

"Yeah. Out there, a lot of info is going to be in people's memories. We'll need to talk to locals to find out more."

"That's what I figured too." He raised a hand as a taxi pulled closer. The cab stopped, and the driver got out to open the trunk.

Ford put his things in the back, then he and Ezra got into the car.

"Where to, gentlemen?" the driver asked.

Ezra gave him the rental house address. The driver pulled away from the curb.

"So, is that everything that's happened? Is your sister okay? You look really—pensive."

"I'm fine." Ezra stared out the window.

"Bullshit. I've spent enough time with you to know something's wrong. And that statement tells me whatever it is has nothing to do with your sister. It's that woman you mentioned, isn't it?"

A muscle in Ezra's jaw twitched, but he didn't look at Ford.

"What happened?"

"Nothing. Don't worry about it."

"Look, I know we're not best buds or anything, but you can talk to me. I think maybe you need to."

Ezra looked at him then. "I appreciate your willingness to listen. But I need to figure this out on my own."

Ford's gold-flecked hazel eyes studied him for a long moment. "Can I offer you some advice?"

"Sure." He wouldn't discount anything Ford said, even if he didn't want to talk about his problems. The man was highly intelligent and a hell of a leader. He usually gave good advice.

"Apologize."

Ezra snorted. "I don't have anything to apologize for. She's the one who left."

"Doesn't matter. Say you're sorry. You can apologize for not understanding how she felt, if you want. The point is to start the conversation in a non-confrontational way."

A frown dipped Ezra's eyebrows. "Aren't you divorced?"

Ford grinned. "Yeah, but that was because I was young and

dumb and married a hag. Since then, I've learned some things."

"You're still single."

"By choice." Ford tipped a finger toward him.

Ezra rolled his eyes and looked out the window again. "I'll figure it out. Once I'm stateside and can go after her. She knows Anna is my priority at the moment. That's not an issue. It's meshing our lives when we live hundreds of miles apart. She doesn't want to set herself up for heartache. Which I get, but—" He broke off and shook his head. "It's complicated."

"Not really. I think you need to think about what you want, and what's needed to achieve that. Make a list of pros and cons. That's what I did after I left the SEALs and was trying to figure out what to do with my life. I listed the reasons why I should and shouldn't stay in the U.S. It helped me see what was most important. Ultimately, my mental health won out, and I bought a boat."

A sardonic smile lifted one side of Ezra's mouth. "Amy's hardly a boat, Ford."

"No. But like my boat, she has an impact on your mental well-being. On your future. Just make the damn list."

Ezra chuckled at the exasperation in Ford's voice. "Yes, Commander."

"That's right. Don't forget it."

Mood lighter, Ezra thought about what Ford said. It probably wouldn't hurt to make a list. He'd already been thinking about it. If he figured out his life, then he could go to Amy armed with a plan.

But first, he had to get Ford up to speed on the problems at Dalton Creek. Once Anna and her family were safe, he would worry about himself.

Thirty-Two

Bright sunshine hit Ezra's face, belying the chilly wind that whipped around beneath the awning at the Nashville airport. It was a big switch from the sweltering weather he left behind in Australia. He turned up his jacket collar and lengthened his stride, heading for long-term parking and his car.

Digging in his backpack, he found his keys, thankful he'd thrown them in his bag and not his suitcase, or they'd have gone up in flames with the Piper. If only he'd left his phone in it and not tucked into the pocket next to the pilot's seat.

It didn't matter, though. He was back in the U.S. and could get a new phone. Which was exactly what he was doing as soon as he got back to Clarksville.

Weaving his way through the sea of cars, he found his truck and unlocked it. After throwing his small suitcase and his backpack in the rear seat, he got in and started the engine. A chill ran down his spine. Winter was fast on its way here. It was in the fifties, but it was windy. He adjusted the heat, then buckled his seatbelt and pulled out of his parking space. With a quick stop at the tollbooth, he paid his parking fee and left.

The tires hummed on the pavement as he maneuvered his way off the airport grounds and onto the loop around Nashville. He tapped his fingers on the steering wheel, edgy. Now that he was home, he had a list of things to do. Number one was to track down Amy. Despite their month together, he hadn't gotten her address. He had her phone number, but he wasn't sure she'd answer if he called. The D.C. area was within a day's drive. Once he had her address, he planned to take a road trip this weekend. He'd leave as soon as he got done at work on Friday. Letting her stew any longer wasn't something he wanted to do. He wished he could go today, but he had to be back on base tomorrow. He'd never make it to D.C. and back before then. Not even if he flew.

Miles ticked by, and soon, signs for Clarksville appeared. Getting off the interstate, he drove to his local cellphone carrier. It was a Monday morning, so he hoped they weren't too busy.

Their parking lot came into view and he gave a mental fist pump. It was virtually empty. Pulling into the lot, he parked and got out, huddling into his coat against the wind. Australia had ruined him. It would take him weeks to acclimate to this weather.

Hurrying inside where it was warm, he glanced around, spotting a free employee.

The young man smiled. "Hello. What can I do for you?"

"I need a new phone. Mine was destroyed in a plane crash."

The man blinked. "I'm sorry. Did you say plane crash?"

Ezra nodded. "I had an iPhone. I'd like the same thing."

"Oh, um, sure. We can do that. Do you have your ID?"

"Yeah." Ezra handed over his driver's license, then leaned against the counter, resigned to being here for a while.

The clerk worked as quickly as he could, finding Ezra's account and setting him up with a new device. Thankfully,

Ezra backed things up to the cloud, so once the phone updated, it downloaded all his apps and files with ease. An hour after he arrived, he walked out with his new device.

Getting in his truck, he started the engine, letting the heat warm him, and opened his email. The icon told him he had several dozen messages that weren't there when he left Darwin for Brisbane.

One from his commanding officer caught his eye, and he groaned. The subject line was "Deployment." Clicking on it, he scanned the text, cursing this time. He was to report to base as soon as he got the message. No other details were provided.

"Dammit." He slammed his hand against the steering wheel. This was not the plan. There was no telling how long he'd be gone. It could be a quick mission that only lasted a week or so, or he could be gone months. Cursing again, he set the phone down and put the truck in gear to head to base.

THIRTY-THREE

Frosty grass crunched under Amy's feet as she walked through the yard at her parents' house toward the pond. Their dog, a black and white Great Dane named Harry, ran ahead, scaring the geese. She stuffed her hands in her pockets, exhaling a breath and watching it fog. It was going to be a cold Christmas in Georgia this year.

Sunlight danced over the ground, reflecting off the ice crystals and creating a golden glow. Steam rose from the pond as the sun warmed the air. Amy closed her eyes and savored the peace. She hadn't had much of that lately.

It had been almost seven weeks since she left Australia. And since she'd heard from Ezra. He'd left a voicemail a few days after she returned, telling her he'd been called up for a mission and that he'd be out of reach for a while.

She wished he hadn't. It took her a month to stop rushing to the phone every time it rang. Which was ludicrous, anyway. She'd made her feelings clear when she left Darwin. She didn't want to talk to him. Wasn't interested in a relationship. Not when they lived so far apart. She never should have let herself succumb to the need that night at Mindil Beach. Her body had overruled her mind, though, and convinced her it was the right move. She wished she'd told it to stuff it. Maybe she could have avoided a lot of this heartache.

Amy opened her eyes and blew her breath out through her nose on a harsh exhale. Why was she thinking about him again? She'd been enjoying the peace and quiet. Now she was edgy.

Rolling her shoulders, she quickened her pace to catch up with Harry. The dog wasn't likely to run off, but she didn't want him to wander into the trees where she couldn't see him. He liked to find birds and squirrels and tree them, then sit there and wait. He'd ignore her calls and be impossible to find.

She whistled as he loped around the back of the pond. "Harry! You stay here."

The dog looked back, then froze. His already erect ears stood straight up. He barked once. It was a low warning sound that sent a chill up Amy's spine and had nothing to do with the bite in the air.

Frowning, she watched him for a moment. His gaze was fixed behind her. She turned, not knowing what to expect. But what she saw wasn't something she'd even fathomed possible.

Her breath froze in her lungs. *Ezra.*

He walked toward her, his long, jean-clad legs eating up the ground. The black parka he wore made his broad shoulders even wider. Aviator sunglasses covered his eyes, reflecting the sun.

She stayed where she was, forcing her lungs to work. What was he doing here?

A low growl from her side drew her attention. She glanced down. Harry stood next to her now, growling at Ezra. "No, Harry. Sit."

The dog's butt hit the ground, but his gaze remained on the man now just feet away. She looked up.

"Hi, Tinkerbell."

Amy studied him, wishing she could see his eyes. "What are you doing here? How did you even know where I was?"

His teeth flashed in a quick smile. "That's quite the story, actually." His expression sobered. "Can we talk?"

Her silly heart sped up and shouted, "He's here!" Gritting her teeth, she told it to shut up. "Why? I said everything in Darwin." She put a hand on Harry's head, needing the anchor. Her heart still wanted to leap out of her chest, despite her best efforts to quell it.

"Right, but you didn't let me speak." He held up a hand when her eyebrows slammed down. "I'm not upset about that or implying anything. I understand where you were coming from. I just want a chance to talk to you. Please?"

She curled her fingers into the dog's fur. That one word was like a knife. It cut open the flimsy box holding back her emotions.

Harry barked.

Ezra took off his sunglasses, giving the dog a wary look. "I'm not about to get eaten, am I?"

Amy rolled her eyes. "No. He looks more fierce than he is." She huffed and started walking, snapping her fingers to call the dog. Harry trotted after her.

"Wait. Where are you going? Is this a no?"

She glanced over her shoulder. "I'm not standing out in the cold for this conversation. If you really want to talk, follow me." She faced forward, not waiting for an answer, and marched toward the house.

In a few strides, he caught up to her. Amy kept her gaze fixed on the white farmhouse. If she looked at him, she'd never be able to keep her thoughts off her face. Seeing as her thoughts were currently one giant jumbled mess, and she couldn't pick one out to save her life, it was probably best to keep them all to herself. At least for the next couple of minutes. She knew, eventually, she'd have to face him.

The crunch of their feet in the grass was the only sound as she led him to the house. When they reached it, she mounted the porch steps and pulled open the screen door. It creaked from the cold. Through the window in the inner door, she saw her mom glance up. Amy bit back a groan. She'd been hoping no one would be in the kitchen. Then she could escape with Ezra upstairs and hopefully send him on his way without her parents or sisters noticing.

Amy pushed the door open. A smile started on her mom's face, then froze as she saw Ezra walk in behind her.

"Mom, this is Ezra. Ezra, my mom, Grace." She didn't stop as she entered the kitchen; just kept going, heading for the stairs around the corner.

"Amelia—"

"I'll explain in a little while," she called over her shoulder. "Harry, stay." She halted the dog and kept moving.

"Hello, Mrs. Preston."

Ezra greeted her mom, but he followed her out of the room.

"Where are we going?" he asked, his voice low.

"My room, so no one will bother us." She rounded the banister and hurried up the steps. Reaching the second floor, she all but ran down the hall. The last thing she needed was for one of her sisters to come out. They'd be much more persistent than her mom. Why did he have to show up here? Why couldn't he have come to her house in Virginia? Then she wouldn't have to explain his presence—and their relationship —to her entire family.

She shoved open her bedroom door and motioned him inside. He closed it behind them. Amy spun to face him, drinking him in. God, he looked amazing.

"This is nice." Ezra's gaze tracked around the room, no doubt taking in the lilac-colored walls, white furniture, and landscape paintings of her youth. Her mom had done little to redecorate any of their bedrooms when they moved out. Normally, it didn't bother Amy. She wasn't here enough to care. And she found the colors soothing. Here, she knew she was always surrounded by people who loved her.

Her heart clenched. Present company was no exception. Though she wondered if that was still true.

She cleared her throat. "Say what you came to say, Ezra. It's Christmas, and I'm here to spend it with my family."

A flash of pain went through his eyes before he schooled his features. "I quit my job."

Her eyes rounded. "What?"

"My commission was up for renewal and I turned it down. I'm not entirely sure what I'm going to do, but in three months, I will no longer be employed by the U.S. Army."

Amy sank onto the bed, staring at him, mouth agape. "Why would you do that?"

He walked closer and sat down beside her. His large hand enveloped her smaller one. "Because I made a list."

"A list?" She frowned.

Ezra nodded. "Of the pros and cons of staying in the Army. You won."

"I won? What do you mean?"

"I mean, that when I had everything written out, the only con to staying in the Army was not being with you. It outweighed everything else."

She blinked, then looked away. Tipping her head, she tried to process that. He'd quit his job. For her? She looked at him. "You quit to be with me?"

"I did. I love you, Tinkerbell. More than anything. The Army—it's just a job. You—You're my life. You and whatever family we create."

"Family?" He wanted a family? They hadn't talked about that.

But she could see it. A cute, two-story house—much like

this one—with a couple of dark-haired kids running around in the yard. Playing in the sprinkler on a hot summer day with a dog. She could see the two of them sitting on the porch, watching the kids frolic. It was an idyllic scene.

Hope lit in her chest. She put a lid on it, not wanting to get carried away just yet. Needing some space, she stood and paced to the window, looking out.

"Amy, I know you're scared that this won't work out. But I'm more scared of life without you. You're all I've thought about for the last month and a half. So much so that it affected my job. My heart wasn't in it anymore. I still did it, but for the first time, there was somewhere else I wanted to be. That's never happened to me before."

She pressed the back of her hand to her mouth, feeling the fear he talked about. "What if you come to resent me? I already told you I didn't want to come between you and your job."

He got up and came to stand in front of her. "You didn't, Tink. I can still fly. Just not Blackhawks." He took her hands. "Sometimes, there are points in our lives that require us to examine our future. I did that, and what I thought I wanted isn't what I want anymore. My career won't keep me company when I'm old. It won't cheer me up when I'm sick. It won't give me mini-versions of myself to keep me on my toes." He arched an eyebrow, a hint of a smile playing with his lips. "It won't give me a life. But being with you will."

"Oh." The word came out on a choked whisper. She pinched her lips together, holding onto the tears that threatened to fall. She swallowed back the lump in her throat. "You make a valid point." She'd never thought of their relationship —or any relationship—in those terms. Now she saw his decision to leave the Army in a different light.

"I know." One corner of his mouth kicked up.

A soft chuckle bubbled from her lips. "I see you didn't leave your cockiness in Australia."

His smile bloomed. "Nope. That's here to stay. Get used to it." He brought his hands up to frame her face. "I love you, Amelia. Will you grow old with me?"

The hope in her heart burst free of its bonds. She didn't bother to hold it hostage anymore. Raising her hands, she grasped his coat. "Yes. I love you, Ezra." She was so very glad he tracked her down.

He lowered his head. Just inches away, a thought struck her.

"Wait." She raised a hand and covered his lips. "You never did explain how you found me."

Ezra arched an eyebrow, then sighed when she continued to give him a curious look. "I had Asher find your address in Virginia and drove there. When I got to your house and you weren't home, I did some thinking, and realized since it was Christmas Eve, you might be with your family. So, I called him back and got the address here."

"Wait. It's still Christmas Eve. You were at my house this morning?"

He nodded. "I left right after work last night. Drove all evening and into the night. It was about three a.m. when I got to your house."

"You knocked on my door at three a.m.?"

"Well, yeah." He lifted a shoulder. "I knew I wouldn't sleep. And I figured after the way we parted in Darwin, you'd be reluctant to talk, anyway, so I figured what did it matter what time it was?"

Amy let out a quiet chuckle. "It would have mattered. I like sleep, remember?"

He grinned. "I was also hoping your sleepiness would make it easier to persuade you. Fewer barriers up around your emotions and all that."

She narrowed her eyes. "I'm going to have to watch you. You're sneaky." She shook her head. "But how did you get here so fast? It's an eight-hour-plus drive. It's only eight o'clock now."

"I have a friend—a guy I flew with at one time—who lives in the area. He owns his own aircraft, so I called him, desperate. I was exhausted and knew I couldn't make that drive without sleep. And flying down commercially was out of the question. I'd never find a seat on Christmas Eve. Once I explained everything, he agreed to fly me down. We landed at the regional airport and I took a taxi out here."

"Wow." That was quite the journey.

"I was determined. Can I kiss you now?"

The perturbed look on his face made her laugh. "One more question."

His lips flattened. "What?"

"How are your sister and Wayne? Did your friends figure everything out?"

Ezra's expression cleared. "Yeah. Turns out Ernest blamed the Daltons for his family's lack of wealth. I guess the section of property Wayne's dad bought in the nineties had more than one bidder. Ernest's dad also bid on it, intending to start his own cattle station, but the Daltons went higher. Apparently, it dashed the elder Ernest's dreams, and he sank into a depression, then drank and gambled the money away."

"Wow. Isn't the son well-off, though? He offered to buy the station, right?"

"Yeah. He wanted to give it to his dad. Restore the old man's dreams. It's kind of sad, really."

Amy agreed. The guy had ruined his life and nearly ended several others in a quest to—

Her thoughts fled as Ezra pressed a hard kiss to her lips. With a grunt of surprise, she wrapped her arms around him and kissed him back.

He lifted his head far enough to look into her eyes. "Sorry. I couldn't wait any longer."

Smiling, she put her hand on the back of his head. "That's fine. Do it again." Her heart full, she pulled his head down, standing on her toes to meet him. He could kiss her whenever he wanted.

EPILOGUE

Amy looked up from her book at the knock on the door and frowned. She glanced at the clock, her frown deepening. Who would be at her door on a Saturday morning?

Putting the book down, she got up. Maybe Ezra locked himself out. He'd gone for a run, wanting to enjoy the cherry blossoms before they were all gone. She shuffled to the door, and grasped the deadbolt. The sleeve of her robe caught her eye, and her shoulders slumped. She glanced heavenward. She was still in her pajamas. If it wasn't Ezra, whoever it was would get a laugh. Like her luggage, her nightwear was—well, colorful. The purple zebra print robe covered her from head to toe, but it was the softest, warmest thing, and she loved it.

"Oh, well." With a sigh, she flipped the locks and opened the door.

It wasn't Ezra.

"Hi." A dark-haired woman not much taller than Amy stood on the porch with a bright smile on her pretty face. She waved. "I'm Brooke McGinty. Is Ezra here?"

Amy frowned. "I'm sorry. Who are you? He's never mentioned you. How do you know him?" She'd better not be some crazy ex-girlfriend. He'd told her about the woman he'd been with before they met and mentioned a few others. None of them sounded insane.

"Oh. Well, that's unfortunate. I was hoping he was considering my offer, but if he hasn't spoken with you—"

Amy waved a hand. "You're making no sense. What offer?"

The woman's smile softened. "A job offer. As a pilot. May I come in?"

"I'm not sure." She glanced past her, hoping Ezra was coming down the street. But she saw no one. That didn't mean he wasn't close, though. He could be coming from a different direction. "He's not here. He went for a run."

"I can wait. And if you'd prefer, I can wait in my car." She pointed over her shoulder to the gray SUV at the curb.

Curiosity got the better of Amy. "If I let you in, will you tell me what offer you're talking about?"

"Of course."

Amy stepped back and let her in. She shut the door, then motioned to the couch. "Have a seat, please. Would you like some coffee or water?"

"A water would be lovely. Airplane air always makes my mouth dry."

Amy walked to the counter that separated the kitchen from the living area. "You flew in this morning?" She rounded the bar and took a glass from the cabinet, setting it in the dispenser in the fridge door.

"Yes."

"From where?"

"Asheville. Ezra really didn't mention anything we talked about to you?"

"No." Amy walked back to Brooke and handed her the glass.

"Thank you." She took a drink.

Amy sat down on the opposite end of the couch. "Fill me in."

Brooke lowered the glass, holding it between her hands. "My family owns a series of mountain resorts throughout the Appalachian Mountains, and we employ several pilots to ferry executives from place to place. We're in need of a new one. A chief pilot, to be exact."

Amy arched an eyebrow. "And you want Ezra to be that pilot?"

Brooke nodded. "He's been—"

The front door opened and a sweaty Ezra stepped through. When he saw Amy sitting with Brooke, the smile forming on his face turned down. "Who's this?" He shut the door.

"Brooke McGinty." Amy pinned him with a look.

The frown on his face intensified. He turned his attention to Brooke. "Why did you come here? I told you I wasn't interested."

She held up a finger. "You told me you weren't interested because there was nothing for your fiancée in Asheville. That her job was here. I've solved that problem."

"What?" Amy looked between them. "Ezra, what's she talking about?"

He entered the room and sat down in the chair across from the couch. "I'm not sure." His expression had turned contemplative. "What are you talking about, Ms. McGinty?"

"After our discussion, I went to my dad and grandpa, and had a talk with them about some goals we'd previously discussed for our main resort. One of those was adding a small museum. Our family's history in the area dates back over two hundred years. The resort is nearly half that age. We have as much history or more in the area as the Biltmore House, yet we have nothing displayed publicly besides a few photographs in the lobby to commemorate that fact." She smiled, turning her gaze on Amy. "But I'm hoping with your help we can change that."

"Me?" Amy pointed at herself. "How?"

"We want to bring you on board to design and implement, then run, a small museum at our Asheville resort."

Amy stared at her, mouth hanging open. "What?" she finally managed to squeak.

"Hold on." Ezra held up a hand. "This isn't some ploy, is it? To get me to say yes? You're not going to hire her, then turn around and kill the project in a few months, are you?"

"No. Absolutely not." Brooke shook her head. "Actually, I should be thanking you. I've been trying to get my family to move ahead with the museum for years, but I always get pushed aside for other projects. But your résumé is so impressive that I finally had the leverage I needed to get it built. Please don't turn me down. I really want this." She gave him a pleading look.

"Um," Amy raised a finger. "Question. How did you even know about him?" She pointed at Ezra. "He hasn't been looking for a new job." She frowned, then looked at him as a thought occurred to her. "Have you?"

He shook his head. "No. The charter flights I've been flying, while not exciting, are fine. I'm home every night, which is what I wanted. She found out about me because the pilot they want to replace is a former commander of mine. His wife had a stroke, and she now needs more care and attention, so he wants to retire. He heard I'd left the Army and mentioned my name to the McGintys." He glanced at Brooke. "When she contacted me about the position, I told her I'd think about it. That gave me some time to look into career opportunities for you. But there weren't any. You'd have to take a pay cut and become low man on the totem pole. I wasn't about to do that to you, no matter how good my job would pay, so I turned her down."

"And now I'm here, as the head of Human Resources for Appalachia Resorts, offering you both excellent jobs. And"—Brooke held up a finger—"it has the added bonus of being closer to your family." She nodded at Amy.

"My—How do you know where they live?" Amy frowned.

"Because I make it a point to learn what I can about our employees. We've run a successful company for almost a hundred years because we pay attention to our staff and treat them well. We're successful because we want our employees to be happy."

"So you dig into our lives?" Amy wasn't sure she liked that.

"Only what's publicly available. I don't do in-depth background checks until we're signing contracts and talking benefits. I want to bring you the best possible offer out of the gate. It saves us all time." Her gaze bounced between them. "So? What do you say? And did I mention we offer relocation services? Moving is on us, and we'll put you up at the resort until you find a house."

Amy's mind spun. This was all overwhelming. Especially for so early on a Saturday morning. She hadn't even finished her coffee.

"Could you give us some time to discuss it, Ms. McGinty? I can call you in a day or two with an answer." Ezra's quiet voice cut through the chaos in Amy's mind.

Brooke smiled. "Of course." She set her glass down on the coffee table and stood. "You still have my number?"

He nodded.

"Perfect. I'm staying in town today and am flying home tomorrow sometime. Feel free to call me if you have any questions. I'll answer what I can."

Ezra rose. "Thank you. I'll walk you out." He held out an arm, gesturing to the door.

"Thanks." Brooke glanced at Amy as she took a step toward the door. "It was nice to meet you."

"You too." A weak smile formed on Amy's face. She was still too stunned to muster anything more.

Ezra walked Brooke to the door and let her out, then shut it. Amy stared at him.

"What the hell just happened?"

He let out a snort and walked back to the living room to sit next to her. "We just got headhunted."

"Is that what that was?" Amy pointed to the door and the woman beyond. "I have to say, she is not at all what I would envision a corporate headhunter to be. She's too nice. And young."

"Yes, well, Appalachia Resorts isn't your typical corporation, either. I did some homework on them when they approached me. They've been family-owned since their inception. Reviews from guests online are great. Other hotel chains the same size don't fare as well."

"Why didn't you tell me about this?"

He lifted a shoulder. "Because I didn't want to bring it to you unless it was a viable option. The only reason I even considered it was because of the salary they offered."

She narrowed her eyes. "Brooke mentioned good pay. How good is good?"

Ezra hesitated, then said a number that made her eyes bulge.

"Ezra! Why didn't you take it? For that, I would have gladly gone back to being a museum technician or even a docent."

He had the good grace to look chagrined. "I already told you I wasn't sacrificing you for a job. Your happiness means more to me than anything, you know that."

"Okay, we need to iron something out here." She shifted and took his hand in hers. "I get that you want me to be happy. And I appreciate that. But this is a two-way street, buster. Part of what makes me happy is when you're happy too." Her brows knit. "Are you happy? With your job, I mean? I know we're good, but outside of us—are you happy?"

He pressed his lips together and glanced away, then lifted a shoulder. "I'm not unhappy." He turned his gaze back to her. "But the charters are dull. It's the same routes every day. And I miss flying choppers. I'd get to do that working for Appalachia Resorts."

Amy nodded once. "Thought so. Go get Brooke's number and tell her to come back."

"What? Wait, you want—"

"To make us both happy. I like my job, but you know the hours suck. Working on the resort's museum sounds exciting. Both of us will go to work energized, ready to see what the day brings."

Ezra studied her for a long moment. His blue eyes searched hers, and she could see his mind working. "She did mention there could be a few overnight trips. More some months than others."

"That's fine. We'll be together more often than not. And you won't be getting shot at, either, on these trips. That alone is a win."

A slow smile spread over his face. "You're sure about this?"

"Yes. **One** hundred percent." She let go of his hands and gave him a soft shove. "Go get the number."

He laughed. Instead of getting up, he grabbed her and pulled her into his lap. "Later. Right now, I need to show my fiancée how much she makes me happy."

Amy's giggled died in her throat as his mouth landed on hers. It would be a long time before he found that number.

The End

Thank you for reading Stranded With Ezra. I hope you loved it! Want to know more about Ford? His story is out now! You can read it **HERE**.

If you'd like to read more about Ezra and Amy (and the other characters in this series), join my mailing list. Subscribers get a bonus chapter or scene after every book! You'll also get access to exclusive teasers, giveaways, and the occasional book recommendation, as well as sneak peeks into my world as I create my stories. Click **HERE** to sign up!

Ford's Fight - Ch.1

Heels click-clacking on the marble floor, the sound echoing through the cavernous foyer and down the hallway, Brooke McGinty made her way through her fiancé's home, brushing a bead of sweat off her forehead. It might be September, but it was North Carolina, and she'd been rushing. When she left her office forty-five minutes ago, she thought she would be late for their dinner engagement. She got hung up with a demanding bride. The resort event planner, Mia, showed up at her office with the woman in tow two hours prior, at her wit's end. The caterer had promised the bride a specific kind of caviar and could now no longer deliver. Mia had called around, but had little luck tracking down the brand the bride wanted. Brooke did her best to console the woman while she sent out emails to all her contacts, hoping someone had a line on a supply of the stuff for the Saturday wedding.

But all that put her behind, and Johnathan hated when she was late. The world operated on Johnathan Cassidy's time-line, and God forbid if you upset the balance. Once she ushered the slightly mollified bride out of her office, Brooke hightailed it to her house and changed clothes, forgoing a shower in favor of some deodorant and a quick spritz of her favorite perfume, then hopped in her car and hurried across the city to the Cassidy's massive estate. She was sure she'd be late, but the traffic gods smiled on her and she was actually a few minutes early.

Raised male voices carried from the rear of the house. She frowned, changing direction for the study rather than the front living room as she recognized Johnathan's voice. Getting closer, she recognized the second voice. It was his brother, Will.

"Are you sure you've thought this through all the way? I mean, hell, John, we're talking about murder here. If we get caught…"

Brooke froze, feet from the doorway. *Murder? What?*

"We won't get caught. It's not like I plan to bludgeon or shoot the old codger. He's ancient. No one will suspect anything but a heart attack."

Leaning against the wall, she edged closer. This had to be a prank. Johnathan saw her coming on the security monitor and roped Will into playing some sick joke on her. He couldn't be plotting the death of someone for real. Right?

A whisper of unease niggled her mind. Johnathan had a temper. He'd never laid a hand on her, but seeing him angry still terrified her. A stillness overcame him that turned his normally handsome face into a cold, emotionless mask.

"Why is this even necessary? You said you want to make sure you take over, but once you marry Brooke, you're a shoo-in. What's the rush?"

Brooke covered her mouth to hold back the squeal that wanted to break free. They were talking about murdering her grandfather! She shuffled closer. Taking her phone from her purse, she opened the camera app and set it to record video, then aimed the receiver at the door with a shaking hand.

"So, you know that blonde chick I brought to the party at Benton's a couple of weeks ago?"

"The one with legs for days?"

"That's the one. I'm not sleeping with her just for her looks. She works in the records room for the old man's personal attorney. I get all the files pertaining to him that come across her desk. We both have a good roll in bed, and she gets some pretty baubles. It's a win-win."

Anger turned Brooke's blood red-hot. She felt heat warm her cheeks as she clenched her teeth together to hold in the growl. The bastard not only wanted to take out her grandfather, he was sleeping around on her too? She shouldn't be surprised. Her relationship with Johnathan Cassidy wasn't a match made in heaven. It was more—expected. Two young people from two prominent families of marriageable age. And they didn't hate each other. He was good in bed. She hadn't seen any reason not to marry him. Love wasn't really one of her requirements for a happy marriage. She'd seen too many couples claiming to be madly in love, only to divorce a few years later because it wasn't enough. Brooke wanted someone compatible and dependable. Johnathan fit that bill.

Apparently, he wasn't as dependable as she'd thought if he was honing his bedroom skills with other women before coming home to her. She rolled her eyes and leaned closer to hear what else he had to say.

"Anyway, she brought me a copy of the changes he wants to make to his will. Brooke inherits his share of the business, but her dad will still become CEO. The old man stipulated, though, that if she sells within ten years after inheriting, she gets nothing from it. All the money goes to the family foundation."

"What happens if she dies before then?"

Brooke clamped her hand tighter over her mouth as she bit back a gasp. Would they want to murder her too?

"Ownership transfers to the foundation. Then it's theirs to do with as they please."

Will cursed.

"Exactly. Which is why we need to act quickly. Before he signs the papers. This is the perfect time to set something up. He'll be out of town two more days."

"What about her dad? He's in line to become CEO."

"Unfortunately, yes. But he's part of this plan too. We'll kill two birds with one stone." He paused to chuckle. "Quite literally."

Of all the nerve! Brooke ground her molars together to keep in the angry growl. If he thought she would let him get away with this, he had another think coming. She would record every word he said, then take it straight to the police. Then, once her family was safe, she'd tell her dad and grandpa. They could have the pleasure of firing him. Right after she threw her engagement ring in his face and told him to shove it where the sun didn't shine.

"Okay, so what do you have in mind?" Will asked.

The phone lit up in Brooke's hand, displaying the name of the bride she'd so recently ushered out of her office, and her ringtone echoed off the hallway walls.

"No! Crap!" She silenced it, but the damage was done. Conversation in the office ceased. Not waiting to see if they came out to investigate, she spun on her heel and hurried back the way she came. Confronting them was not part of her plan. Especially without backup.

"Brooke!"

She glanced back, heart pounding. Johnathan barreled down the hallway after her, that cold, emotionless mask on his face. Dread filled her belly, and she let out a short squeal, quickening her pace until she ran down the hall. She slammed into the front door in her haste to exit. Battling with the lever-action handle, she yanked it open and scurried down the steps, thanking the heavens she wore heels every day. She could run almost as well in them as she could in tennis shoes.

At the bottom of the steps, she turned right, heading for her silver BMW convertible, gleaming in the bright September sunshine. Reaching the car, she yanked on the door handle and fell inside. A quick glance back showed Johnathan and Will exiting the house. Will pointed at her car, and they ran down the steps.

A sob broke free of her throat as she jammed her foot on the brake and stabbed the start button. The engine roared to life. Brooke didn't bother with her seatbelt. She put the car in drive, and with a squeal of tires, shot around the bend in the circular driveway. The car fishtailed as she straightened the wheel, exiting the curve.

Getting the car under control, she sucked in a breath through her nose. She needed to get it together.

Think, think, think! She needed a plan. After seeing Johnathan's face, she had no doubt he knew she'd heard every word. But who could she go to? Her grandfather? But he was in Asia. What could he do half a world away? Right now, she needed someone who could help her.

She hit the button on her steering wheel to place a call. "Call Dad." The phone rang through the car speakers several times before her father, Elliott McGinty, answered.

"Hi, pumpkin. I'm getting ready to head into a meeting. Can I call you back?"

She bit her lip, making a quick decision. "Actually, I just called to ask if I could borrow the jet. I need to do some scouting for a client's destination wedding. Mia's booked solid and asked me to help." She needed some time to figure out what to do. Telling her dad what she overheard—and without further evidence—would just create a sense of panic. And with what she knew, Johnathan would probably put his plan on hold. He'd want to silence her before he went after her family. Staying silent would keep them safe.

"Oh. Well, sure. When do you need it?"

"Today, if possible."

"Today?"

Brooke could almost see the frown form between his eyebrows. She had the wheels turning in his brain. But she didn't want to involve him in this. Not yet. The less her family knew, the better.

"I know it's short notice, but so is her wedding. She's in the family way, so they're wanting to get married as soon as possible." She thanked her lucky stars she was good at thinking on her feet. She just prayed she could remember all these lies.

"Oh, well, that's understandable. I'll call Ezra and have him head to the airport. Where can I tell him you're going?"

She scrambled for an answer, not really sure where she wanted to go, just that she needed to get away. Going to the police wasn't an option yet. All she had was a recording of them talking. Johnathan had powerful friends. The entire case would get swept under the rug, and Brooke would be at his mercy. She needed time to think, and the only way to do that was to run and hide.

Gulping a breath, she responded. "French Polynesia." That should get the staff at the airport to put plenty of fuel in the jet. She'd come up with a more specific destination when she got there. Brooke didn't plan to tell anyone except Ezra where she was headed, and that was only because he had to fly the plane.

"Okay. I'll let him know."

"Thanks, Daddy." She felt tears threaten and rolled her lips in as her voice fell off on the last word.

"Anytime, pumpkin. Have a safe trip."

She let out a shaky breath, then sucked in another one,

forcing a cheery note into her voice. "I will. Talk to you soon." He bade her goodbye, and she hung up.

Turning out of the Cassidy's neighborhood, she headed for the freeway. Her mind raced as fast as her car. She didn't dare go home. That would be the first place Johnathan would go. But she needed her passport, and it was in the safe at her house.

Brooke uttered another epithet, grumbling about countries and their laws, and pressed harder on the gas pedal. She'd get there, run in and get it, along with some extra cash, then head to the airport. Clothing and toiletries were easy to buy wherever she went.

Cars flowed down the highway at a steady clip. Rush hour was just ending, thankfully. Brooke wove in and out of traffic, going much faster than the posted speed limit. She prayed for no police and kept an eye out. The sign for her exit loomed, and she breathed a sigh of relief.

Her fingers drummed a nervous beat on the steering wheel as she slowed, queuing with the other cars at the red light. She willed it to change. Once it did, she followed the line through the intersection, then resumed weaving in and out of traffic.

At her house, she didn't bother pulling into the garage. She parked haphazardly in the driveway, then ran in through the front doors, pausing only long enough to fumble with her keys.

Stumbling over the threshold, she threw the locks into place—because even though she practically flew here, she didn't trust that Johnathan wasn't right behind her—then ran into her office to open her safe.

Brooke swung open the painting behind her desk to access the recessed safe and spun the dial on the lock to open it. Her fingers shook, and she missed the second number. When she did it again, she forced herself to take a deep breath and slow down. She needed to stay calm. Letting her emotions rule would only hinder her effectiveness in getting out of town before Johnathan caught up to her.

After her third attempt, the door swung open. She reached inside and withdrew her passport, as well as the bundle of emergency money she kept on hand. Her family was quite wealthy, which meant there were always people out there who disliked them. Her father had always cautioned her to be ready for anything—and that included having cash on hand. If he were here with her now, she'd give him a big kiss. It was saving her ass.

She shut the safe and spun the dial, then put the picture back in place. With the items she came for in her hand, she headed for the door, stuffing them both into her purse as she went. Exiting the house, she ran down the walkway to her car. Her heels clacked on the concrete, keeping pace with her thundering heart.

Pulling open the car door, she dove inside, throwing her purse onto the passenger seat. She buckled up, then started the engine, backing away from the house and onto the road with a quick squeal of her tires. Out of sight of her house, she gunned it, making her trip to the airport a quick one. She hoped Ezra was there and ready to go. The sooner she was in the air, the safer she'd feel.

Thankful for her family's status, Brooke bypassed the main airport entrance and went through the private gate. Her dad had alerted the guards, so when she showed her ID, they waved her through. She pointed the car toward her family's hangar, doing her best to keep her speed slow as she crossed the tarmac. Parking beside the building, she got out and hurried toward the plane, which was sitting just outside the hangar.

The tall man walking around it with a clipboard and pen in his hands glanced at her with a smile. "Hi, Brooke. We'll be ready to go soon. If you bring your luggage over, I'll load it once I finish my pre-flight checks."

"I don't have any luggage. Do you mind if I sit inside the plane to wait?"

He frowned. "No luggage?"

Brooke felt a bit like a bug under a microscope as Ezra's gaze sharpened and he stared at her for a long moment.

"What's wrong?"

She fought to put a blank mask over her face. "What makes you think anything is wrong?"

One dark eyebrow shot up. "Spur of the moment trip, no luggage, deer in the headlights look on your face—I'd say something's wrong."

She'd always liked Ezra Chastain, but right now, she was rethinking that position. "I'm fine."

"Bullshit."

Brooke wrung her hands together and glanced away.

Ezra crossed his arms and arched that eyebrow again. "We can stand here all evening if you'd like."

Anger drew her eyebrows together. "You work for my family. Dad gave me permission to use the jet. Your job is to fly it."

A smile cocked one side of his mouth. "Gee, I think I'm feeling a little too tired to fly. Maybe even a little sick. Might be coming down with something." He took a step toward the hangar. "I'll go call the reserve pilot. You can wait a few hours for him to get here from San Antonio, right?"

Brooke ground her molars together and shot a hand out to snag his sleeve. "Fine. You win." Her eyes darted around again, and she sighed. "I overheard—something—and I need to get out of town while I figure out what to do."

That sharp gaze pierced her again. "What did you overhear?"

She refused to meet his eyes, knowing if she did, she'd spill her guts. No one else needed to be involved. She didn't want to put anyone else in danger.

"Brooke, tell me what's going on. I can help."

She hesitated. Ezra was former military. She didn't doubt his ability to keep her safe, but she wasn't sure it was wise to involve anyone else at this point. And he had a family to think about. She didn't want to put his wife, Amy, and their new daughter, Gretchen, in danger.

"Brooke, you need to tell me what's going on. Whatever it is, I can help."

It was the confidence in his tone that made her tongue loosen a little. She looked at him. "I'm in danger. Can we just leave it at that, please?"

"No. What kind of danger? From whom?"

"The deadly kind. And from Johnathan."

He frowned. "Johnathan? Your fiancé?"

She nodded.

He raked his gaze over her, and a banked anger flared to life in his eyes. "Did he hurt you?"

The steel in his voice warmed her a little. It was nice to know someone wanted to go to bat for her. "No. Not yet. Look, I just need time to figure out what to do. Please. I just want to get on the plane and get out of here."

"To French Polynesia?"

She threw up her hands. "Sure. There or anywhere else out of the country. I don't really care, so long as it's not here."

He studied her for another moment. "Okay. But we're not going to French Polynesia."

Brooke frowned. "Then where are we going?"

"Costa Rica."

About the Author

After spending most of her adulthood moving around the U.S. and Europe, romantic suspense author Ashley A. Quinn has settled in her home state of Ohio with her husband, two kids, and a menagerie of pets. She started writing in her teens and never stopped. Her first novel, Smoky Mountain Murder, came out in 2016, and she has since published more than twenty titles. When not writing, you can find her with her nose stuck in a romantic thriller or binge-watching baking shows and British TV dramas. She is an avid baseball fan and also enjoys crafting and puttering around her garden.

Smoky Mountain Judge

Wagner Brigade

Stranded With Ezra: A Prequel to the Wagner Brigade

Ford's Fight

Dean's Dilemma

Jordan's Journey

Sam's Salvation (coming June 2024)

Asher Assignment (coming September 2024)

Max's Mission (coming December 2024)